The Book of Life
The Greatest Story Ever Told

The Book of Life

The Greatest Story Ever Told

Heather Rae Hutzel

The Book of Life
The Greatest Story Ever Told

Copyright © 2012 by Heather Rae Hutzel

All rights reserved. No part of this publication may be reproduced, stored in a retrieval system, or transmitted by any means – electronic, mechanical, photographic (photocopying), recording, or otherwise – without prior permission in writing from the author.

Printed in the United States of America
ISBN: 978-0-9885036-9-4

All scripture verses, unless otherwise noted, are taken from the Holy Bible, New International Version®, NIV® Copyright © 1973, 1978, 1984, 2011 by Biblica, Inc.™ Used by permission. All rights reserved worldwide.

Scripture quotations marked ESV are taken from The Holy Bible, English Standard Version® (ESV®) Copyright © 2001 by Crossway, a publishing ministry of Good News Publishers Used by permission. All rights reserved.

Scripture quotations marked TNIV are taken from The Holy Bible, Today's New International Version® TNIV® Copyright © 2001, 2005 by Biblica, Inc.™ Used by permission. All rights reserved worldwide.

Scripture quotations marked AMP are taken from the Amplified® Bible, Copyright © 1954, 1958, 1962, 1964, 1965, 1987 by The Lockman Foundation Used by permission. All rights reserved.

Scripture quotations marked GOD'S WORD are taken from GOD'S WORD®, © 1995 God's Word to the Nations. Used by permission of Baker Publishing Group. All rights reserved.

Learn more information at:
www.His-wordpress.com

To my King,
The Author and the Perfector, the Beginning and the End.

Thank You for sharing Your story of unrelenting love. I pray I have recorded it just as You told it to me.

{Acknowledgements}

Thank you to my wonderful family and friends for all your love and support. You have played such an important role in the story of my life. I can't thank you enough. I love you all!

Thank you to my husband, David, for being the true picture of love in my life. I honestly believe that I may never have come to understand just how much God loves me without the example you gave me. You are amazing in every way, and I'm honored to know that you are the person I will always have by my side no matter where this life takes us. Thank you for always supporting my hopes and dreams. There have been many, yet you never shy away when I come to you and say, "Hey, I have this great idea!" Thank you for letting me dream with my head in the clouds while always keeping my feet planted firmly on the ground. I don't know what I'd do without you. I love you!

Thank you, Momma, for being such a support throughout the entire process of writing this book. You have read, edited, re-read, and re-edited countless times. You have seen the best days of this adventure and the worst days, and you always listened even when I knew I wasn't making any sense! You believed in me this whole time, even when I stopped believing in myself. Thank you for being my "guinea pig" and sharing what you've learned by going before me. But most of all, thank you for being my friend.

Thank you, Dad, for instilling in me the value of being a hard worker. You've taught me integrity by the way you live, and you set an example of what it looks like to set your mind to a challenge and succeed. I can't remember a time you ever doubted my ability to achieve what I set out to do. You have always been there for me. Thank you for being my biggest fan.

Thank you, Ben, for playing a special role in this journey. You are more than a brother to me, you are an amazing friend. Thank you for sharing your graphic creativity and bringing my ideas to life on the computer screen. I'm so proud of you and can't wait to watch you achieve your dreams.

Thank you to my editor, Adele, for polishing my manuscript and playing such an important role in getting this book ready for print. I appreciate the many hours you devoted to this novel.

Last, but certainly not least, thank You, Jesus. Thank You for sharing with me this amazing story and for bringing me on this adventure. Only You could bring Your dream to life in someone like me. Thank You for the certainty of love and life that I have in You. I can't wait to see what You have in store next, and I can't wait to watch lives change by the power of Your story. It is truly "the greatest story ever told."

{Dear Reader}

If you are indeed reading this book, then a very grand dream has come to fruition. Writing this book, or any book for that matter, was never my personal intent or vision for my life, but sometimes we are given dreams bigger than our own and with them, the responsibility to carry them out. *The Book of Life* is one of these dreams. It is something that has far surpassed my own humble aspirations, and I have accepted the calling with honor and humility.

The Book of Life is a novel, fiction based on the words of the Bible. Throughout this story are themes, details, and even direct quotes from the pages of Scripture, and many aspects in this story are accurate to the writings and teachings of the Bible. As you are reading this story, you will notice number endnotes throughout the text. Every time you see one of these references, this is a place where I have used one or more verses of Scripture from the Bible in entirety or in paraphrase. I have definitely taken my creative liberties as a writer, so I encourage you to look up some of these references once you have finished reading *The Book of Life*. All of the endnotes are included in the back of the book. While many elements in this book are "fiction" and are not illustrated specifically or in such detail as they appear in the Bible, I can't help but wonder if the story didn't actually go a little something like the one I'm telling.

As a follower and servant of my King, Jesus, I believe with all my heart that the words of His Bible are true and accurate recordings of history. It's as if the Bible is a puzzle, with all its pieces scattered on a table, but God has shown me how to put the pieces together, and the picture it creates is His story.

The Bible is God's Word and within those words His truth. Therefore, this book, *The Book of Life*, contains the very words of God. The story of His kingdom, His creation, His power, His love, His redemption, and His return are all true.

If you are uncertain of God's story and the trueness of His words, I encourage you to allow God to tell you His story through the words contained within these pages. Then, once you have finished, grab a Bible and read for yourself the *real* Book of Life.

Sincerely, the Messenger (not the Author)

Heather Rae Hutzel

"These are the things God has revealed to us by His Spirit. The Spirit searches all things, even the deep things of God."

1 Corinthians 2:10

Part I

Rebellion

{Prologue}

THE LORD BROUGHT ME FORTH as the first of His works, before His deeds of old. I was formed long ages ago, at the very beginning, when the world came to be. When there were no watery depths, I was given birth. When there were no springs overflowing with water, before the mountains were settled in place, and long before the hills, I was given birth. Before He made the world or its fields or any of the dust of the earth, I was given birth. I was there when He set the heavens in place and witnessed Him marking out the horizon on the face of the deep. With my own eyes, I saw Him establish the clouds above and fix securely the fountains of the deep and give the sea its boundary so the waters would not overstep His command. That was when He marked out the foundations of the earth. Then I was constantly at His side. I was filled with delight day after day, rejoicing always in His presence, rejoicing in His whole world, and delighting in mankind.[1]

{~}

It was a beautiful day like no other, like no day that had ever occurred before. More beautiful than the day before, yet somehow not as beautiful as tomorrow promised. This is the way it used to be before the happening.

The air was thick, warm, and sweet, delicious even. The sky was clear, clearer than the clearest sky man has ever seen, a color that can only be described as a harmonious blend of all the hues in a rainbow. It sparkled as if it were made with some precious stone, reflecting light and color in a splendid display of illumination.

In the whisper of the wind could be heard a soft melody, a sound so sweet and pure that it gave life to the body. In the distance, could be heard a chorus of voices, a humming tune that I couldn't quite pick out, but knew it was the most striking song my ears could ever taste. It was a tune that reverberated in my very core and moved me in ways beyond understanding. This day was more beautiful than any day man has ever known, simply because this day took place in a time before man has ever known.

This was the time of the beginning and the end.

It was on this day like no other, that I was summoned to the throne, not an unusual event in and of itself. I had been summoned times before. Yet, this day was different. I sensed an oddity. Something had shifted in the winds. There was a feeling in the air I could not describe, a sensation I had never before experienced.

As I would later learn, an event of monumental importance was about to take place, altering history in ways beyond my own comprehension. No amount of wisdom and understanding could have prepared me for what was about to take place. No one but the One could have predicted such an upheaval.

I prepared myself to enter into the throne room where I had been summoned. Never have I felt worthy of this act, and I never shall. It was an event that always took my breath away, much like every other experience in this land. This occasion, however, surpassed them all.

How could I stand in the throne room and not be entirely struck with awe and wonder of the majesty before me? The rush I felt before the throne was one of sheer pleasure and complete humility. It weakened and exhilarated me all at once. Even the strongest and bravest would fall on their knees.

"Enter!" the voice boomed from the throne room just beyond where I stood. It was the most beautiful sound to my ears, harmonious and melodic all at the same time.

On passing through the regal doorway, I felt a warm sensation flooding my very being, an awareness of my body weakening despite my will. I fell prostrate. Never could I bring myself to look upon the Holy of Holies, the Alpha and the Omega, the Beginning and the End.

The room itself is beyond description. Towering walls that reached to the sky were covered with every precious stone ever known, and their prisms reflected a pure light that emanated from the One seated before them. The reflection alone was enough to steal a being's sight.

Chaste voices filled the throne room with a royal song, the harmonious blending of four perfect voices singing, "Holy, Holy, Holy, is the Lord God Almighty, who was and is and is yet to come."[2]

I began to unify my own voice with theirs in song, the song I knew so well, a song all heavenly hosts recognized in their hearts and loved to sing day in and day out, never tiring of its splendid chorus.

I knew the source of these voices without even glancing. At the center of the room, surrounding the throne, were the four strange creatures that chanted, never ceasing day or night.

"You are worthy, our Lord and God, to receive glory and honor and power, for You created all things, and by Your will, they were created and have their being."[3]

They were unlike the warriors or cherubim. Each one was unique to the others yet similar at the same time. Upon each creature were six pairs of wings that were covered with pairs of eyes all around, front and back, and each had a face unique to the others: one like a lion, one like an ox, another like an eagle, and the forth with a head remarkably resembling the image of the Almighty himself.[4]

"Arise!" The voice shook the throne room with the rumblings and peals of thunder, and I trembled under its power.

"I cannot, my Lord. I am unworthy; for who is like You, O Lord? Your understanding no one can fathom."[5]

"Arise, Michael, for the time has come. You must assemble My armies, for we are going into battle. The time has come for you to fulfill your purpose and role as Archangel, leader and commander of the Army of God."

Slowly, I lifted my eyes, gazing first upon the sea of crystal that stood between the Almighty and me. Then my eyes met His. Never have I seen something so beautiful, so powerful, and so indescribable.

His presence was brighter than the purest light, and from the throne came flashes of lightning. His appearance was that of jasper and ruby, yet even more remarkable and lovely to gaze upon. A rainbow encircled the throne and shone like an emerald. I rose to my feet as a command from my Lord, but I could look upon His beauty no longer. I bowed my head in humility.[6]

"I will serve You with honor, my Lord. Show me the way I should go, for to You I lift up my soul."[7]

"Very well, Michael. Now listen to Me closely. Evil has been found in the realms of Heaven and on the Mountain of God. Wickedness has been found in Lucifer, the guardian cherub full of wisdom and perfect in beauty. His heart has become proud on account of his splendor. He is full of violence and has sinned against me."[8]

Humbly I fell to one knee, "Forgive me, my Lord, but I do not know of this sin and evil of which You speak."

"Of course you do not, Michael. No one does. Lucifer is the first of his kind. He declared in his heart, 'I will ascend to the heavens. I will raise my throne above the stars of God. I will sit enthroned on the mount of assembly, on the utmost heights. I will ascend above the tops of the clouds. I will make myself like the Most High.' Lucifer is full of selfish ambition and envy against Me, and these, Michael, are sin and evil. For I am God, and there is no other. I am God, and there is none like Me."[9]

I could scarcely believe what my ears had heard. How could anyone believe he was greater than the Almighty? My mind could not even begin to comprehend the words spoken to me.

My Master continued, "The guardian angel Lucifer was blameless from the day I created him until today when wickedness has been found in him. He, who was once full of my wisdom, my mysterious ways, and understanding, will be cast from the Mount of God. He is expelled from my presence forevermore!"[10]

{~}

On the Mountain of God assembled all of the Almighty's warriors, a great and mighty throng of muscled bodies preparing to fight for the Great King. Rows and rows of towering, winged soldiers, as far as the eye could see, began preparing for combat, outfitting themselves with the armor provided to them by the Lord Almighty.

In grounding for the war, I announced to them, "For these are the words the Lord, your God, sends.

"'Warriors, our struggle is not against flesh and blood, but against the rulers, against the authorities, against the powers of the dark world and against the spiritual forces of evil in the heavenly realms. Put on the full armor of God, for today, the day of evil comes. Heed my words,' says the Lord, 'So you may be able to stand your ground, and after you have done everything, to stand. Stand firm then, with the belt of truth buckled around your waist, with the breastplate of righteousness in place, and with your feet fitted with the readiness that comes from the gospel of peace. In addition to all this, take up the shield of faith, with which you can extinguish all the flaming arrows of the evil one. Take the helmet of salvation and the Sword of the Spirit, which is the Word of God.'"[11]

The warriors drew their flaming swords and took to the sky. We were heading into battle.

{~}

In his wickedness, Lucifer engaged one third of Heaven's angels to follow him and to strike up armies against the Lord. They were deceived by the corrupted wisdom Lucifer had been feeding them. They had sealed their doom the moment the declaration of Lucifer as their lord touched their lips.

They too made ready for battle by his commands, knowing in-full their rebellion and sin but never presuming the fate that awaited them. This was the day of the beginning and the end, the start of the greatest war ever to be fought and that would ever be known.

{~}

Thunder shook the Mountain of God, and lightning pierced the sky. The very heavens seemed to revolt at the atrocity taking place. Clouds rolled in and darkened the land as the warriors of God filled the air, their sheer numbers blanketing the sky in strength and power. The sound of their beating wings shook the mountain in an upheaval of the peace that once filled the land.

War broke out in Heaven, and my angels warriors and I fought against Lucifer. He and his angels wrestled back, but they were not strong enough against the power of the Almighty God.[12]

The armor of the Lord surrounded us and strengthened us as we proceeded to drive the rebelling cherub from Heaven. Lucifer and his angels were no match for the Sword of the Spirit, the very Word of God that once filled Lucifer with great wisdom. On that very day, he and his angels lost their place in Heaven.

As I myself used the Sword of the Spirit to deliver the final blow to Lucifer, I declared in a mighty voice, "All those gathered here will know that it is not by the sword or spear that the Lord saves, for the battle is the Lord's, and He will give all of you into our hands!"[13]

My warriors and I lifted our voices in a piercing battle cry as I thrust forward, using the Sword of the Spirit to pierce through the heart of Lucifer.

Then the voice of the Lord rang out through the air, and all became still. "You, Lucifer, were the seal of perfection, full of wisdom and perfect in beauty. Every precious stone adorned you: carnelian, chrysolite, emerald, topaz, onyx and jasper, lapis lazuli, turquoise, and beryl. Your settings and mountings were made of gold. On the day you were created, they were prepared. You were anointed as a guardian cherub, for so I ordained you. You were on the holy Mount of God, and you walked among the fiery stones. You were blameless in your ways from the day you were created, until today when wickedness was found in you. You are full of violence, and you have sinned against Me, so I am driving you in disgrace from the Mount of God, and I expel you, o guardian cherub. Your heart became proud on account of your beauty, and you corrupted your wisdom with envy and selfish ambition because of your splendor. All wisdom you once knew is now confused with the knowledge of evil. The truth will be far from you, and you will not know reality from deception."[14]

At the Lord's words, a burning fire overtook Lucifer and consumed him, reducing him to ashes on the ground in the sight of all of us who were watching.

"You have come to a horrible end, Lucifer, and will be no more. From this day forth you shall be called Satan. All your pomp has been brought down to the grave, along with the noise of your harps. Maggots are spread out beneath you, and worms will cover you. You will be brought down to the realm of the dead, to the depths of the pit."[15]

Thunder shook the land and lightning blinded the sky as the shrill cries of Satan and his angel demons pierced through the thick air. It was the most horrific sound ever to be heard, a sound so sinister and vile, it could only be the howling of evil itself.

The Lord God hurled Satan and his army out of Heaven and into the depths below. As the final cry faded, a chill swept over the Mountain of God, a sensation never experienced by any of the heavenly hosts.

The chill brought with it a silence so thick we could reach out and touch it. Then, all went black and darkness enveloped the land.

And God said, "Let there be light."[16]

{Chapter 1}

AND THERE WAS LIGHT. It was the brightest purest light I had ever seen. It pierced through the thick dark that enveloped the Mountain of God and warmed the souls of all who were present.[1]

My Lord and Master looked upon my face with hope shining in His eyes and said, "Michael, this is good."

There had never been darkness before the day the Great War began. It was terrifying and foreign. Even the strongest warriors' knees trembled at the cold, blackness that shrouded us. Never before had we been so grateful and in awe of the light that God's presence provided. We had never been without His light. The darkness was a first for us all, one of many firsts that we would encounter over the course of history.

I was reminded in this moment that God is still God, and nothing can shake Him. Nothing is beyond His wisdom and understanding. His ways are not my ways, and His thoughts are not my thoughts. I realized the future would be forever changed beyond my own comprehension, yet my King foreknew the events to come. I vowed that day to stand by His side and fight valiantly, serving my King until the end. But this was just the beginning.[2]

{~}

In the beginning, I watched my King create the heavens and the earth. In this time, the earth was without form and empty. Below the Mountain of God, shrouded in darkness, was the great deep, and the Spirit of God was hovering over the waters.[3]

The darkness that had been over the surface of the deep retreated in fear when the thunderous voice of my Lord commanded, "Let there be light!" And there was light, and I watched in wonder as my King swept His mighty hand across the piercing illumination and created a great division, one half a brilliant and warm beam, the other the coldest, darkest void.[4]

The Lord spoke again to me. "Michael, in remembrance of this day, I am creating night. Night shall be a period of darkness that will occur every day from this day forth. Whenever night falls, and darkness covers the land, My creations will be reminded of the events that took place on the Mountain of God, and they will recall the day evil was found in the realm of Heaven."

Night fell over the land, and there was evening, and there was morning. This was the first day.[5]

{~}

On that morning my King commanded, "Let there be a vault between the waters to separate water from water."[6]

I watched in reverence as the Lord God raised His hands high above His head in a grand sweeping motion. The waters before Him swelled and rushed upward like a massive geyser.

The Lord held His hands high with outstretched fingers, His arms trembling at the power coursing through them.

The water was held captive before Him. I could hear the sound of it roaring and see the white of the waves pulsing through it, yet the tower itself appeared motionless in the presence of the King. Its color was as blue and deep as precious sapphire, and it ascended high as if it were trying to touch the apex of the Mountain of God. It was so strange; even though the water soared above the Lord, it somehow appeared to be cowering before Him.

My King's eyes were raised high as if He were staring deep into the face of the great pillar of water. Of course, the water did not have a face in the sense that the angel warriors and I have a face, yet somehow it seemed to be humbly lowering its eyes from the Master who held it.

In an instant, the Lord cast His hands downward and pressed them out to either side in the same force and power He used to command the waters upward. As He did, a great force could be felt through the land. It pressed hard against my body and stole my very breath away. It caused a great, sweeping wind to rush through the Mountain of God, piercing through the center of the pillar of water and causing it to split in two. As the waters roared past me, rushing to the east and to the west, I silently wondered, "Who is this that even the winds and the waves obey Him?"[7]

I watched as my Lord, God the Father, stood there majestically holding the waters apart with His very presence and power. His body was straightforward with His legs and feet pressed together beneath Him, supporting His commanding frame. His head was held high, and His face was turned upwards, His strong, masculine arms extended out to the sides as if reaching to the farthest breadth of east and west, His palms open with outstretched fingers.

He stood there for what seemed like eons, and a strange emotion swept over me. I could not place it, but a sense of foreshadowing overwhelmed me, and a single, hot tear rolled down my cheek.

Slowly and softly, my King rotated His outstretched arms, one upward and one downward, until they pointed north and south. Without any spoken command, the waves before Him followed, creating a sea above and a sea below, mirroring the position of the Lord's outstretched arms. In between the waters was the vault that separated the water under from the water above, and God called the vault "sky."[8]

Night fell over the land. There was evening, and there was morning. This was the second day.

{~}

In the morning, the Spirit of the Lord was hovering over the waters. He had taken to calling the water below, the sea. It was a beautiful masterpiece created by the Lord's hand, with colors of sparkling sapphire and emeralds. During the day, the brilliant light created by my Master reflected off its glass-like surface. It was mesmerizing to watch; for with its rhythmic motion of ebbing and flowing in a constant current, it seemed alive.

The sea was vast and immeasurable; it stretched far below the Mountain of God and extended to the east and the west, its depth known only by the Lord. It seemed to stretch into eternity. It was only in comparison to God Himself that the sea seemed small.

On this day, I watched as the Lord reached down and scooped the sea into His mighty hands. Up until this moment I believed it would be impossible to contain the sea. Of course it would be, except that with God, all things are possible.[9]

The Lord's hands are strong and powerful, yet soft and gentle, and it was in these hands that my King shaped the earth. He took the sea and rolled it into a large sphere. Slowly He shaped it in His hands, turning it this way and that, until it was smooth, round, and perfect. Finally, He stretched out His arms and placed the indigo orb back into the sky. Where once there had been two vast oceans separated by the great vault of sky, now hovered a globe of water, surrounded by a layer of sky, and above that, a canopy of water.

I then witnessed My King reach out His strong hands and cup one on either side of the earth and rest them softly above the water. And God said, "Let the water under the sky be gathered to one place, and let dry ground appear."[10]

Suddenly, beneath His hands, the sea began to bubble up. It started slowly with little flecks of air arising from the depths of the sea and floating to the surface; it quickly picked up pace. The bubbles rapidly rose and seemed to multiply before my very eyes. They broke the peaceful surface and foamed along the top of the once serene sea. The whole sphere shook and trembled under the might of the King's hands, and a low rumbling could be heard throughout the land. The sea became more violent, and water started sloshing and shooting skyward. Large waves formed and retreated from beneath God's commanding hands.

Slowly, something began to rise from the waters. It started small at first and grew, peeling back the waters around it and forming into a large mass that was situated in the middle of the sea. Unique compared to the water, it was solid and massive, a dry ground. God called the dry ground land, and it was surrounded by the gathered waters of the sea. I watched in awe as the waters began to calm, and a tranquil feeling settled back over the sea. Finally, My King pulled His hands back and lowered His arms to His sides.

Then He turned to me, grinned, and said, "Michael, this is the earth, and it is good."

I beamed back at the Lord, for these were the first words He had directed toward me since the day He brought back the light. And they were the same words, "Michael, this is good."

"My King," I began to inquire, "What is this good You speak of?"

For you see, before the Great War began, the word "good" did not exist, simply because there was no evil or bad in comparison. There was no need to explain. Everything was good, and it was understood, but things were different now, and always would be, as I would later come to realize.

"Michael, everything that I create, everything that comes from Me and My perfect wisdom is good, for My wisdom is pure. I do not create anything that is less than perfect. There was never a need to distinguish, but now that evil exists, you must remember this, Michael: I am good; therefore, everything that is of Me is good. Remember the former things, those of long ago and never forget. I am God, and there is no other. I am God, and there is none like Me."[11]

"I will never forget, my King."

"You see, Michael, I am doing a new thing. The old is gone, and the new has come!" His eyes sparkled even more than usual as He spoke those words. God the Father looked deeply into my own eyes, peering into my soul, searching for my understanding. It felt as if my heart had stopped.[12]

"Forgive me, my King, but what is this new thing You are creating? I do not understand Your ways."

I could not even begin to comprehend what my Master's plan encompassed. I had watched Him over the past two days, and words still escaped me as I tried to describe what I had witnessed.

My King's smile broadened as He spoke. "I have a Son, Michael, an heir. This new thing I am building is a Kingdom, a Kingdom that I am creating for My Son. He is the Prince of Peace, and I must create for Him a Kingdom over which He will one day reign. He will rule over the earth and all that is in it, and the earth and all its inhabitants will worship and adore Him, just as they worship and adore Me, for the Son and the Father are One."

If I thought I didn't understand my King's ways before, I was even more mystified now.

My Master recognized my confusion. "Michael, I do not expect you to understand what I am doing here. There is no way you could comprehend my infinite power. One day, you will know in full what you now know only in part. There are only three things that remain, Michael: faith, hope, and love. And the greatest of these is love."[13]

"Love? My King, what is love?"

"Watch and see, Michael. Watch and see."

The words of the Lord infected me with anticipation, and I stood eagerly beside my King as He turned to admire His creation.

{~}

Sometime later, my King came to me and said, "Come with Me, Michael. Let us walk upon the earth I have created."

I followed my Lord from His place on the Mountain of God to the earth below. I stood there with Him on the shore of the dry ground that He created and looked out along the vast sea. Never had I seen something so beautiful, yet somehow I knew that my King was about to do something even more amazing.

We stood there for minutes, or perhaps it was hours, I don't know, for in the presence of the King, it's as if time stands still, and nothing else matters. A sense of calm, quiet peace enveloped us as we admired the Lord's creation. My Master smiled as He gazed out across the surface of the brilliant sea He had created.

After some time, He turned away from the sea and looked back out across the immense plain of dry ground, the very land He had caused to rise from the depths that once contained it. I stood silent and observed as He walked a few paces forward, away from the shoreline. He stooped down and reached His mighty hands in front of Him and scooped a handful of the dust of the dry ground. He held it for a moment, looking at it in the light that emanated from His very presence. It was brilliant. The dust was like crushed precious stones that reflected little flecks of colored light.

Slowly and steadily, my King let the dust slip through His fingers until only a small amount remained. He brought His hands up toward His mouth and cupped His hands together to conceal the particles of the ground. He closed His eyes and whispered something over His hands that contained the dust, hushed words that I strained to hear but could not quite make out. I watched as my King slowly opened His eyes and rose to His feet. His hands were still close to His lips as He uncurled His fingers with palms facing upward. The glimmering dust lay still in His hands. As He stood there, a soft breeze began to blow, rustling the King's hair.

Gradually the wind began to pick up, and with its growing intensity God said, "Let the land produce vegetation: seed-bearing plants and trees on the land that bear fruit with seed in it, according to their various kinds."

And it was so.[14]

The Lord blew upon the dust in His palms, and as it left His mighty hands, it found its place among the winds and was carried to every corner of the earth. Everywhere the dust fell, the land produced vegetation. The wind became stronger and caused widespread pollination among all the vegetation. Seed-bearing plants multiplied according to their kinds, and trees bearing fruit with seed grew in population according to their kinds.[15]

Before my very eyes, the most lush, magnificent foliage multiplied around me and blanketed the earth. The plants brought with them splendor and thick, aromatic fragrances. The vivid colors that were reflected in the flecks of dust were now adorning every tree and plant across the earth, and the flowers were as stunning as the most precious emeralds, sapphires, and rubies. Each was unique and lovely beyond anything I had ever seen before.

In turning toward me, the Lord saw the look of awe and amazement upon my face. He began to smile and chuckle, which turned into a laugh, a deep hearty laugh that warmed my soul.

He placed His hand upon my shoulder and said, "Michael, this is good."

We spent the afternoon wandering across the land admiring the King's creation and the birth of His Son's Kingdom. As we walked along, the Lord caused streams to bubble up from the earth, and they watered the whole surface of the ground and all of the vegetation that covered it. It caused a warm mist to rise up from the ground and surround the plants, making everything appear so enchanting, as if the earth and all that was in it was shrouded by a veil, like a bride on her wedding day.[16]

As dusk began to fall over the earth, my King and I made our way back to the shoreline. Then darkness crept in and covered the land, and there was evening, and there was morning, the third day.[17]

{~}

The next morning, I found my King once again standing on the shore of the sea. This time, however, rather than gazing out upon the vast ocean, my King had His eyes fixed above on the great vault He called the sky.

The light was always brightest at this time of day, so I was amazed the Lord could fix His eyes upon the light for so long. It was the purest, whitest light, the kind that could only be from God Himself; therefore, was it any wonder that it was only He who could look upon it? I approached, walking closer to the Lord, and took a seat on the sandy shore near His feet. I longed to spend my days just sitting at the feet of my Master, watching Him in all of His splendor create the Kingdom that would one day belong to His Son. My Lord did not acknowledge my presence. Instead, He continued His examination of the light in the sky before Him. As He stood there, He was silent and motionless, except for the faint breeze that moved through His hair. The King was so handsome to gaze upon, so powerful and magnificent in stature that no words could ever describe His majestic presence.

After some immeasurable amount of time passed, God said, "Let there be lights in the vault of the sky to separate the day from the night, and let them serve as signs to mark sacred times, and days and years, and let them be lights in the vault of the sky to give light on the earth."[18]

With these words, the Lord reached His arm skyward and swiped His mighty hand across the light, gathering in His palm a handful of the pure, white beams. He brought the light to His chest and cupped His other hand on top, containing it. I watched Him as He began compressing the light between His powerful hands. When small beams escaped through His fingers, I could barely continue to watch because of their piercing radiance. Unfazed, my God continued to condense the light, forming within His own two hands a glowing orb.

After what seemed like hours, I watched as the King reared back with His arm and launched the lighted globe into the great vault of the sky. The power of God's hand caused the glowing ball to fly through the vault for an immeasurable distance until He held up a halting hand, signaling it to stop. It ceased its voyage and hung there, suspended in the bright sky. This was the sun, and God created it to be a great light to govern the day.

The Lord also created a lesser light that was to govern the night. He called it the moon. The King created the moon in the later part of the day when the light from the sky was beginning to fade. He scooped the less intense light out of the vault and molded the moon in the same way, using less force in compressing the light to create a dimmer glow. When He finished, the Lord tossed the moon into the sky, just as He had done with the sun. He made the sun and the moon to provide light on the earth to govern the day and the night and separate light from darkness.[19]

Just as the last bit of light was fading from the day, my Lord surprised me with one more magnificent creation. Of all the moments I've had with my King, this one I will treasure for all time. The sun that my Master created slowly slipped below the horizon, and night began to fall. My King and I stood on the shore of the sea and watched the grandest display ever to take place, the very first sunset.

Since that day, I have never seen a more breathtaking sunset, nor will I ever behold one like it again, and I had the privilege of witnessing it, standing side by side with the God and Creator of the universe.

I cannot even begin to describe the very first sunset the Lord's hands created, for no words could ever give it justice.

The great Artist painted the sky with an explosion of colors that have never been seen since that moment. I could feel the warmth and radiance pouring over my body; the reflection of the colored light moved in waves across my skin. I was amazed to find that the lilies and flowers of the earth that God created only one day before paled in comparison to the splendid display above them.

The sunset brought life to all the senses. Not only was it the most wonderful sight my eyes had ever seen, but it also awaked my ears to a heavenly chorus, a song of pureness and color. I could taste it on my tongue and feel the vibration of the light pulsing through my being. A sweet aroma pierced my nostrils.

The sun began to make its final descent below the sea, scattering diamonds of light across the surface of the water. They mirrored off the sea and bounced into the sky above, fleeing from the darkness. Before the last bit of light disappeared from the day, my King reached out once more with His powerful hands and scooped up the final glow of the day. Gently He brought His hands to His lips and drank the light from His cupped hands. He didn't swallow the light, but spat it out across the darkness, leaving tiny glowing flecks of light hovering in the vault of the night sky. He had created the stars. The moon arose from the other side of the earth and hung in the blackness, now surrounded by all the stars and other heavenly bodies.

I stared in awe at the great night sky above me. The darkest night ever seen was punctured with bright diamonds of light, and the moon stood out in contrast against the black. It reminded me that, even in times of darkness, the Lord's light still shines. No evil can compare to the pure, holiness of the Lord.

As the Lord turned and began walking towards me, He noticed the smears of light that remained on His hands. He looked down to examine them, then lifted His eyes to meet mine, and smiled. Once more, the mighty King turned His face upward toward the night sky and wiped His hand across the velvet black, leaving smears and swirls of dancing illumination amongst the stars – the galaxies.

Finally, my Master turned back toward me. He clasped an arm around my shoulders and began leading me down the shoreline. A warm laugh erupted from deep within as He turned His face upward. He took His opposite arm and gestured up at the nighttime display and said boldly, "Michael, this is good!"

And there was evening, and there was morning, the fourth day.[20]

{~}

Before the morning sun rose over the sapphire sea, the Lord led me to the far side of the land. We walked all night across the shore and through the thick foliage that now encompassed the earth. It was a quiet walk, guided by the light of the moon and stars the Lord had created, the silence being broken only by the sound of the wind dancing gently over the leafy vegetation. We could just begin to make out the far horizon as the sun began to slip back up over the water and into the great vault above – the first sunrise.

It was almost as breathtaking as the sunset I had witnessed the night before. The sunrise was lovely in a completely different way; it brought the promise of a new day and a new beginning. The most radiant shades of orange, red, yellow, and pink flooded the sky and melted into a pale blue expanse as the colors wrapped themselves around the earth.

Our toes touched the refreshing water of the sea when we reached the far side of the land. My King stooped to gather some water in His hands and brought it to His lips for a drink.

"Michael, whoever drinks the water I give them will never thirst. Indeed, the water I give them will become in them a spring of water welling up to eternal life."[21]

Having spoken that promise, He bent down again, cupping the water in His own hands and pouring it into mine.

"What is life, my King? What is eternal life?" Again I found myself baffled by the mysterious ways of my Master. I eagerly searched for answers, for His wisdom.

"I am life, Michael. I am the Alpha and the Omega, the Beginning and the End. To the thirsty, I will give water without cost from the Spring of the Water of Life. I am the light of the world. Whoever follows Me will never walk in darkness, but will have the light of life."[22]

With the recent events that had taken place in the realm of Heaven, I suddenly began to understand the words of wisdom from my King. In the way that God Himself is light, the absence of Him is darkness. In the same way, my Lord was proclaiming that He is life, and the absence of Him is the farthest thing from life. To have eternal life would be to remain in the presence of the King for all eternity. If the darkness was even a faint foretaste of the nonexistence of God, then I wanted no part in it.

I brought my hands to my own lips and drank the water the Lord had given to me.

The King smiled at me, and in that moment, I knew exactly what He was thinking, *Michael, this is good.*

As I finished drinking the water, the Lord turned away from me to gaze back out across the infinite blue ocean. He began advancing out, wading until He was almost waist deep in the waters. I ventured no further, choosing to remain on the shoreline where the waves quietly lapped at my feet.

He stood there and let His arms drop to His sides, His fingers dangling in the fresh water. Suddenly, God proclaimed, "Let the water teem with living creatures."[23]

As the words left His lips, the water surrounding my Master's body began to churn and slosh as a multitude of sea creatures suddenly appeared in the sea directly beside and under Him. It was as if they had been stowed away in His legs and at His very command began to emerge from their hiding place.

In mere moments, the ocean waters were teeming with living animals of all shapes and sizes. There were small finned animals made of brilliant colors. They swam together in what appeared to be a dance for their King. Schools of tiny, spear shaped, diamond-colored beings darted and moved with such a rhythmic motion that their song could be heard from the shore where I was standing. Giant watery beasts leapt from the depths of the sea, and the blue waters parted to release them into the sky above. Droplets fell from their mighty bodies, glimmering like crystals in the sunlight and guiding the beasts as they plummeted back into the ocean below.

The Lord's laughter rang throughout the land as He raised His hands high above His head, looked up toward the sky, and called out, "And let birds fly above the earth across the vault of the sky!"[24]

At His words, the branches of the nearby vegetation began to shake and bounce as large flocks of winged creatures emerged from the forest and took to the sky. They danced in an aerial display of beauty and grace, dipping down and nearly touching the sea before lifting back up to the blue expanse. Their voices rang out and carried across the waters, blending with the beating of the waves and the rhythm of the swimming creatures. A magnificent symphony surrounded me, coursing through my being. It was as if the King had become the Conductor of a perfect melody. His power spilled over into His creation. The earth and all that was in it became a living song.

I could feel the beat underneath me, vibrating through the shoreline. I didn't dare blink, for fear I might miss even a single moment of the marvelous events that were taking place before my very eyes.

"Be fruitful and increase in number and fill the water in the seas, and let the birds increase on the earth." The Conductor's voice carried across the water and through the sky, His blessing falling upon the beings He created.[25]

Accompanied by the night display of dancing colors and rising moon and stars, the harmonious song continued into the evening. An emotion I had never before experienced swept over me as I lifted my hands and my heart in worship. I wanted to give my King praise for all I could see, for it was I who was with Him when He spoke the world into being. I couldn't help but raise my voice to blend in harmony with the song of life all around me. The heavens declared the glory of God. The skies proclaimed the work of His hands. Day after day they poured forth speech, and night after night they revealed knowledge. They had no speech, they used no words. No sound was heard from them, yet their voices went out into all the earth, their words to the ends of the world.[26]

My King and I stood there on the shoreline, watching the panorama in wonder and silence. No words passed between us, but before the final colors of the sunset had faded from view, my King uttered in a hushed voice, "Michael, this is good."

There was evening and there was morning, the fifth day.[27]

{~}

As the sun rose the next morning, I could hardly hold back my anticipation for the day. What wonderful and miraculous feats would my Master accomplish today?

It was later that morning when I finally found my King wandering through the thickness of the forest. I saw Him at a distance, facing away from me. The sun was behind him, surrounding him in a halo of honor, and the mist of the ground enveloped Him in a golden haze of pure radiance. The fruit-bearing trees surrounded Him, their silhouettes creating a lovely vignette. It was such a striking scene, for one would think the King Himself should be silhouetted as the trees, but no! His presence beamed with warm rays that created a white glow that was brighter than the sun rising behind Him. This grand view was joined by the heavenly song of God's creation that continued to sing to Him day and night.

As the song persisted, a soft breeze swept in and flooded the forest. It rustled the branches, and I felt it glide across my skin and over the tops of my wings. The wind billowed away from me and carried itself across the land to where the Lord was standing. It rose up through the mist, causing the golden haze to swirl and dance around the presence of the mighty King. I saw my Master close His eyes, a smile playing on the corner of His lips. He lifted His face upward and extended His arms to the sides.

And God said, "Let the land produce living creatures according to their kinds: the livestock, the creatures that move along the ground, and the wild animals, each according to its kind."

And it was so. [28]

Out of the landscape emerged creatures of all kinds. Some with four legs and hooves, others covered with dense hair, and still more with thick, scale-like skin. They bounded across the forest floor and traveled in herds across the land. They came in all different shapes and sizes, reflecting my Master's love for beauty and variety. I couldn't help but stand there, watching and taking in the miraculous sight as my King basked in the joy of His creation. Moments passed as all variety of creatures materialized from the forest, coming forth to receive their blessing from the Lord.

I was lost in thoughts of wonder when I heard it, a steady rumble in the distance. It grew louder and closer, shaking the tallest of trees as it approached. Finally, it reached the center of the forest. My eyes widened in awe as, to the right of the Lord, the trees parted to make an entrance for the largest of the Lord's created beasts.

What strength it had in its loins, what power in the muscles of its belly! Its tail swayed like a cedar, and the sinews of its thighs were close-knit. Its bones seemed to be made of tubes of bronze, and its limbs were like rods of iron. It had a neck that stretched to the height of the forest, and its head traveled among the top of the canopy. It was covered in a thick hide of skin that wrinkled and creased as its monstrous frame moved over the earth.[29]

The beast slowed as it neared the presence of the Lord, and I watched in wonder as it stopped before Him. The motion started up above, shaking the top of the forest, as the animal's head and neck lowered down through the canopy. The largest of all the created land animals, lay down its mighty neck until its head rested at the feet of the King. It bowed respectfully before Him, seeking the blessing of the Lord.

In response, the mighty King reached out in front of Him and laid His royal hands on top of the beast's massive head.

Without moving or retracting His hands from their resting place, the Lord lifted His face and turned in the direction where I was standing and watching from a distance.

My King's face widened with a broad grin, and I heard His voice ring out as the Lord of all creation proclaimed, "Michael, this is good!"

{Chapter 2}

Now the Lord God had planted a garden in the east of the earth in Eden; it was called the Garden of Eden. It was in this garden that I found my King, walking amongst the foliage. I began to approach. I wanted to praise Him for His mighty works and creation. I longed to fall at His feet in honor as the great beast had done. Slowly, I began walking toward Him, approaching my Master quietly in reverence.[1]

Although His back was to me, and He was still a ways off, somehow I knew the King sensed my presence. Still He did not turn to face me. Instead, the Lord turned His face to the left and fixed His gaze on something beside Him.

I stopped suddenly as two figures, much like His own, emerged from the garden to stand beside the Lord. My heart stopped, and my breath caught in my throat. Standing there before me, in the center of the garden, were three forms that appeared nearly identical. They all shone with a piercing brightness that caused me to shield my eyes and avert my face.

The Lord was in the center, His light glowing with the color of the purest diamonds – God the Father. The figure directly to the left of the Lord burned with just as much intensity, and at the center, its light was white like the Lord's, but as its brilliance dispersed, it cast shades of deep emerald and sapphire across the entire garden. It was God the Holy Spirit. I sensed His presence in the wind, during the days before, as my Master created the earth and all its great wonders.

At the right hand of my Master stood the third figure. Again, this body beamed with the white intensity of the Lord, but the outer ring of its light blended into a deep crimson, redder than the reddest of rubies. It was breathtaking.

The King smiled in acknowledgement of the emerald figure on the left and then turned toward the crimson beam on His right. He placed His hands upon its shoulders, leaned forward, and planted a kiss on top of its head.

I fell to my knees in wonder and amazement as I realized this was the Son! This was the Heir for Whom the Kingdom was being built! I could scarcely believe what I was witnessing, the Godhead, Three in One.

Then God said to Them, "Let Us make mankind in Our image, in Our likeness, so that they may rule over the fish in the sea and the birds in the sky, over the livestock and all the wild animals, and over all the creatures that move along the ground."[2]

The Lord God stooped down, reaching out before Him to gather the dust of the ground into His strong hands. The Spirit and Son stood on either side of God the Father to watch the creation of mankind unfold.

God the Father reached out with cupped hands in front of Him, holding the dust between the Spirit and the Son. Simultaneously, They extended Their Own arms with cupped hands held high as if They were holding something precious. Gently, God the Spirit and God the Son opened Their fingers, allowing the contents to slip through and pour over the Lord's hands. It was water, the same life-giving water from the Spring of the Water of Life. God Himself was pouring His very life, His very being, into this creation.

When the water ceased to fall, the Lord began to work the dust and water in His strong yet gentle hands, molding and shaping the mixture until it became a thick mud-like paste. Both the Spirit and Son joined in, kneeling down beside the Lord to take part in this creation. With heads bent forward, They labored, giving careful attention and thoughtful preparation to Their work. It was like watching an artist create a masterpiece.

After what seemed like an eternity, the three figures rose to their feet and gazed down at the molded dirt before Them. Seemingly satisfied, They turned Their backs toward me and bonded together, side by side, creating a curtain with Their bodies. No longer could I see what was taking place. I realized a moment such as this was far too sacred for a humble Archangel warrior such as myself to witness. So I waited.

And I waited some more as a seemingly endless amount of time passed, yet I knew without a doubt that my concept of time was distorted, for the sun was still high in the sky. The bright orb crept slowly across the blue vault, teasing me with the anticipation of the creation I would soon see.

Finally, after an uncertain amount of time, God the Father, Spirit, and Son parted Their bodies, and I was once again granted view of Their magnificent display of power. There, lying on the ground before Them was a form that looked remarkably like the King, except smaller and dull. This being did not glow with the light of the Lord. It had no life. Motionless, it lay before the Trinity.

After a final inspection of the form, God the Father looked to His two companions and smiled. They too marveled at the work of Their hands. With a slight glance over His shoulder,

God the Father looked back across the garden. His eyes met mine and pierced into my soul, as if to say, *Watch and see, Michael. Watch and see.*

I held my breath, afraid that even the exhale of my lungs might disrupt the moment. Silently, I watched as the Creator of the heavens and the earth fell to His knees beside His creation: it was God the Father. Then, as if on cue, both God the Spirit and God the Son placed an authoritative hand upon the shoulders of the Father. As They did, the three bonded together again. Piercing light flashed through the garden and shook the ground with the rumblings of thunder, forcing me to squeeze my eyes shut and cover my ears. I nearly tumbled to the ground at the power that coursed through the land. Then, just as quickly as the surge began, it subsided to a soft glow. I leaned forward with bated breath, straining my eyes to get a better view as the Lord of Lords leaned forward in His Spirit form and breathed the breath of life into His creation's nostrils.

At that moment, the man became a living being.[3]

I heard a gasp, a sharp intake of breath as the living being filled its lungs for the very first time. As if this sound were a signal to Their departure, the Spirit and the Son vanished from sight.

The man's chest expanded as the breath of life continued to fill his lungs, giving vitality to his body. Slowly, he opened his eyes and looked upward to gaze upon his Maker. A smile crept across his face. I had seen that smile before. It was the same smile that had been directed toward me time and time again by the mighty King Himself. This man looked just like his Creator, like the Son of God.

Radiant and ruddy, how handsome the man was. His head was like purest gold, a warm and beautiful complexion, framed by his wavy hair, black as a raven. His eyes were like doves by the water streams, washed in milk, mounted like jewels upon his striking face. His cheeks were flushed like beds of spice yielding perfume and his lips soft like lilies dripping with myrrh. His arms were sturdy like rods of gold set with topaz, and his body like polished ivory decorated with lapis lazuli. His brawny legs were pillars of marble set on bases of pure gold.[4]

The Lord extended His hand to the man and helped him to his feet.

"You shall be called, Adam," the Lord said to His creation.

The man peered back at his Maker, recognizing something within the Lord that resonated within him, something familiar, something that resided in the Lord was also within this man.

"And You are my Creator and my King, my Father," Adam replied. "I will worship and adore you all the days of my life."

The Lord smiled warmly back at Adam, for He loved the man as Himself.

{~}

There in the Garden of Eden, the King placed the man He had formed to work the land and take care of it. Out of the ground in the garden, the Lord God made all kinds of trees grow. Trees that were pleasing to the eye and good for food for the man.[5]

In addition to caring for the Garden of Eden, the Lord also gave the man, Adam, the task of naming every living creature the King had created. The Lord God Himself had formed all the wild animals and all the birds in the sky, but He brought them before Adam to see what he would name them. The Lord delighted in watching the man, for He loved to witness his expression as each creature went before Him, more unique and beautiful than the one before. The man was just as in awe as I had been when I watched my God create these beings.[6]

As the man gave names to all the livestock, the birds in the sky, and all the wild animals, My Lord and I stood near Adam and listened as he imparted names to each one. Whatever the man called each living creature, that was its name. The Lord and I laughed and smiled at the titles the man gave the animals. We overflowed with joy at the parade of His creations.[7]

As the procession of animals continued, Adam's smile began to fade. His face no longer matched the King's expression of happiness. Adam was full of an emotion I had never seen before. His eyes were dark, and his shoulders slumped forward. He appeared to have the weight of the world on his back. I watched my King's smile slowly disappear as He realized the lack of joy in His creation.

The Lord God said to me, "Michael, it is not good for the man to be alone. I will make a helper suitable for him. I have brought My creation before him, but there is no helper fitted for him. Look Michael, He is lonely and sad. This is not good."[8]

The mighty King approached the man and laid a gentle hand on Adam's shoulder. It was only then that the man looked up. He peered up into the eyes of his Creator and, for the first time in hours, smiled. It was as if Adam already knew the King's plan. He seemed to sense that the Master was about to make things right for the man and provide for his deepest longing, love and companionship.

The Lord God raised His other hand, and slowly and softly He covered the man's eyes, causing him to fall into a deep sleep. Gradually, the Lord moved His hand from Adam's shoulder and placed it on his back, supporting the weight of the man's body as He lowered him to the ground. I watched my Master kneel beside His creation and place His strong hands on the man's abdomen. The Lord let His hands rest there for a moment. They moved up and down with the rising and falling of the man's chest as the breath of life coursed through him.

I shifted on my feet and wondered if I should respectfully step away or avert my eyes from the scene that was about to take place. The Lord noticed my apprehension and reassured me by saying, "Michael, do not be afraid. I am about to do something good."

An overwhelming sense of peace swept over me, and I remained loyally by His side as the Lord created a helper for Adam.

While the man was still sleeping, the great Creator pierced Adam's side and removed one of his ribs. Water spilled out from the opening. It was the very life-water the Lord had poured into Adam when He created him. Now the man was giving up His own life-water for His soon-to-be bride. The water fell to the ground and landed in the dust, the very same dust the King used to create the man. While the man's eyes were still closed, the King took Adam's rib and placed it gently beside him on the ground. He used the life-water from the man that mixed with the dust and gently began molding and shaping it until it became a soft and pliable clay.

My Master split the clay-like substance in two. One half He lay on top of the rib and the other He laid on top of Adam's pierced side. God placed His hands on top of the substance and at the same time whispered something over Adam. With His spoken word, the substance changed beneath His hands. It became flesh. The Lord spoke, and His words became flesh.

At this moment, the King's form began to illuminate even brighter than before. The diamond white light grew in intensity and warmth; it pierced straight through my core. As the light reached its surging point, the Lord kept one hand on Adam's side while placing His other hand on the rib. The King's voice boomed through the garden, "I am the Light of the world.

Whoever follows me will never walk in darkness, but will have the light of life!" With these words, the light grew to a greatness of unknown power. Lightning flashed and the rumblings of thunder shook the ground where I was standing. I could no longer see anything but pure white filling the land. The symphony that all creation sang subsided, and a hush fell over the earth. Then, just as abruptly, the brilliance diminished. The song of the earth began again, and the Lord's creation continued on as if nothing unusual had taken place.[9]

I regained my sight and the Lord's light dimmed to a faint glow. I looked to where He was kneeling beside the man. There, next to Adam, lay a second figure.

How beautiful she was. Her eyes were like doves, soft and gentle, and her skin the color of the dust from which she was taken. She was lovely like a lily of the valley, and her long, dark hair tumbled from her shoulders as if it were descending from the hills. Her lips were a scarlet ribbon curled upon her lovely face, and her voice? Oh how sweet! Her graceful legs were jewels, the work of an artist's hands. She was altogether beautiful. There was no flaw in her.[10]

Upon finishing His handiwork, the Lord God woke the man and revealed the beauty beside him. This creation was to be the man's helper. Adam sat up and rubbed his eyes to gaze upon the lovely figure lying next to him. He reached out and touched her. At the soft contact of Adam's hand, the beautiful being's eyes fluttered and then slowly opened. The man extended his hand and lifted her to her feet.

Adam spoke, "This is now bone of my bones and flesh of my flesh. She shall be called 'woman,' for she was taken out of man. You have stolen my heart, my bride. You have stolen my heart with one glance of your eyes. How delightful is your love!"[11]

The man was beaming with joy. At last a helper had been found for him. The Lord God smiled at them both, and Adam embraced the woman as the Lord stood beside them. He placed one hand on each of their shoulders.

And God said, "This is why a man will leave his father and mother and be united to his wife, and they will become one flesh. The wife will submit in love to her own husband as to the Lord God, and in this same way, the husband will love his wife as his own body, for she is your body. For I, the Lord God, made a woman from the rib I have taken out of the man. He who loves his wife loves himself. You will love her as yourself because that is how I have loved you."[12]

God continued to bless them and said to them, "Be fruitful and increase in number. Fill the earth, subdue it and have dominion over it. Rule over the fish in the sea and the birds in the sky and over every living creature that moves on the ground. I give you every seed-bearing plant on the face of the whole earth and every tree that has fruit with seed in it. They will be yours for food. And to all the beasts of the earth and all the birds in the sky and all the creatures that move along the ground, everything that has the breath of life in it, I give every green plant for food."[13]

The King then removed His hands from their shoulders and completed His blessing upon them. Adam pulled away from his wife and held her at arm's length. He smiled at her beauty and looked deep into her eyes.

"You shall be called Eve," Adam said to her, "for you have life in you, and from you, life will be passed down. You will be the mother of the living."

Adam and his wife were both naked, but they felt no shame.[14]

As the man embraced the woman again, I turned to look at my King. He was smiling broadly, and His eyes crinkled in the corners from the joy that filled the garden.

The Almighty Creator turned to me and said, "Michael, I told you once before, and I will say it again. One day, you will know in full what you now know only in part. There are only three things that remain, Michael: faith, hope, and love. And the greatest of these is love. And this, Michael, is love, that a man lay down and give His own life that another may have life."[15]

The great King placed His mighty hand on my shoulder and led me out of the garden where the man and the woman would live. With one final glance, the Lord peered back over His shoulder and saw what He had created: mankind in His own image, in the image of God He created them; male and female He created them. He turned back to me and pulled me a little closer in a one arm embrace as we made our way out of the garden.[16]

"Michael, this is very good."

And there was evening, and there was morning, the sixth day.[17]

{Chapter 3}

THUS THE HEAVENS and the earth were completed in all their vast array. By the seventh day, God had finished the work He had been doing, so on the seventh day He rested. Then God blessed the seventh day and made it holy, for on it He rested from all the work of creating that He had done.[1]

{Chapter 4}

Lucifer's head was spinning. He slipped in and out of consciousness as memories of his downfall drifted through his mind, haunting him like a bad dream.

Thunder shook the Mountain of God and lightning pierced the sky. The very heavens seemed to revolt at the atrocity taking place. Clouds rolled in and darkened the land as the warriors of God filled the air, their sheer numbers blanketing the sky in strength and power. The sound of their beating wings shook the mountain in an upheaval of the peace that once filled the land.

War broke out in Heaven, and the great army of the Lord, led by the Archangel warrior Michael, fought against Lucifer and his fallen angels. The corrupted guardian cherub and his followers wrestled back, but they were not strong enough against the power of the Almighty God. Lucifer was furious!

The armor of the Lord surrounded His mighty warriors and strengthened them as they drove Lucifer and the other dishonored angels from Heaven. They were no match for the Sword of the Spirit, the very Word of God that once filled Lucifer with great wisdom. Now he was full of violence. His heart had become proud, and he corrupted his wisdom because of his splendor. That very day, he and his angels lost their place in Heaven.[1]

Michael delivered the final blow, thrusting forward with the Sword of the Spirit to pierce through the heart of Lucifer as the Lord's army lifted their voices in a piercing battle cry. All became still.

Then the Lord spoke. His words rang out as He poured out a curse on Lucifer. A burning fire overtook him and consumed the fallen one, reducing him to ashes on the ground in the sight of all who were watching.

Because of his envy and selfish ambition, all wisdom he once knew was confused with the knowledge of evil. The truth was far from him, and he no longer knew reality from deception. Now he was Satan.

Satan was cast from Heaven and fell from the Mountain of God like a star falling from the sky to the earth. He was given the key to the shaft of the Abyss, and when he fell, smoke rose from it like smoke from a gigantic furnace. He was brought down to the realm of the dead, to the depths of the pit, and the sun and sky went black.[2]

Thunder shook the land and lightning blinded the sky as the shrill cries of Satan and his demon warriors pierced through the thick air. It was the most horrific sound to ever be heard, a sound so sinister and vile it could only be the howling of evil itself.

The Lord God hurled Satan and his army out of Heaven and into the depths below. As the final cry faded, a chill swept over the Mountain of God, a sensation never experienced by any of the heavenly hosts.

The chill brought with it a silence so thick, they could reach out and touch it. Then, all went black and darkness enveloped the land.

The last thing Satan remembered before fading into a state of darkness was the Lord's voice echoing in his head.

"You have come to a horrible end. All your pomp has been brought down to the grave, along with the noise of your harps. Maggots are spread out beneath you, and worms will cover you. You will be brought down to the realm of the dead, to the depths of the pit."[3]

{~}

When Satan woke from a state of unconsciousness, he found himself on the shore of the sea that the Lord had created. Rage filled him as he came-to and started to recall the events that had taken place on the Mountain of God. Satan cursed the Lord under his breath.

As he began stomping his way across the sandy shore, Satan realized his surroundings were very different from what he last remembered, the violent battle between his own followers and the Lord's army. Satan clenched his jaw at the thought of his downfall.

What was this place anyway? It was sickeningly beautiful, like the Heaven he remembered. *I don't want to remember that place.* Satan fumed, his fury nearing its boiling point. He had never felt anger and hatred so strongly.

That was when he saw it. Satan's body stiffened as he caught a glimpse across the shore. Two figures were walking through the thick, lush garden that was hedged by the pristine coastline. They were mere yards from where Satan was standing. His mouth fell agape, and his eyes widened at the vision before him. Satan wasn't sure what, or whom he was looking at, but he swore he had seen these creatures before. It was from his dream. *Or was it a dream?* Satan couldn't tell. The vision seemed so real, *so foreboding.*

Sometime after being cast into the fiery furnace of the Abyss, Satan had a vision.

A great sign had appeared in Heaven: a woman clothed with the sun, the moon under her feet, and a crown of twelve stars on her head. She was pregnant and cried out in pain, for she was about to give birth.

Then another sign appeared in Heaven: an enormous red dragon with seven heads, ten horns, and seven crowns on its heads. Its tail swept a third of the stars out of the sky and flung them to the earth. Then the dragon stood in front of the woman who was about to give birth so that it might devour her child the moment He was born. She gave birth to a son, a male child, who would rule all the nations with an iron scepter. Her child was snatched up to God and to His throne, and the woman fled into the wilderness to a place prepared for her by God, where she might be taken care of.[4]

Satan burned with fire and anger as he mulled over the dredged up visions in his mind. He now realized their meaning: the Lord had a child, a Son. All of it made sense now: this place, all the creations, and this despicable beauty. Here the Lord was creating a Kingdom for His heir, a Kingdom for His Son.

A Kingdom that should be mine, Satan fumed.

"Demons!" Satan barked at his minions.

They were hiding in the shadows, terrified of the light of the Lord that exposed them. They shivered and cowered as they crawled from their hiding places.

"We'll see about this so called Kingdom the Lord is creating for His Son. We all know that the Lord's inheritance is rightfully mine. After all, I was once his lovely creation, His elite guardian cherub until he banished me!" Satan sneered and touched his hand to his now mangled face.

"I should be the one receiving all the glory! I will make His creation worship me as you have. I will steal away the Lord's honor and take it for myself!"

Satan pounded his fist into his open palm and glared back across the shore toward the garden. He shook his head in disgust. *They look just like Him.*

The sound of the waves crashing rhythmically behind him brought Satan's attention back to the mission at hand. He turned back toward his wretched demon followers and began to scheme how he would corrupt the Lord's Kingdom by destroying His heir.

{Chapter 5}

IN THE BEGINNING, the man and the woman spent most of their days working and tending to the land in the Garden of Eden. They delighted in taking care of God's great creation.

They looked after the creatures the Lord had made and cared for all the beautiful plants that grew in the garden.

Daily they went out into Eden to harvest fruit from the seed-bearing plants that the King had provided for their food. At the rising of the sun, Adam and Eve gathered only enough for that day, and each morning, they went out for more. They never worried what they would eat, for the Lord always provided for them, just as He did with the birds of the air. They had no store room or barns, yet God fed them, for how much more valuable were the man and the woman than the birds.[1]

They never worried about their bodies or what they would wear, for they were naked and unashamed. Their figures were lovely and created in the image of God Himself. They were altogether lovely just as the Lord created them. The Lord made them unclothed and beautiful because the King does not look at things such as outward appearance. The Lord looked at their hearts.[2]

When they were not working in the garden, Adam and Eve journeyed out to the farthest corners of Eden and even beyond the garden walls to discover the mighty works of the Lord's hand. They loved to explore the land their Creator had made, and they never ceased to be amazed at the grand displays before them.

On the sixth day of every week, Adam and Eve gathered enough food for two days, for on the seventh day, the man and the woman rested. The Lord God had blessed the seventh day and made it holy because on it, He rested from all the work of creating that He had done.[3]

On the seventh day of every week, Adam and Eve spent their time in the Garden of Eden. It was on this day, the Sabbath, that the Lord went to the garden to spend the day resting with His beautiful, created ones. I would often go with my Master to the garden on these days, for wherever my Master went, there I wanted to be also.

On the Sabbath, the great King rested with the man and the woman, sitting in their presence, laughing and conversing with them. They would lie back and watch the birds of the air dance through the pale blue sky or refresh their feet in the cool tides of the seashore. Their Maker watched the man and woman as they slept under the mid-day sun, the breeze moving along their bare skin while the afternoon dew clung to their eyelashes. The drops glimmered with the fluttering of their eyes as they dreamed of the Lord's great wonders.

I embraced these days, for they reminded me of the days of old when I worshiped my King on the Mountain of God. It was strange that I did not long for that place. It was the land I called home for so long, but I soon realized that home was where my King was. As long as I was in the presence of His Majesty, I was at home. Now the Lord was here on the earth. He came to the earth to dwell among men, to live in unity with His created ones whom He loved as Himself.[4]

I never ceased to marvel at the King's creation. This was the royal Kingdom He was building for His Son Who was coming to reign over all the earth. This Kingdom was to be His inheritance. All of God's creation was to be passed down to His Son, the great Prince of Peace.

The man and woman were created by the Lord to have dominion over the earth and to build it up into a mighty Kingdom for the King's Son. They were made in the image of God, out of love, to reflect that love in relationship with God the Father, the Spirit, and the Son. The Son would love and adore the created ones, just as His Father loved Him, by lavishing on them gifts of untold treasure. For no eye has seen, no ear has heard, and no human mind can conceive the things the Lord God has prepared for His created ones who love and adore Him.[5]

Adam and Eve remained in the King's love by obeying His every command. This obedience brought great joy to the man and the woman, for the Lord's yoke is easy and His burden is light. The man and woman loved to serve the Great King, and there was never a reason not to. Adam and Eve loved the Lord with all their hearts, with all their souls, with all their minds, and with all their strength. Tending to the Garden of Eden was their part of honoring the King and, in turn, His Son, the Prince. They were stewards of the Lord's creation. Adam and Eve were preparing the Kingdom for the Son.[6]

Not only had the King commanded Adam and Eve to subdue the earth and rule over the fish in the sea and the birds in the sky and over every living creature that moves on the ground, but also, He blessed them saying, "Be fruitful and increase in number and fill the earth." The man and the woman honored the Lord with their bodies, and the woman was with child.[7]

This mystery was yet another astonishing work of the King that I anticipated. Through love, life would be birthed. It was just as Adam had said to his wife on the day she was taken out of him.

"You shall be called Eve. For you have life in you, and from you, life will be passed down. You will be the mother of the living."

{~}

Taking daily walks throughout the land with the Lord had become a custom I anticipated each day. Of all the time I have been with the Lord, not a day has gone by when I did not have the pleasure of walking side by side with my Master.

On this particular day, the Lord and I were strolling through the Garden of Eden, just as we had time and time again, for He loved to watch His created ones enjoying the life He had given them. It was another remarkable day, created by the hand of the Lord. The birds of the air were singing their creation song, the waves of the nearby shore kept a steady beat, and all the other animals of the land sang along in their own unique and mysterious voices. The honey-colored rays from the sun warmed the earth and caused a thick mist to veil the ground in a lace-like curtain. It parted as we walked through, dancing around the King's legs.

On this particular day, I knew that Adam and Eve were off exploring the vast earth the Lord had created, so I was unsure as to why we had traveled to the garden. Adam and Eve could spend an eternity discovering the earth's beauty, never once tiring of the glory that filled the land, for the King's earth was infinite and so full of wonder. The Lord was not expecting them back until dusk.

My King and I began to make our way through the inner garden, and as we traveled along the path, I noticed a sense of apprehension from my King. I stayed close to His side, vowing to stand and fight for the Lord's honor and glory, just as I had done on the Mountain of God when evil was discovered in the realm of Heaven.

Finally, we neared the center of the Garden of Eden, the very place where God the Trinity breathed life into the man. My King stopped and stood silently as if He were waiting. Unsure of what to do, I peered around the garden, searching for any explanation for my Lord's uneasiness.

I had just finished scanning our surroundings and was about to turn back to my Master when I heard it, a strange noise. It was nothing I had heard before. The sound did not come from one of the animals or beasts of the earth. It was different. An odd emotion began to pulse through my being. I felt cold, and the tiny hairs stood up on the back of my neck. *What creature could have made such a sound?* I turned to my King with a quizzical look and watched as His once jovial appearance faded.

"What is it, my King?"

The Lord held up a halting hand, signaling my silence, and slowly turned to stare off into the thick of the garden.

"Come forward, Satan!" the King's voice bellowed and thundered through the garden, sending chills up my spine.

You see, the Lord is the God of love, but He is also a God of wrath. I was reminded in this moment how the King expelled Lucifer and won the battle over him. It was this thought alone that brought me comfort as I witnessed the most horrific-looking creature I had ever seen. It crept forward out of the garden foliage.

In stark contrast to his former self, the now mangled and disfigured Satan stood there in the midst of the Holy of Holies and all His splendid creation. I gasped at Satan's appearance, for it bore no resemblance to the handsome guardian cherub he once was.

"Where have you come from, Satan?"[8]

Satan crossed his arms over his chest. "From roaming throughout the earth, going back and forth on it."[9]

The King stared Satan in the eyes, His wrath boring through to the demon's core, yet the Lord remained steadfast and composed before the enemy.

"Did you not learn your lesson, Satan? I am the King of Kings and the Lord of Lords. All honor and praise and glory belong to Me. You cannot overturn the power of the Lord, so what do you want, Satan? Why do you approach Me now in the center of all My created glory?"

I was surprised at the question the King directed toward this hideous creature, for the Lord God knows all things. Nothing in all creation is hidden from His sight. He is all knowing and all powerful. He knew Satan's words before he even spoke them. It seemed God was asking more for the benefit of Satan than for Himself.[10]

"I have come to make a deal with you," Satan sneered.

I cringed at his tone and demeanor toward the King of the universe. This monster had no respect at all toward the Lord God.

"A deal?" The Lord repeated. "Who are you to proposition the Lord of all creation?"

"What's the matter?" Satan jeered, "Don't you think you can win against me again? Or do you fear me now that I have been condemned to the realm of the Abyss and have taken one third of your warrior angels with me?"

I drew my flaming Sword of the Spirit and posed, ready to strike down this disgrace before me.

"Put your sword away, Michael." The Lord spoke boldly as He held up a commanding hand, "Satan is no match for My power, the divine authority of the Lord God." He turned back to the beast and said, "Very well, then, what is your offer?"[11]

An evil grin spread across Satan's face, and he rubbed his gnarled hands together in some sort of sick delight. "Do Your created ones worship You for nothing?" Satan asked. "Have you not put a hedge around them and blessed the work of their hands? But tempt them with something that is evil, something that is not good, and surely they will fall." [12]

"I, the Lord God, cannot be tempted by your evil, Satan, nor do I tempt anyone. Do not put the Lord God to the test."[13]

The King turned abruptly and began to walk away, but Satan was not finished. Suddenly he shouted, "Then let me tempt them! I bet I can lure them to disobey your commands. When the desire for evil gets ahold of them, they will be enticed and lured away. Then their souls will belong to me! Death will be sent against them, and they will be separated from You for all eternity."

The Lord stopped in His tracks. He glanced over at me and then slowly turned to stare evil in the face. The King looked upon Satan with disgust and bewilderment. Who did this monster think he was? Then the Lord spoke the most powerful words I have ever heard.

"Do you not know, Satan? Have you not heard? I, the Lord, am the everlasting God, the Creator of all the earth. I do not grow tired or weary, and My understanding no one can fathom. I Am the great I Am. I will be victorious over you, mark My words, Satan, this war is not over. Very well then, you may tempt the man and the woman, but on them you may not lay a finger. Away from Me, Satan!"[14]

Then Satan went out from the presence of the Lord.[15]

{~}

Now in the middle of the garden was a tree that the Lord God caused to grow up from the ground. It was a magnificent towering tree, full and vibrant, covered with lush greenery, succulent fruit, and beautiful branches that overshadowed the forest. It towered on high, its top above the thick foliage. The waters of the earth nourished the tree, deep springs made it grow tall. Their streams flowed all around its base and sent their channels to all the trees of the field, causing it to tower higher than all the other trees of the garden. Its limbs increased, and its branches grew long, spreading because of the abundant waters. All the birds of the sky nested in its boughs, all the animals of the wild gave birth under its branches, and all the creatures lived in its shade. With its spreading boughs, it was majestic in beauty. The cedars in the garden of God could not rival it, the boughs of the junipers could not equal its boughs, nor could the plain trees compare with its branches. No tree in the garden of God could match its beauty. The Lord made it beautiful, the envy of all the trees of Eden. This was the Tree of Life.[16]

Beside the Tree of Life was the tree that the Lord God had allowed Satan to grow, the tree of the knowledge of good and evil. It was a dark tree with gnarled branches, dying leaves, and rotting fruit; for anything that does not come from God is not good. Anything not from God is evil. Satan, however, is crafty and is the master of disguise, for his wisdom is confused with the knowledge of evil. Even he believes his own lies. So Satan took on the form of a serpent and hid among the branches of the tree of the knowledge of good and evil. He waited in silence for the man and the woman, waiting for his moment to strike.

{~}

As dusk was approaching, the man and the woman returned to the garden from their adventures of the day. Their skin glowed from the kisses of the sun, and expressions of pure joy danced across their faces. The man, Adam, held tightly to his wife's hand as he led her back to the inner garden to their home.

The Lord and I were waiting for them. It was such a blissful moment to have them back. I could feel my heart grow with happiness. They looked so beautiful. I never failed to marvel at their resemblance to the Creator. And Eve, she looked so radiant, her stomach already beginning to swell with the life growing inside her. I turned to my King to witness His own joy, but something was different.

He had a smile upon His mouth, but His eyes reminded me of Adam's on the day he was created, before the Lord gave him Eve. It was sadness. The Lord's eyes did not sparkle as they usually did, the way they had before the earlier encounter in the Garden of Eden.

"Come, My children," the King said to them, "and let us dine together by the shore of the sea."

The Lord led them each by the hand to the edge of the Garden of Eden to the place where the sea met the land. The Lord had been to the shore earlier in the day and carried with Him choice fruits from the various trees of the garden. He had gone and prepared a place for them to sit and eat together, a place where they could watch the sunset over the waters and take in the night's display as the moon and stars rose to their rightful place in the sky.

I followed at a distance, not wanting to interfere on this intimate moment. When they finally reached the shore, I stopped at the edge of the forest and stood guard.

"Please sit, My created ones, and let us eat." My Master gestured for Adam and Eve to take their places along the sandy shore.

So the Lord dined with Adam and Eve on the seashore, and I listened as they laughed and talked about the great wonders they had witnessed that day. Adam and Eve were so full of excitement and love for the Lord. They were awestruck by the work of His hands.

I listened as Adam described in detail the majestic mountains. I watched Eve's face light up as she told the Lord of the flowers she had gazed upon. She spoke of their colors, their fragrance, and their beauty.

I listened to the Lord's responses to His dear created ones. He reacted with just as much enthusiasm and surprise as the man and the woman did when they told their stories. The Lord's joy matched the man and the woman's so closely, I thought the Creator of the universe Himself had never gazed upon such wonders.

As my King smiled at His children, I noticed the sadness that filled His eyes. Something was troubling Him, and it cut to my heart to see His sorrow.

The meal came to an end, and as the sunset faded to deeper reds and purples, the King lowered His voice a little, changing the tone of their conversation.

"Adam and Eve, do you know that you are free to eat from any tree in the garden?" the Lord softly asked the question.

"Yes, my Lord." Adam answered. "You said on the day You created us, 'I give you every seed-bearing plant on the face of the whole earth and every tree that has fruit with seed in it. They will be yours for food.'"[17]

The Lord smiled at the man, "Yes, Adam. You remember; this is good, but today I tell you, My created ones, you must not eat from the tree of the knowledge of good and evil, for when you eat from it, you will certainly die. Death will be sent against you. Watch and pray so that you will not fall into temptation. The spirit is willing, but the body is weak."[18]

"Death?" Eve leaned forward as she spoke up. "My King, what is death?"

The Lord looked down, and sorrow filled His face.

"My sweet Eve, death is separation from Me, your Lord and King. It means we will never be together again."

Adam and Eve looked to each other and then back to their maker. Their faces fell, and the elation they had, just moments before, disappeared. They were so much like Him. They even experienced His sadness.

Before they could utter a word, the King looked to Adam and said, "Adam, My created one, whom I love as Myself, do you love Me?"

"Yes, my Lord," Adam replied with conviction, "You know that I love You."

The King replied, "Obey My commands."

The Lord then turned to Eve and spoke. "Eve, My sweet daughter, do you love Me?"

"Yes, my King," Eve leaned in closer, "You know that I love You."

"Obey My commands."

The third time the Lord said to them both, "My precious created ones, created in My Own image, do you love Me?"

Both Adam and Eve looked hurt because the Lord asked them a third time, "Do you love me?" Adam reached over and took the hand of His wife and leaned in closer to the Lord. He placed a hand on his Maker's shoulder as he spoke for the both of them.

"My Lord, You know all things. You know that we love You."[19]

As Adam's words faded into the night, a soft, sad smile appeared on the King's lips. The sun dipped below the horizon, the last colors fading from the day as the Lord said, "Obey My commands."

{Chapter 6}

ON THE DAY BEFORE the Sabbath, my King and I began making our journey to the Garden of Eden to spend the seventh day resting and delighting in the Lord's created ones. I had expected this day to be just like all the others, joy-filled and lovely, a celebration of life and of all the Creator's majestic handiwork.

All creation sang out to Him as we made our journey across the land and through the forest that led to the garden. I embraced every moment, looking all around me as we traveled, admiring the wonderful displays of the Lord.

The sun was rising now, and the dew-covered leaves sparkled with the radiance of the new day. The morning sunrise was magnificent; it seemed as though the sky itself had noticed the King walking below it and, therefore, danced and swirled with a song of color. It was the sky's own way of bestowing honor and praise on the One Who created it. It was in these moments when the Lord lit up the sky, that I felt closest to Him. I basked in the glory of the King. His very presence warmed my soul and caused my face to glow with pure elation.

I was so overwhelmed with the wonderment of all creation that at first I did not recognize the preoccupied look on my Master's face. His lips were smiling like mine, expressing the joy of our walk together, but His eyes seemed far away.

Normally during our walks, the King would describe to me in great detail the plans He was making for the Kingdom He was preparing for His Son. He would tell me of the great wonders that were yet to come and of things my own humble mind could not even begin to conceive. But today was different, and the King and I walked in silence as we made our way to the Garden of Eden to see the created ones.

I knew full well that the mind of the God Who created the universe would be concerned with matters I couldn't even imagine. I could not begin to comprehend His understanding and omniscience. I realized the Lord would be consumed with other matters from time to time, but still, I was certain my King's mind would be revived when He was able to rest and delight in the ones He loved.

I did not offer up any words to my King, but rather allowed the silence to remain between us as we continued making our way to the Garden of Eden, walking side by side, Master and servant.

{~}

Meanwhile, in the Garden of Eden, Adam and Eve were just waking up to the same beautiful sunrise the King and I had witnessed as we journeyed toward them. They both sat up from their restful night and began making preparations for the day. That morning, Eve was to go out into the garden to collect fruit from the seed bearing plants, enough for two days, for the following day was the Sabbath. Adam stayed back to tend the garden and animals.

As she made her way to the center of the Garden of Eden, Eve collected fruits of various shapes and sizes. There was so much variety for food! The Lord provided far beyond the needs of the man and the woman, for He loved them as Himself and longed to lavish them with gifts of His love.

The fruits were brilliantly colored, plump, and ripe, bursting forth from the vine with all the colors of the morning sunrise. They practically begged to be picked and savored. There were those with soft edible flesh and others that required peeling to reach the mouth-watering juices on the inside. Each fruit burst in the man's and woman's mouths with variations of sweet and tart while the deliciousness of the Lord's variety dripped down their chins. They could never tire of the bounty the Lord God provided.

Sweet floral aromas welcomed Eve when she finally reached the center of the garden. She continued along, selecting choice fruits for herself and her husband, each time plucking a piece of fruit from one of the many surrounding trees and placing it in her cupped arms. She created a makeshift basket supported by her protruding abdomen. Eve felt the life moving inside her pressing hard against her arm as she continued strolling through the dense foliage. The idea that life was to be brought forth through her brought inexpressible joy to Eve. She was delighted at the grand role she had been given as a part of the Lord's Kingdom.

The soft melody of the bubbling springs accompanied by the tune of the birds, lulled Eve into a sweet daydream of the coming Kingdom and Prince, the Lord's Son, Who would one day reign.

It wasn't until a plump, citrus-colored fruit entered her field of vision that Eve was shaken from her thoughts. It looked so delicious. Rising up on tiptoes, Eve felt the muscles in her calves tighten as she stretched to grasp it. She desperately strained to lengthen her fingers, trying to close the small gap between her and the fruit. Eve's fingertips brushed its fuzzy skin right as her balance failed her. As she stumbled to regain composure, one of the pieces of fruit that was cupped against her stomach tumbled and landed with a soft thud. It rolled slightly, just before stopping at her feet.

Eve stooped to pick it up, but right as her fingers reached the small piece of fruit, there was a rustling above her head. Eve jumped back with a start and peered up into the tree above to see what kind of creature had startled her.

There hanging from the branch was a serpent.

It was not like any of the serpents Eve had seen before. It had the same slender body like the other serpents, but this one's colors were strange. It had ten horns on its body, starting on its head and traveling down to the tail. Its face was wide like a viper, but it had a mane of spikes like a lion surrounding its head. Its eyes, dark as night, bore straight through the woman. They were captivating.

Now the serpent was more crafty than any of the wild animals the Lord God had made, and he used his deception to change the appearance of the tree of the knowledge of good and evil. Of course, he could not change the tree literally, for Satan does not hold that kind of power, but he used his words to change the way the woman saw the tree.[1]

"Hello there, Eve," the serpent hissed as his long body uncoiled and moved closer to the woman's face. "Look at this tree I have found. It has beautiful branches that overshadow the forest, it towers on high, and its top above the thick foliage is even higher than the Tree of Life!" The serpent was feeding lies to the woman, pouring them out thick and syrupy like honey. He knew what he spoke was not true. The serpent would stoop to any level in an attempt to persuade her that he offered something better than the tree God provided, even if that meant making something evil appear to be from God. "Look!" He continued. "The waters nourish it, and deep springs make it grow tall. Their streams flow all around its base and send their channels to all the trees of the field. You see, this is why it towers higher than all the trees of the garden!"[2]

Eve's eyes widened as she listened to the words of the entrancing creature dangling from the branch in front of her. As she soaked up the lies of the convincing serpent, the tree's appearance began to morph before her very eyes.

The serpent said to the woman, "Tell me, Eve, did God really say, 'You must not eat from any tree in the garden'?"[3]

His tail curled tighter around the branch, as he confused the words of the King, just as his wisdom was confused when he was cast from the Mountain of God. Cocking her head to the side, the woman took in the serpent's words.

Finally, she replied, "We may eat fruit from the trees in the garden, but God did say, 'You must not eat fruit from the tree that is in the middle of the garden, and you must not touch it, or you will die.'"[4]

The serpent snickered at the woman's response, for he knew those were not the words the Lord had spoken to His created ones. Eve was already buying into the lies he was feeding her.

A sickeningly, delightful smirk spread across the serpent's face. "You will not surely die," the serpent lied to the woman, "for God knows that when you eat from this tree, your eyes will be opened, and you will be like God, knowing good and evil!"[5]

Eve stared back at the cunning creature before her, her eyes searching those of the serpent. Eve knew her King had commanded her not to eat from the tree that was now towering ominously before her. The Lord had specifically told her and her husband they would die if they ate of its fruit. Their

Creator said three times to obey His commands, yet still... Eve peered upward into the boughs of the tree, shielding her eyes slightly from the blinding sun above.

Eve pondered the words of the serpent. Maybe God was holding back from her and Adam. Maybe this tree offered something that God was trying to keep from them. Did He not want Adam and Eve to experience the knowledge of good and evil? *What is evil?* she wondered. The serpent's lie about God's character began to take root. *Is God not Who He says He is?* Eve's eye twitched ever so slightly as the thought crossed her mind that maybe, just maybe, God was trying to keep something wonderful from them.

She was still wrestling with this idea when a familiar voice from behind broke into her thoughts.

"Eve, there you are." Adam's voice came from behind her. "I just finished tending to the garden and the animals. I've been searching everywhere for you. What are you doing in the middle of the garden?"

Adam approached his wife shrouded in the darkened shadows cast by the dying tree. "Eve, this is the tree from which the Lord commanded us not to eat. Remember, He told us to obey His commands."

Eve fidgeted nervously, "Yes Adam, but look!" She gestured upward at the gnarled and perishing tree before her, but to Eve the tree was beginning to look more and more appealing as she considered the deceptive words of the serpent.

"The serpent has shown me this tree, Adam. Don't you see it? The serpent has told me that it has beautiful branches that overshadow the forest. It towers on high, and its top above the thick foliage is even higher than the Tree of Life! The waters nourish it, Adam, deep springs make it grow tall. Their streams flow all around its base and send their channels to all the trees of the field. This is why it towers higher than all the trees of the garden!"⁶

The serpent nearly fell from the tree with excitement. She believed every word he was saying.

Adam again glanced upward at the tree, scrutinizing it carefully.

"Eve, please, come back with me. The King, our own Creator, told us not to eat from the tree of the knowledge of good and evil, or we will certainly die. We would be separated from our Lord for all eternity. Please, Eve…" Adam tugged gently on his wife's arm.

"But, Adam," Eve pulled away, "we will not certainly die. The serpent told me that God knows when we eat from the tree, our eyes will be opened, and we will be like God, knowing good and evil."⁷

The serpent recognized the exact moment the wave of doubt washed over the man's face. Suddenly, he too began to question the words of his Maker. Seizing the opportunity, the serpent crept across the branches in the direction of Adam.

"Look closer!" he hissed. "Its limbs increase, and its branches grow long, spreading far because of abundant waters. All the birds of the sky nest in its boughs, all the animals of the wild give birth under its branches. All the creatures live in its shade. The cedars in the garden of God cannot rival it!" the serpent practically shouted.⁸

Adam glanced back at his wife who was smiling in agreement with the serpent. She stared back at her husband for confirmation, wondering if he now saw the tree as she did.

The serpent looked back and forth between the two, desperately trying to convince the man of his lies. He coiled backward as if ready to lash out and strike his prey. As the man turned back toward him, the serpent delivered his final blow, appealing to Adam's and Eve's human natures. The man and the woman were created in the image of God, but now the serpent was going to convince them otherwise and embed in them a desire to be like God in a way that they were never meant to be, the judge between good and evil. The serpent prepared to plant his own envy and selfish ambition into the man and the woman by convincing them of a lie, not only about God, but also about themselves.

"Look at its fruit; it's delicious and lovely!" The serpent lurched forward at the man. "You will not certainly die when you eat it, for it will give you power! You will become like God, knowing good and evil!"[9]

As the words left the serpent's mouth, the sound of all creation went quiet. Everything became still. Even the wind was silenced as the serpent's words echoed in the mind of the man and the woman.

Eve padded quietly over to where her husband was standing. She grabbed hold of his hand and looked up into his eyes, searching for a response, but none came. She stepped forward and strained upward, selecting a piece of fruit from the branch above. Adam watched closely, but no word of protest left his lips as he too began to desire the power of the tree before him.

Eve examined the fruit closely. When she saw it was good for food, pleasing to the eye, and also desirable for gaining wisdom, she brought it up to her parted lips and ate of it. She reached up with her forearm and wiped the dripping juice from her chin as she turned back toward Adam. Then she gave some of the fruit to her husband, who was standing there with her. And he ate it.[10]

Slowly they chewed the flesh of the fruit, which was surprisingly tough and gritty like sand. They waited for the smooth, sweet flavor to flood their tongue, as it did with all the other fruits of the garden. Instead, a sharp taste oozed from the fruit. It was a sensation like nothing they had experienced before. Bitter and rancid flavors poured into their mouth. It was a biting feeling, as if the serpent himself had lashed out to strike their tongues.

Instantly, the eyes of both of them were opened, and the man and woman realized they were naked. They were immediately ashamed because their own wisdom and knowledge of good that the Lord God had given them, was confused with the knowledge of evil. Suddenly they began to think it was wrong to be naked and turned from one another. They felt critical of their bodies and were embarrassed of how they must look to one another. Something that was once beautiful, the picture of perfection, was now corrupted by evil and lies that could never be true.

Adam's and Eve's minds were now like the serpent's. All wisdom, they once knew, was confused with the knowledge of evil. The truth was far from them, and they did not know reality from deception.[11]

Slowly they swallowed the fruit in their mouths and then began gathering fig leaves. They sewed them together and made coverings for themselves.[12]

{~}

How I longed to see the man and the woman. I had anticipated our reunion all morning as the Lord and I made our way to the Garden of Eden. We finally arrived in the early afternoon, while the sun was still high in the sky. It was such a spectacular day, just like every other day the Lord had created; it could not be more perfect. Yet, as I scanned the garden, the man and the woman were nowhere to be found. Every other time we had journeyed to the garden, Adam and Eve had been waiting and ready to greet us as we joined them for the Sabbath.

My mind raced to the only logical conclusion, "My King, maybe the man and the woman are out journeying across the land. Maybe they are out discovering your mighty wonders." My own mind began to drift to the far corners of the world, exploring the great and unsearchable mysteries of the King.

My Master glanced down at me and smiled that same sad smile, as if He knew what I suggested was not true.

After hesitating a moment, He finally tore His gaze from mine. "Yes, Michael. Perhaps they are."

{~}

In the cool of the day, the Lord decided to wander through the Garden of Eden in search of Adam and Eve. I fell in stride with Him, allowing Him to lead us to the center of the garden. The leaves and the branches rustled as we made our way through the thick foliage, and the birds sang joyfully, making known the presence of their Creator.

The man and his wife must have heard the sound of the Lord God approaching, for they hid among the trees from the King. While my Master never said that He knew where the man and the woman were hiding, I remembered His understanding of all things. The Lord God wanted the man and the woman to come to Him, but He never wanted to force them to love Him.

The King called out to the man, "Adam, where are you?"

There was no response, only the soft sound of the insects humming along to the tune of the birds. The Lord God called out again.

"Adam, My beloved, where are you?"

After a few more moments of only the sounds of the forest answering the Lord's call, Adam finally answered, "Here I am Lord, You called me?"[13]

Adam and his wife, Eve, revealed themselves from their hiding place among the thickly covered trees and now stood to face the Lord God. The tree of the knowledge of good and evil towered ominously behind them. The King's face turned downcast as He realized the man and the woman had covered themselves with fig leaves.

Recognizing the question in the King's stare, Adam timidly offered, "I heard you in the garden, and I was afraid because I was naked… so I hid."[14]

The Lord's voice was even and calm, but I sensed the emotion burning behind His eyes as He said to them, "Who told you that you were naked? Have you eaten from the tree that I commanded you not to eat from?"[15]

Adam, sensing the King's disapproval, succumbed to the encompassing nature of his sinful acts. "The woman you put here with me, she gave me some fruit from the tree, and I ate it."[16]

"What is this you have done?" The Lord directed the question to Eve who had been standing beside her husband with her eyes turned toward the ground.[17]

Her hair covered her face with shame as she meekly replied, "The serpent deceived me, and I ate."[18]

Hearing Eve's confession, the King's wrath burned inside Him. He stormed over to the tree of the knowledge of good and evil.

Throwing His hands upward toward the knotty, leafless branches of the tree, the Lord's voice boomed, "Show yourself, Satan!"

Slowly the serpent uncoiled itself from among the top branches and made its way down to the lower limbs, near where the King was standing.

The King pointed an accusing finger at the serpent and declared, "Because you have done this, cursed are you above all livestock and all wild animals! You will crawl on your belly and you will eat dust all the days of your life. I will put enmity between you and the woman and between your offspring and hers. He will crush your head, and you will strike his heel."[19]

At these words, the life inside Eve kicked, producing a piercing pain in her side.

The King turned sharply and walked back toward the man and the woman. They were both cowering with shame and humility before the King, for they knew they had sinned against the Lord. They did not keep His commands. When the Lord faced Eve, His appearance became solemn and sad at the realization of the impact her actions would have.

To the woman he said, "Because of this, I will make your pains in childbearing very severe. With painful labor you will give birth to children. Your desire will be for your husband, and he will rule over you."[20]

My Master then turned to Adam and said, "Because you listened to your wife and ate fruit from the tree about which I commanded you, 'you must not eat from it,' cursed is the ground because of you. Through painful toil, you will eat food from it all the days of your life. It will produce thorns and thistles for you, and you will eat the plants of the field. By the sweat of your brow, you will eat your food until you return to the ground, since from it you were taken; for dust you are and to dust you will return."[21]

The man and the woman both fell at the feet of the Lord. Desperation and anguish flooded their being as waves of guilt and sadness sank in, emotions that were never meant to be experienced by Adam and Eve. They had brought evil upon themselves.

The Lord God looked up from the man and the woman, and there in the thicket was a ram caught by its horns. My Master went over and loosed the ram. He took it and sacrificed it. The Lord slaughtered the ram in order to make garments of skin for Adam and his wife, to clothe them and provide for them.[22]

In that moment, for the very first time in history, blood was shed.

I was horrified at the sight as I watched the life-water pour from the animal's wounds and puddle on the ground in a deep crimson red, such a stark contrast to the thick, white wool that once covered the animal. Eve's small frame shuddered as she sobbed, clinging to her husband while the Lord continued to use the animal's hide to make coverings for them. The Lord provided for Adam and Eve as He always had. Even in their sin, the Lord provided.

The Lord completed the garments for the man and the woman as the sun was beginning to hang lower in the sky. The day was coming to an end. His face was downcast and despairing as He handed over the clothing to the man and the woman. The Lord watched as they donned the ram skins and wiped their wet eyes. Adam and Eve now realized the fullness of what they had done. They had broken their promise to keep their Maker's commands. It was no different than if they had said they did not love Him. The penalty of their sin was death, the ultimate separation from their Creator God.

As they finished dressing, the Lord turned to me and spoke softly, "The man has now become like one of us, knowing good and evil. He must not be allowed to reach out his hand and take also from the Tree of Life and eat and live forever."[23]

My mind started racing as I tried to understand what the King was saying. "My Lord, what will become of the man and the woman? What is going to happen to them?"

My Master slowly turned from Me to look upon the very creation that had rebelled against Him.

"You are banished, My created ones. You must leave now. You are expelled from Eden, and you will work the ground from which you have been taken. You may not live here any longer."

A small gasp escaped from Adam, and Eve buried her face on her husband's shoulder as she cried for what had been lost. Adam slowly wrapped a comforting arm around his wife and turned her to make their way out of the Garden of Eden.

With sad eyes, the Lord watched after them as they began making the long walk out of the garden.

Without turning His eyes from them, my King whispered, "Michael, I need you to call on one of the cherubim, one of your guardian warriors from My army. Have him placed on the east side of the Garden of Eden with his Sword of the Spirit. Tell him to flash his flaming sword back and forth to guard the way to the Tree of Life. They must not return."[24]

{~}

Just about the time evening was beginning to creep over the land, I made my return from assigning the guardian cherubim to his post. The stars were emerging from their hiding places and making their appearance in the dark blue twilight. To me, they did not shine as brightly as they had the night before. In fact, all of creation seemed solemn as a result of the day's events. Little did I know, the Lord's creation would never be the same again.

When I finally arrived back at the center of the garden, I found my Lord standing in the same place where I had left Him. He hadn't moved at all. I held back in the shadows, wondering what it was that held my Master's gaze so captive. I followed His eyes to the where He had them fixed. That's when I realized. He was watching the man and the woman. He had continued to watch them the entire time as they made their way to the garden entrance. Slowly and somberly they shuffled, never glancing back, too heartbroken at the curse they had brought upon themselves. They were nearly there.

Ever watchful, my Master stood there as Adam's and Eve's silhouettes shrank against the horizon. The sorrow on my King's face pierced through my heart like a sword. Never had I experienced such emotion, such pure, raw grief. I dropped my head and clutched my chest, wishing the hurt to stop. I couldn't even imagine the sadness that must be overwhelming my Lord, for they were His created ones, created in His own image, a piece of Him.

I longed to run to Him to console my Master in His grief. I took a cautious step, preparing to move forward from my hiding place among the shadows and into the flood of amber light that poured from the slowly descending sun, but something caught my attention from the corner of my eye. I hesitated.

Hovering forebodingly behind the King was the tree of the knowledge of good and evil, and dangling from one of its lower branches was the serpent. It began to make its way down. Silently I drew my sword and posed, ready to fight if he made one wrong move.

The serpent slithered along the ground and made its way to where the King was standing, announcing its presence by the scraping sound of its belly dragging along the ground. The Lord heard his approach, yet not once did He take His eyes off of His created ones, not even when the serpent reached the King's feet and rose up to stand in his demon form.

Satan stood beside the Lord and crossed his arms over his chest. He followed the gaze of my Master and stared over the horizon, straining his eyes to see the man and the woman in the distance. With arms still crossed over his puffed chest, Satan cocked his head, focusing his attention on the Lord standing beside him.

"I told you I could tempt them." Satan mocked with a devious grin. "I lured them to disobey your commands, and now they belong to me. Death has been sent against them, and they will surely be separated from You for all eternity." Satan chuckled to himself at the thought.

A long moment passed with only a silent response from the King. His eyes remained fixed on the fading vision of the man and the woman. Softly, He said, "I want them back."

The sound of evil rang through the garden as Satan's shrieking laughter erupted, "You cannot have them back," he spat, "They are mine now. The price to get them back would be too steep. You could never pay to get them back."

As if on cue, a suffocating silence enveloped the land, and for a split second my Master looked away from His beloveds to stare directly into the eyes of Satan.

"To be with them, I would do anything. No price is too steep for my created ones whom I love."

Satan's mind raced, mulling over the Lord's statement. *No price was too much?*

Suddenly, Satan's eyes widened at the realization of the depth of the King's words. He clasped his gnarled hands together in front of him and narrowed his beady eyes on the King.

"Name your price," the Lord declared, boring His eyes into the ugly beast.

"Your Son. The price to get them back is the cost of Your one and only Son."

My breath caught in my throat. I nearly choked at Satan's words.

Before I could advance, my King slowly turned back toward the entrance of the garden, catching the last glimpse of the man and the woman as they finally made their exit out of the Garden of Eden.

They were no longer in sight. They were gone.

For a brief moment, my Master continued to stare off into the distance at the place where Adam and Eve disappeared over the horizon. Then, without turning His eyes from the place where they vanished, the Lord declared in a deep voice, "Done."

With the Lord's spoken word, Satan disappeared, vanishing into the imposing night.

I stayed back in the shadows of the garden foliage, unsure of what else I could do, so I stood watch over my King as His guardian warrior. I would stay there all night.

Little did I know at the time, it was this very night that would set the course of history and the future. Since that moment, I have not once stepped down from my position. I have never left His side, not that night and not for all eternity. For it is the way it has been since the beginning, it has been my calling to serve my Master and King.

Night rushed in as an oppressive weight, stealing the last colors of the day. All hope seemed to fade from the sky. Just before the land was lost in complete blackness, I saw the final light of the day fall over my Master. It was the last thing I saw.

The Lord buried His face in His hands and wept.

Part II

Redemption

Approximately A.D. 33

{Chapter 7}

A BLINDING FLASH of lightning pierced the darkening sky; its crackle penetrated the silence, and the ensuing growl of thunder rolled through the land. The Lord's army of angel warriors and I crowded around the portal, the doorway that divided the spiritual realm from the earthly world below. Since that fated day when the Lord's created ones chose against the King's love, there had been a separation of the natural world as we once knew it, leaving two realms, the earthly one and the spiritual.

It was not even noon yet, but the sky was dark and heavy. Clouds blanketed the sun with an oppressive and eerie charcoal-green haze. A chill swept through the land as we watched the event unfold below.

Sweeping through the sky in the earthly realm, but unseen to the human eye, was the dark winged hoard of demon warriors. They were more hideous than ever with their twisted, fanged mouths and dark yellow eyes. Each was equipped with a set of tattered bat-like wings and gnarled talons with hooked claws upon each toe. Horns emerged from their darkened heads and twisted to a sharp point, framing each grotesque face.

I could no longer see the ground beneath the swarm of Satan's followers. They were too thick. I reached for my hilt, preparing to give the battle cry that would bring all of the Lord's army into assembly. My Sword of the Spirit blazed with piercing brightness as I drew it from its sheath; its hilt flashed as light caught the engravings. Just as I raised it high, about to shout the declaration of war, a thunderous voice boomed from behind me.

"Put your sword away, Michael."[1]

A vast ocean of cherubim warriors as far as the eye could see had gathered as spectators around the portal, ready at a moments notice to engage in battle for the King's honor. As if they were the Red Sea themselves, the crowd parted, making way for the King as He approached me, the commander of His army. Upon reaching the front of the crowd, the entire assembly fell to their knees before the great I Am. Each and every forehead kissed the floor in reverence. I too bowed humbly before my Lord, displaying the honor He so rightfully commanded.

It was not until I felt the heaviness of His strong hand on my shoulder that I dared look up.

"Rise, Michael."

Slowly, in obedience, I rose to my feet and gestured to the King's warriors to follow my lead. My Master nodded to me in approval and then turned to face all who were present, His face solemn and untelling.

His mighty voice echoed throughout the Mountain of God as He indicated to the portal, where the demon soldiers swooped past. "You will not have to fight this battle, My brave warriors, for this is My battle."[2]

A hush fell over the assembly as the King paused, a look of deep concern washing over His face. He seemed to be recalling a memory of long ago.

Addressing the crowd, He broke the silence. "I the Lord will fight for you. You need only to be still.[3]

"I tell you, do not fix your eyes on what you see here today, My great army, but fix your eyes on what is unseen; for what is seen is temporary, but what is unseen is eternal. I am telling you these things today so that in Me you may have peace. In the world there is trouble," He paused, glancing down through the portal at the creation that had long ago forgotten Him, "but take heart. I have overcome the world!"[4]

A deafening silence hung thick in the air. The King's words, they seemed so… final. His last statement lingered over us, but we did not understand it.

The King turned to face the portal, and with a look of utter pain on His face, He waved His hand over its surface. It was a grand sweeping motion that caused a forceful gust to whip through the Mountain of God. It rushed past the Lord and over the top of the portal. Flashes of emerald and sapphire erupted, blinding us all. I restrained from shielding my eyes and instead fixed my gaze solely upon the eyes of my Master. *What is He doing?*

The piercing light grew in intensity and was accompanied by a roar, like the sound of water being pulled down a drain. Finally, the wind died, the light subsided, and the sound softened until it was no more. I kept my eyes fixed on my King, and slowly the other warriors let their hands down from their burning eyes. There was a great uproar and commotion as each warrior regained his sight, and the entire assembly charged forward, rushing the portal.

I then knew what He had done. I didn't even have to look. My Master's eyes said everything. The Lord had sealed the portal, locking it up so that nothing or anyone could pass through to the earthly world below.

The warriors surrounded the sealed gateway and cried out in anguish. The portal that had once been a doorway, stood now only as a window, impenetrable to anyone who dared pass. I questioned the Lord with my eyes until He finally tore His gaze from mine. Immediately, I turned and began pressing through the crowd. I struggled through the wall of angelic beings and pushed my way to the front where my strongest warriors continued to close in around me, all of them desperately trying to see past each other and catch a glimpse of the event unfolding below.

Leaning forward, I pressed my hands on the portal's cold, glass-like surface. The very touch of it sent chills up my spine. My breathing felt labored, as if oxygen had turned to nails. Finally, I gained the courage to look.

As I peered through to the world beneath, the great swarm of demons parted momentarily, allowing us full view of the scene below.

There on a hill was the King's Son.

He was nailed to a cross.

{~}

The angel warriors and I charged the portal in a desperate attempt to break through and rescue the King's Son from the dominion of darkness. Somewhere, in the depths of my soul, I knew our attempts were in vain, but still I could not will myself not to fight for the King and His Son's honor. It was ingrained in me. My very purpose, since the beginning of time, was to serve my Master and fight for Him at all costs.

I cried out above the crowd in desperation, pleading with my King for any hope that was left. "My Lord! It's your Son!

Quickly, we must go to Him! Just give command to Your angels concerning Him, and we will lift Him up in our hands. He will not even strike His foot against a stone!"[5]

The King's saddened eyes searched mine, as if pleading me not to make this situation any harder than it already was. He shook His head slowly and then began to approach me through the sea of warriors. The crowd parted, making way for the Lord as He stepped back up to the portal. He stopped directly in front of me, placed a consoling hand on my shoulder, and fixed His eyes on mine. I tried to focus, but everything melted before me as tears pooled in my eyes. Desperation overwhelmed me. I longed to burst through to the world below and rescue the Lord's Son.

"Michael, you are a brave warrior. I know you will fight for Me to the ends of time, but please, you must listen to me closely." The Lord's voice was calming and tender. It washed over me with a sudden peace, a sense of calm in a moment of utter turmoil, a time in my life that was completely outside my control.

"This thing must happen in order to fulfill a debt," my King continued, "the debt of sin. For the wages of sin is death, but the gift of God is eternal life in Christ Jesus. Michael, My Son has been sent to redeem My created ones whom I love. He has come so that they may have life again and have it to the fullest. He will rescue them from the dominion of darkness and bring them into His Kingdom, the Kingdom of My Son whom I love, in whom they will have their redemption, the forgiveness of their sins. They will be redeemed with the Tree of Life...My Son's life, given on a tree."[6]

The Tree of Life. My mind started racing. It flashed back to the Garden of Eden on that monumental day that forever changed the course of history. I could see the man and the woman in my mind's eye. They were standing there beneath the Tree of Life, looking up into the full glory of God. I peered down through the portal at the scene below. A gathering of people, descendants of the Lord's created ones, now looked up to stare full into the glory of God, His Son, life itself hanging on a tree.

Solemnly, we stood there, side by side, Master and servant. Once again, My King placed His calming hand on my shoulder. I wondered, *How is it that the Father consoles me in such a time as this?*

We could do nothing now but watch and pray as the King made the greatest sacrifice in order to provide for His created ones. In my mind, I was again transported back to the garden, on the day my Master sacrificed the first animal, a ram in order to provide for His children. Now here was my King, again providing for them, for the Lord does not change. Even in their sin, the Lord provided. The same stark contrast was evident. The King's Son, perfect in all His glory, whiter than the ram's wool, was stained with His life-water. His very blood was being poured out as a sacrifice for the Lord's created ones.[7]

I watched in horror as my Lord's Son hung there on that cross. Where once stood a majestic and powerful presence, now hung a weakened and wrongly accused man. Below His widespread arms, His limp body drooped. His legs and feet were pressed together beneath Him, supported by the nails the Roman soldiers drove through His feet. With the last ounce of strength He had, the Son held His head high and turned His face upward as if searching for His Father. His once strong, masculine arms now strained to hold up His heavy body. They tensed in agony, lifting His chest to breathe. The Son's arms extended out to the sides as if reaching to the farthest breadth of east and west. His palms were open with outstretched fingers, and dagger-like nails pierced His perfect flesh.

I stood there watching for what seemed like eons when a strange emotion swept over me. I could not place it, but it haunted me like a memory of long ago. It overwhelmed me, and a single hot tear rolled down my cheek.

{~}

Thunder rattled the earth, and the sky darkened with the increasing cloud cover.

"The time has come!" was the cry of Satan to His demon warriors.

The people in the earthly world were unaware of the evil presence that abounded. They remained completely oblivious to the war waging all around. They did not realize the impact of their actions. They did not understand, for if they had, they would not have crucified the Lord of glory. Those who passed by hurled insults at the Son, but their words could not even begin to match the curses that Satan's followers unleashed. The thick mass of dark and evil creatures swarmed around the cross, taunting and jeering the King's Son as He hung there in agony. They shouted obscenities and took turns delivering blows to His frail body as they swooped past. One rather large winged demon launched itself at the Son and delivered a shattering blow to His cheek. Sadly, I watched as my Master's Son turned His head to offer up the other.[8]

"Come down from the cross and save Yourself!" the people of the earth sputtered.[9]

In the same way, the chief priests and the teachers of the law mocked him among themselves. "He saved others," they called out, "but He cannot save Himself! Let this Messiah, this King of Israel, come down from the cross that we may see and believe."[10]

The Son began to whisper to Himself, desperately clinging to the words of His Father. "I must have steadfast patience and endurance, so that I may perform and fully accomplish Your will." He looked upward, searching for His Father. "You have Me endure many terrible troubles, but You will restore Me to life again. You will bring Me back from the depths of the earth."[11]

The swarm of demons grew thicker as He spoke. They circled the ever-weakening human body of the King's Son and reached out with lashes from their talons, in an attempt to bring Him to His demise. The demons knew that this was the Lord's Son, but what they didn't understand was why He had been sent. In the fullness of all their evil, Satan and his fallen angels could not understand love, the kind of love that the King had for His created ones, the kind of love that would cause Him to give up His one and only Son. Satan had always known that the Lord's Son would one day be given over to him for the fulfillment of a debt, but what he didn't know was when or how. In this moment, it appeared to Satan and his army that the King had made His first mistake, for in His human form, the Lord's Son appeared conquerable. The infinite power and authority of the God of the universe had become finite in this Man. It seemed to Satan that he would win.

I thought so as well.

For hours, the King's Son endured the taunts and torture that were becoming more and more violent with each passing minute. I slumped over the portal, pressing my hands and face against the surface. All strength had gone from my legs. With tear-filled eyes, I witnessed the gentle movement of the Son's lips as He continued whispering to Himself, "For I know the plans You have for Me; not My will, Father, but Yours."[12]

Suddenly, one of my own cherubim warriors burst through the crowd and ran to where I had fallen on my knees. He pulled me from the portal and vigorously shook my shoulders.

"Archangel Michael, please! We must save the King's Son!"

I lowered my head in despair, for I felt as though I had abandoned my purpose. Still, in my heart, I knew that the Lord God was in control, for His understanding no one can fathom.[13]

I mustered up all the strength I had left and turned my face toward my comrade. "Trust in the Lord with all your heart, great warrior, and lean not on your own understanding. For the King's ways are not our ways; neither are His thoughts our thoughts."[14]

The mighty warrior's eyes darkened with sadness. Realization set in and slowly he released his grip on my shoulders, allowing me to turn back to the portal and the desolation that it held.

Under my own breath, I whispered to myself, "O Lord, my God and Master, what is to become of Your Tree of Life now?"

I stared down through the portal, but my eyes did not focus on the vision below. Instead, I replayed the memory of the day Satan approached the Lord in the Garden of Eden and the proposition he made to my King.

With every last ounce of hope I had, I clung to the memory of my King's words.

Do you not know? Have you not heard? I, the Lord, am the everlasting God, the Creator of all the earth. I do not grow tired or weary, and My understanding no one can fathom. I Am the great I Am. I will be victorious over you, mark My words, Satan, this war is not over.[15]

{~}

Minutes passed like years as the totality of mankind's sin was heaped upon our Lord's Son. From the spiritual realm, we could physically see the human sin clinging to the Son's body. A Man without sin, He was perfect above all. He obeyed His Father's will to redeem the first act of disobedience to save what was lost.

Somewhere in the depths of my soul, I heard the soft echo of my Master's voice, the mysterious words I had long ago forgotten. Now they resurfaced with surprising clarity.

Michael, I do not expect you to understand what I am doing here. There is no way you could comprehend my infinite power. One day, you will know in full what you now know only in part. There are only three things that remain, Michael: faith, hope, and love. And the greatest of these is love.[16]

The world below melted before me, my eyes pooling with tears. This is what my King meant when He spoke of love. There has never been and never would be a greater love than this... a Man laying down His Own life for all of mankind.

{~}

In the earthly world, it was about three in the afternoon, and the people on Golgotha watched as Jesus' body weakened with the pain and struggle. They could not see their sins upon Him. They did not realize He came to be their savior. Those who were present were unaware of the sin that increased upon Him, becoming more dense and heavy with each passing second. It swarmed His body like locusts and ate away at His perfect flesh. My stomach tightened with sickness.

I looked to my right, where my Lord had been standing watching over His Son, enduring the most painful experience a Father could ever bear. His shoulders sagged, and His head slumped forward in grief. He didn't realize I was watching.

Finally, He could bear no more, and the King turned His face. Slowly, He shook His head and stepped away from the portal, turning His back on His Son. The sin of mankind was too heinous and thick. The perfect Maker of Heaven and earth could no longer look upon His only Son.

I allowed my gaze to follow my King as He quietly escaped the crowd, His shoulders shaking as anguish took over.

The King disappeared, and at that very moment My Master's Son cried out, "Eloi, Eloi, lema sabachthani?" which means "My God, My God, why have You forsaken Me?"[17]

Silence followed. There was no reply from the Lord.

Satan looked to the sky as if waiting for the very heavens to burst forth, releasing the Lord's wrath in a battle of untold fury. When no response came, he took this as his cue.

What happened next I cannot be certain. I suppose I will never know, but for a brief moment it appeared as if Satan locked his gaze with mine. The corners of his mouth twitched in what appeared to be a sly smirk. Furious, I pounded my fist on the portal just as Satan turned away to face his army.

"Finish Him!" he shouted.

The demon warriors shrieked and latched onto the Son's body, pulling at His flesh and tearing at His soul.

Desperate cries erupted from the angel warriors as we pounded and charged the portal, frantically straining to reach the Master's Son.

Groans and cries of sheer anguish escaped from the Lord's Son as the demons tore the last ounce of life from His body.

"Father," He managed to utter, "Into Your hands I commit My spirit." As the words left His mouth, the demons bonded together and heaved on the Son's soul, desperately straining to rip it from His human body. With all the strength they could muster, the demons gave one final tear, and with a loud cry, Jesus breathed His last. The demon warriors tore the Son's life right out of Him and dragged His soul down into the Abyss below.[18]

{~}

Thunder erupted from the heavens above and lightning pierced the darkened sky. A chill swept over the hill of Golgotha, and in that very moment, the curtain of the temple was torn in two, from top to bottom. The chill brought with it a silence so thick we could reach out and touch it. Then all went black, the sun stopped shining, and darkness enveloped the land.

{~}

Three Days Later

And God said, "Let light shine out of darkness. I will make My light shine in all their hearts to give them the light of the knowledge of God in the face of Christ."[19]

{~}

I stood with my King in the heavens in front of the portal, the very portal where we all grieved only three days earlier. The wound to our hearts was still fresh, and the pain so unbearable. My Master peered into the portal, watching the earthly world below, the very world that had murdered His one and only Son.

The past three days had been a mourning period for all the heavenly hosts. Even our King grieved with us. I was still sick in my heart over the atrocity that had occurred, unable to look at the humans of the world below. They did not seem fit to bear

His image after what they had done. Strangely, my Master seemed renewed and vibrant.

"Please forgive me, my King, but how is it you can find joy in such a time as this."

My Lord turned slowly from His viewing place at the portal, His eyes bright with hope.

In a mighty voice, He began to speak, pouring into me His own faith and joy.

"Michael, the first man, Adam, became a living being, the last Adam, a life-giving spirit. The spiritual did not come first, but the natural, and after that the spiritual. The first man was of the dust of the earth. The second Man is of Heaven. As was the earthly man, so are those who are of the earth, and as is the heavenly Man, so also are those who are of Heaven. Just as they have borne the image of the earthly man, so shall they bear the image of the heavenly Man."[20]

My confusion must have shown, but my Lord held up a halting hand as if waving off my questions. Instead, He continued.

"My Son, Who being in very nature God, did not consider equality with God something to be used to His own advantage; rather, He made Himself nothing by taking the very nature of a servant, being made in human likeness. And being found in appearance as a man, He humbled Himself by becoming obedient to death, even death on a cross! Therefore, I will exalt Him to the highest place and give Him the name that is above every name. At the name of Jesus, every knee will bow, in Heaven and on earth and under the earth, and every tongue will acknowledge that Jesus Christ is Lord, to the glory of God the Father.[21]

"Consequently, just as one trespass resulted in condemnation for all people, so also this righteous act will result in justification and life for all people. For just as through the disobedience of the one man the many were made sinners, so also through the obedience of this one Man, the many will be made righteous." [22]

I felt my eyes widen with wonder at the mystery of His words.

"I will make known to them the path of life, Michael. I will fill them with joy in My presence, with eternal pleasures at My right hand. He is risen, Michael! My Son is risen from the dead. I have conquered death! For love conquers all, and My love will always win!"[23]

"Look!" the King gestured to the portal before us. "He is coming with the clouds, and every eye will see Him, even those who pierced Him, and all people on earth will mourn because of Him. So shall it be!"[24]

With a bubbling enthusiasm from my Master's words, I rushed to the edge of the portal. I pressed my face and hands against its surface, desperately searching for the hope my Master described. I didn't see anything, but just as I was about to turn to my Master, the sky opened up. It flashed with the purest, most brilliant light I had ever seen!

The exuberant voice of the Lord came from behind me, "We have won the war, Michael, but the story is not over yet."

{~}

"Father, My prayer is not for them alone. I pray also for those who will believe in Me through their message, that all of them may be one, Father, just as You are in Me, and I am in You. May they also be in Us so that the world may believe that You have sent Me. I have given them the glory that You gave Me, that they may be one as We are one, I in them and You in Me, so that they may be brought to complete unity. Then the world will know that you sent Me and have loved them even as You have loved Me.[25]

"Father, I want those You have given Me to be with Me where I am and to see My glory, the glory You have given Me because you loved Me before the creation of the world."[26]

Part III

Re-creation

Present Day on the Island of Maui

{Chapter 8}

APPLAUSE FILLED THE AUDITORIUM as Dr. Gardner stepped down from the podium, nodding his gratitude to the audience as he made his way off stage.

"Another spectacular presentation, Dr. Gardener." One of his colleagues met him at the edge of the stage and pumped his arm with a vigorous handshake.

"Thank you, Dr. Stevens. Hopefully the audience agrees. You never know what kind of response you will get with a crowd of this size. There are a lot of different backgrounds and beliefs represented in this room."

Dr. Stevens raised his eyebrows, "Speaking of which…" he nodded in the general direction behind Dr. Gardener.

"Well, well, well," came a familiar voice. Dr. Gardener cringed and Dr. Stevens slipped away quietly as Dr. Todd, a professor from the university on the island of Maui, stepped forward and clapped Dr. Gardener hard on the back.

"I have to say, Gardener, I heard you were a brilliant man, but never would I have expected such biblical insights from a professor, let alone a scientist!"

Dr. Todd taught biology at the university with Dr. Gardener and, like most of the other science professors, was known around campus as a devote atheist. Dr. Gardener sensed the sarcasm in his voice.

"Thank you. I figure I might as well put my research skills to work. You know... challenge the students and give them something to make them really think."

His words were kind of meant as a jab. Dr. Todd was known for his dry lectures on the theories of evolution. From what Dr. Gardener had gathered from the students, Dr. Todd lectured straight from the textbook and offered little insights or supporting evidence to what he taught. Dr. Gardener was somewhat irritated that traditional science professors could get away with this kind of behavior because evolution was the accepted theory of the university. He, on the other hand, had his work cut out for him. Teaching the subject of creationism wasn't exactly easy in a secular university where most professors felt the need to explain little more than, "And then there was a big bang." Dr. Gardener always felt that if students had the opportunity to compare both theories side by side, they would see the holes that science poked in the evolutionary model. Thus, the "Studies of Science and the Bible" elective was born, and Dr. Gardener was made an adjunct professor, for a semester anyway. The university had agreed to Dr. Gardener's terms for a semester-long trial run. After that... who knew? Dr. Gardener considered the possibility of introducing his self-developed course to other universities. Not only would it provide him the selfless opportunity to spread the life-altering message that he believed to his core, but it would also offer him the opportunity to satisfy his dream to see the world. After all, he was young, single, and completely sold out to his purpose in life. It didn't get much more freeing than that.

Dr. Todd scrutinized his younger colleague, seemingly still unsure of what to make of the newbie. Finally, he shrugged his shoulders. If he had caught on to Dr. Gardener's slight blow to his teaching style, he hid it well.

Instead, he simply replied, "Well, hell, I might just have to start going to church if we've got an Armageddon to look forward to," Professor Todd laughed a little too loud at his lame attempt for a joke. Dr. Gardener cringed. He hated the flippant way people used that four letter word. *If only they really knew.*

The professor chuckled again and glanced around nervously, as if looking to see who might be watching his little encounter with "the enemy." Once he was seemingly satisfied that no one of importance was around, he abruptly halted his uncomfortable laughter. His smile faded with it, and he dropped his voice, taking on a more serious tone.

Now it was Dr. Gardener's turn to look around uncomfortably. Quickly, he located his nearest exits, just in case Dr. Todd had noticed his little comment and decided to take offense. Dr. Gardener had heard stories of his tenured colleague's temper. *Why do I always have to speak my mind?* What happened next came as even more a surprise than if Dr. Todd had punched him square in the jaw.

"I have to say," Dr. Todd's voice was a near whisper, "that was by far the most convincing lecture I've ever heard on the topic." He looked Dr. Gardener directly in the eyes as he spoke. "But still, I just don't know..." Dr. Todd's voice dropped off as if he were hoping Dr. Gardener would fill in the blank.

Dr. Gardener recognized the honesty in Dr. Todd's questioning eyes and suddenly felt very guilty for his mocking comment. Even he, someone who studied and now taught the Bible for a living, was guilty of judging and forgetting his true purpose. After all, he was human just like the rest. Silently, he offered up a brief request for forgiveness then took a deep breath. "Well, why don't we do lunch one day next week. We can talk more about the topics from the lecture today and..."

"Dr. Gardener!" A call from across the room interrupted his thoughts as one of his students pushed his way through the crowd. Dr. Todd seemed to be jolted from their conversation as well, and a sudden look of self-consciousness washed over his face as Dr. Todd realized his insecurities were about to be revealed. He saw his brief opportunity to sneak away and took it, disappearing into the crowded room of faculty and students.

Realizing how difficult, and even embarrassing, the conversation must have been for the professor, Dr. Gardener made a mental note to touch base with Dr. Todd privately at a more appropriate time. He turned his attention in the direction of the voice that called out to him.

It belonged to Ikaia, a native to the islands and a student from Dr. Gardener's class. He was one of the few students who had taken a great interest in Dr. Gardener's teachings. He even spoke of desiring a career in the same profession. Dr. Gardener had taken Ikaia under his wing in a mentoring way. He was a brilliant young man with a huge faith in God. Ikaia reminded Dr. Gardener of himself when he was in school. He was incredibly inquisitive and would make an exceptional researcher, not to mention another messenger to the beliefs that Dr. Gardener so desperately wanted to spread.

Dr. Gardener met Ikaia for the first time just two weeks before when the young man introduced himself immediately following the first class. Because it was the doctor's first time teaching, the two men agreed to help each other. Dr. Gardener would be a guide for Ikaia in his studies and pursuing his career, and in turn, Ikaia would help the doctor make a great first impression during his semester at the university. After all, having a positive impact would be critical if Dr. Gardener wanted to share this course with other universities.

Throughout the first two weeks of the spring semester, Dr. Gardener discovered that he thoroughly enjoyed both the students and the fact that he was able to instill in them what he so passionately believed. Still, to him, the whole teaching scene was so new. He was a scientist who, occasionally in the past had given lectures similar to today's, but for most of his career, he did research and wrote books on the scientific relationship between the natural world and the Bible. Teaching had never been his desire until this past year when Dr. Gardener sensed God leading him in this direction, and with all the changes at home, everything seemed to just fall into place. When the opportunity finally did come up, the timing couldn't have been more perfect, so he jumped on it. Desperate for a change in routine and a change in scenery, Dr. Gardener knew a whole semester in beautiful Maui was just what he needed to take his mind off the rough year he had.

Although he was enjoying this new adventure in life, some days, like today, Dr. Gardener wondered how he could make it through the next several months. His grueling schedule was utterly exhausting. *What have I gotten myself into?* As a part of his proposal to the university, Dr. Gardener not only promised to teach the elective course Monday through Thursday, but he also offered a Friday lecture series that was open to all students, faculty, and staff. Dr. Gardener thought it would be an excellent way to whet the appetites of students and professors whose interests were piqued, but maybe not ready to commit to a full course on creation science. Every Friday during the semester, Dr. Gardener chose a different topic to present in a lecture format with a question and answer session at the end. Although the sessions were only two hours long, much shorter than a traditional teaching day, he found them much more draining.

Because the lectures were open to the entire campus, the Friday sessions left Dr. Gardener with an audience full of varying beliefs and levels of understanding. Dr. Gardener had always found it nerve racking to present to a group of peers back home, but these were not even his fellow believing scientists from his research group. This was a group of people who likely had strong convictions against the teachings of the Bible, and a few, such as Dr. Todd, had proven to be slightly confrontational. Just last Friday, Dr. Todd had made an attempt to trip-up Dr. Gardener by hounding him with questions in front of the crowd. Fortunately, Dr. Gardener remained composed and unfazed as he delivered solid evidence, answering completely and honestly each and every question Dr. Todd threw to him. Based on the brief conversation he just had with Dr. Todd, he'd say their little debate had a pretty major impact on the guy. This was Dr. Gardener's favorite part of the job, watching people who, just days before, were adamant against the existence of a Creator, now question their own beliefs.

"Dr. Gardener," once again his thoughts were interrupted as Ikaia finally reached the professor. "What was that all about?" Ikaia gestured in the general direction of where Dr. Todd disappeared.

"Oh, nothing." Dr. Gardener tried to hide his smile, but he failed. Ikaia questioned the doctor with his eyes until sudden realization set in. The young man flashed a knowing smile in the direction of his professor and nodded as if to say, *you're good.*

"I'm impressed. I never would have expected to see Dr. Todd speaking with you in such close quarters. I think he believes he can catch it!"

"Catch it?" the doctor questioned.

"You know, catch it, like Jesus is a cold or something." Ikaia chuckled, "Let's hope for his sake he ends up with a bad case of it."

Dr. Gardener tried hard not to laugh, wondering whether or not it was appropriate. Finally, he succumbed to the wit of his student, believing that if Jesus were standing next to him that very minute, he would have been nodding in agreement and saying, "That's a good one!"

"You know," Dr. Gardener calmed his laughter and became serious, "he did seem to be coming down with something!" He lightly punched his student in the arm, and they both had another good laugh. This type of camaraderie was one of the advantages Dr. Gardener had with being the youngest faculty member, ever, at the university. His students were not much younger than he, and he was able to develop true friendships with them. Friendship was something he certainly needed during this time in his life.

Their conversation lingered a few more minutes as the students and faculty filed out of the auditorium, leaving with more to ponder than they anticipated. Burning questions filled their eyes. It was not what they expected. As they slowly drifted back out into the world, their solemn faces revealed their innermost thoughts: *if this guy is right, then what he said changes everything.*

The crowd finally dispersed, and Dr. Gardener began gathering his materials. *Another week under the belt*, he thought.

Ikaia noticed his tired expression. "Dr. Gardener, you look like you could really use a day to relax. You know, unwind and all. You've been going non-stop since you arrived two weeks ago."

Ikaia was right. Dr. Gardener was not used to this kind of work schedule, not to mention the fact that his internal clock still refused to adjust to the time change. He was beginning to crave one of those quiet days, spent in his home office, studying and writing. *Maybe I'm just not cut out for this type of thing.* He shrugged. *I guess I'll just see where God takes me from here.*

Out loud he said, "You are so right. I think I just need a little time to relax, do something, I don't know... island-style." He smiled at his friend.

Ikaia shook his head in mock distaste at the "island-style" comment and then continued on like he never heard it.

"Well, I have just the thing for you then."

"I'm listening."

"I know you haven't done much sight-seeing since you've been on the island, and if there is one thing that you have to do during your stay on Maui, it's take the road to Hana. Trust me, you have never truly seen the awesome work of God's hands until you take the road to Hana. It will revive you like nothing else."

Dr. Gardener had heard of this infamous road, with its hairpin turns and treacherous terrains, but he also heard of its matchless beauty, vistas so awe inspiring, an observer would think they had stepped into a painting. The road to Hana sounded a lot like life to the doctor. Sometimes hard and full of tragedy, but God is able to use all these things for His good. Dr. Gardener often found he had to go through the bad and the ugly to get to the beautiful in life. After the rough year he had been through, he could really use some beautiful right now.

"I think you're right, Ikaia. That sounds exactly like what I need."

{~}

Silence enveloped the mountain side. The only sound to be heard for miles was the soft breeze rustling the leaves of the forest and the turquoise waves crashing below. The aroma of flowers hung thick in the air, and a song of crickets and other forest life accompanied the percussion of the ocean against the shoreline.

Dr. Gardener stood on the edge of the cliff that framed the infamous road to Hana and peered out at the endless azure before him. Blue waters stretched as far as the eye could see, and white foam danced across the top of the waves. The sky looked almost like a reflection: pale blue marked with the fluffy accents of the clouds, mirroring the whitecaps below. The edge of the cliff came to life with rainbow inspired flowers, colors so brilliant, Dr. Gardener imagined an artist spilling his pallet across the countryside to create such a picturesque scene.

Out across the water, Dr. Gardener stared at what seemed to be a physics defying rock formation, a natural archway formed by the continual buffeting of the seas. Dr. Gardener had heard of these wonders but had never seen one himself. Against the deep blue, an ominous peninsula of rock once stood, appearing strong enough to withstand the waves and weathering of the element, but portions of the mineral substance itself were porous and fragile. Over time, the weakest pieces of the rock formation broke off from the battering waves. The particles were then washed away into the ocean and carried out to sea. In time, all that was left behind was a beautiful archway structure, supported only by the strongest portions of the plain rock that once jutted out into the sea. It was in moments like this that Dr. Gardener realized the mighty work of God's hand. He gazed at the rock, mesmerized by the harmonious blend of science and art that God used to create this magnificent world. *No man could have created such an impossible structure.*

Lost in his own thoughts, Dr. Gardener was reminded of the storms and waves that God used to chip away at him. He often felt God using difficult scenarios to break and wash away his own sin and humanness. Considering the rock formation before him, he wondered if one day his own life might resemble something beautiful, but that hope seemed impossible, except where the hand of God might do something remarkable. Looking back on his life, Dr. Gardener could already identify the many testimonies to the transformation that was being worked in him.

At only twenty-eight years of age, Dr. Gardener was the youngest of his colleagues, not only at the university where he was teaching for the semester, but also among his fellow scientists back home. He was what many would refer to as a genius, brilliant beyond his years. He was the topic of discussion among many of the men and women with whom he worked, fellow scientists who weren't even finished with their schooling by the time they were his age. It was truly an act of God that had brought him into such successful circumstances. *I certainly haven't done anything to deserve all that I have.* Silently, Dr. Gardener thanked his Maker once again for His unrelenting love and grace.

It was this same love and grace that led him to be so passionate about his job. Dr. Gardener felt like, after all he had been through and all God had forgiven him for, the least he could do was to let others know of the second chance God offered. After all, Dr. Gardener was an expert in the field of second chances. He had a rough past for certain, the kind of upbringing you wouldn't expect from such a young success.

Dr. Gardener's story began twenty-eight years ago as an infant in an orphanage. As far as he knew, he had no parents. Even the orphanage staff claimed no record of parents to the bright eyed little boy they raised for so many years. One of the caretakers at the orphanage used to tell him he was special because he belonged to God, and because he had no earthly parents, God had claimed him and adopted him as his own. This explanation was no comfort to the little boy, who in turn, acted out in rebellion against the orphanage, his no-show parents, and ultimately God. As a child, he spent countless hours wondering why a "loving God" would leave him with no family, no home, and no life. As a result, he spent three years of his so-called life in and out of a juvenile detention center, where no amount of correction or rebuke could change his fate.

At the impressionable age of thirteen, he began searching for a place to belong. As is the fate of many children who grow up without loving parental influences, he succumbed to peer-pressure and fell in with the wrong crowd.

To this day, he could still remember every detail of that life-altering night, the night when all his past actions came to a head in an event so monumental, it changed the course of his life forever. He was never the same. The memories of that night haunted him like a dark nightmare. As he stood there on the edge of the road, all the beauty before him began to fade away as his mind drifted back fifteen years ago to that cold October night. *The darkness,* he shuddered at the thought. It was so dark that night, darker than any other night he could recall.

Again, he saw himself as a thirteen year old boy, pulling the hood of his sweatshirt tightly around his face, blocking the chill of the night air as he crept among the shadows of the downtown alleyways. The outline of dilapidated buildings took form in his mind, and the stench of dank corridors wafted into his nostrils. The muffled shouts of a domestic dispute escaped through the paper thin walls. Every so often, the sound of sirens pierced the oppressive blackness, signaling secrets revealed, secrets once hidden under the cover of night.

The image brought to mind a Bible verse he had long ago memorized. It was one of his favorites, learned shortly after he, himself, was rescued from the darkness of his own life.

For you were once darkness, but now you are light in the Lord. Live as children of light (for the fruit of the light consists in all goodness, righteousness, and truth) and find out what pleases the Lord. Have nothing to do with the fruitless deeds of darkness, but rather expose them. For it is shameful even to mention what the disobedient do in secret. But everything exposed by the light becomes visible, for it is light that makes everything visible. This is why it is said: "Wake up, O sleeper, rise from the dead, and Christ will shine on you.[1]

Dr. Gardener felt a brief calm as he played the words over in his head, but shivered again as the memories came flooding back with more intensity. The recollection of his past swept an icy chill over him. To this very day he longed to take back his actions from that night, but then again, it was that very tragedy that God used to make him into the man he was today. *Why you forgave me, I still don't know.* A twinge of guilt burst in his stomach. He thought he had long ago dealt with this remorse, yet here he was again, drowning in his shame. It was strange how recent life events had dredged up old pains and emotions. Silently, Dr. Gardener wondered if he really did ever put closure to them. His mind drifted away, and once more, he was transported to the blackest night he had ever known.

His senses were heightened as he crept his way through the sinister black. His ears were on alert. His eyes searched the dark, desperate to make out the objects in the murky alley surrounding him. He was pretty sure he could smell his own fear as he finally reached the location where he would complete his mission.

The back entrance to the downtown studio art gallery was completely shrouded in darkness. Pressing his back hard against the building wall, he tried to disappear into the cold bricks of the surrounding doorway. He thrust his hand into the front pocket of his sweatshirt, rubbing his fingers nervously against the cold gun barrel. It made him feel like a man to have such a powerful object in his possession. Still, fear gripped him in a way he had never known. "I can't believe I'm actually doing this," he whispered. Desperation for acceptance had led him to make many poor choices in the past, but even he knew what he was about to do was crossing the line.

In his mind, he played over the instructions he had been given. Again, he absentmindedly brushed his hand against the gun, as if it might have some fear of its own and abandon him on this mission. Cautiously, he reached into his other pocket and pulled out a small folded piece of paper. It was a newspaper clipping, an image of a painting. That month, a well-known local artist was exhibiting his newest collection in the gallery. One of the pieces, the one featured in the article, was valued at over fifty thousand dollars. *Fifty thousand dollars!* He couldn't even imagine what that kind of money would look like in cold, hard cash. He double checked the photo. There was no way he was going through all of this trouble for the wrong painting.

As he secured the newspaper clipping back into his pocket, a sudden wave of emotion washed over him. He thought he heard a voice calling him from somewhere within. *Turn around,* it urged. *You shouldn't be here.* He hesitated, considering for a moment the impact of his choices. It called again, *Turn around. This isn't who you are. You are more than this!* With the defiance that only a teenage boy could muster, he stifled the annoying voice of his conscience and shook the conflicting thoughts from his head. A deep breath refocused him on the task at hand: *break in, grab the painting, and get out!* He imagined the satisfied faces of those whose approval he so desperately longed to capture. Then he would be accepted, when he returned with the prize they sent him to retrieve.

He reached for the crowbar that was wedged under his belt and inhaled deeply, attempting to steady his hands as he lifted the cold piece of metal to the doorframe. *Now or never*, he thought. He had just wedged it in and was straining to gain leverage when he heard something in the alley behind him: something had moved.

Someone was there. Someone was watching.

He slipped down into a crouching position, his breath catching in his throat as he slowly reached for the gun. With trembling hands, he pulled the cold piece of machinery from his pocket and raised it to eye level. Ever so quietly, he lowered the crowbar to the ground, freeing his other hand to help steady its mate.

The rapid pulsing of his heart pounded in his ears. He could feel it rattling his ribcage. Time seemed to stop as his body tensed, and icy-like adrenaline coursed through his veins. The pungent smell of metal from the revolver pierced his nostrils. Slowly, he chanced a look around the wall of the recessed doorway.

His eyes scanned the darkness, nothing. He held his breath and waited. Nothing happened. There wasn't another sound, just the soft, faint hum of the freeway a few miles in the distance.

Just my imagination. Slowly he lowered the gun in order to replace it in the front pocket of his hooded sweatshirt. He was rising to his feet and nearly had the gun secured when a deafening crash erupted from behind him. A box had tumbled from the dumpster where he had been aiming only moments before. It sent his feet in the air and his heart into his throat. In an instant, the gun was poised in front of him, shaking against his will in his trembling hands.

Before he had time to contemplate the consequences of his next move, a scrawny-looking, grey and white cat leapt from the top of the dumpster where several other boxes were perched. The cat landed softly on its feet before slinking away into the darkness. *A dirty old alley cat!* He was incredulous. *What has gotten into me? Who am I?* he wondered. *Now I'm afraid of cats?* Silently, he hoped this would never make it back to the guys he so desperately tried to impress.

He shook his head at his own embarrassment and steadied his hands before lowering the gun. He could have kicked himself at his own cowardice. Anger and determination set in, replacing any insecurity he had left. Desperate to finish what he started, he reached down to reclaim the crowbar and what was left of his dignity. The gun was still in his hands, his finger loose on the trigger. It was not until he was standing that he heard it, the sound that changed his life forever.

"Click."

Suddenly, Dr. Gardener was brought back to the present where he stood gazing out over the vast Pacific Ocean. *How long have I been standing here in a daze? And what was that?*

"Click."

There it was again. The sound was familiar to Dr. Gardener, but it seemed out of context in the given surroundings. He couldn't place it. He turned around, scanning the setting to locate the noise, when he finally…

"Click."

Dr. Gardener finally located the source of the sound. Behind him and a little to the right stood a bulky-looking tripod. A large, black camera was mounted on top, facing the magnificent view Dr. Gardener had been observing just moments before. He peered into the wide opening of the lens where he could see the archway formation and crashing waves reflecting from the grand vista behind him.

"Click."

The shutter closed again, and Dr. Gardener tried not to stare as he realized the most awe-inspiring view had been behind him the entire time. Rising from her crouched position behind the camera was, quite possibly, the most breathtakingly beautiful woman he had ever laid eyes on. *So this is what Ikaia meant when he spoke of the beauty on the road to Hana*, Dr. Gardener silently chuckled to himself.

She was stunning. Her skin was the color of a hot cup of coffee with a splash of milk, and long, dark hair tumbled around her slender shoulders. She had the most stunning features, full red lips, and slate grey eyes that were striking against her dark complexion. Her golden, toned legs stuck out from beneath her slightly-on-the-short-side shorts. Dr. Gardener caught himself staring when her sweet voice called to him from behind the camera.

"I thought you were going to jump," she laughed, somewhat nervously.

"Huh, jump? Oh!" Suddenly, he realized what she meant. "Oh, no, I was just lost in thought, I suppose. I mean…" Dr. Gardener had never been at a loss for words before. Normally he was quick witted, but some strange power emitting from this woman, had overtaken him. He took a cautious step forward toward the lovely being before him. His head was a foggy mess. No woman had ever had this effect over him.

She hesitated, perhaps a second too long, before stepping out from behind the protection of her camera. Slowly she moved forward to greet him.

"Beautiful, isn't it?" She smiled nervously at Dr. Gardener as her eyes drifted past him to the striking display that unfolded behind him. Soft wisps of dark hair danced around her forehead as a gentle breeze floated off the ocean and over the hillside. She appeared lost in thought, and Dr. Gardener found himself getting lost in her beauty.

Before he could censor his thoughts, Dr. Gardener whispered under his breath, "Yes, you are."

Shaken from her trance, the lovely stranger abruptly snapped her head back, locking her gaze on his, "What was that? I didn't quite hear you." Her questioning eyes revealed to Dr. Gardener that she hadn't caught his little slip. *There I go again,* he thought. *I swear I have no filter.*

"Oh, I just said yes. I mean, the road to Hana is known for its beauty, isn't it?" Dr. Gardener flashed a coy grin, pleased he had worked his way out of that little blunder.

She didn't respond. She remained standing there poised with arms crossed tightly over her chest, as if guarding herself. Her eyes squinted slightly, and she just continued to stare back at him for a moment, as if trying to figure out this mystery man, like maybe she could sum him up in the next fifteen seconds.

Finally, when she seemed satisfied there was no initial threat involved, the tension faded from her face. She simply shrugged her shoulders and extended a delicate hand.

"Well, it's a pleasure to meet you. My name is Evelyn."

Returning the polite introduction, Dr. Gardener closed the gap between them with one final step as he reached forward and took her soft hand in his. The instant their skin connected, they both felt it, an almost electrical shock, a rush of energy that went from one hand to the next. Surprise overwhelmed their faces as they stared down at their joined hands. At the same moment, they both lifted their eyes to the other's, peering into the soul of the one who had sparked such power.

"Nice to meet you, Evelyn. My name is Adam."

{Chapter 9}

EVELYN YANKED HER HAND BACK, surprised by her own reaction to his touch. *He is quite handsome*, she timidly thought.

Adam, too, seemed stunned by the strange energy that passed between the two of them. He stepped back abruptly and casually removed his shades, revealing for the first time his piercing, bluish-grey eyes. His dark, wavy hair was somewhat disheveled from enjoying the open-air ride in the Jeep, which was now parked on the side of the road. Evelyn didn't dare mention that she had been watching him since he pulled over to take in the spectacular ocean view.

Adam's cheeks were slightly flushed from the heat of the day, *or was he blushing?* Evelyn couldn't tell, but it stood out noticeably against his olive-tone skin, which was much lighter than her own café au lait coloring. She loved the fact that her ethnic appearance left everyone wondering whether or not she was a local to the islands. She wasn't. He certainly didn't seem to be from around here. Evelyn wasn't quite sure what gave it away, she just... knew. Although Evelyn had never seen this man before, there was something in his eyes that seemed all too familiar. Whatever it was, something about this mysterious tourist left her desiring to know him more, a feeling she hadn't experienced towards a man since, well…never.

She noticed his tanned, muscular legs from beneath his khaki, cargo shorts. *Runner?* Evelyn silently wondered. His well-defined, bronzed arms were crossed in front of him, pulling his shirt tight across his chest and biceps. She had a weakness for the athletic type. *That sure got me in trouble a time or two in college.*

Adam cleared his throat and flashed a crooked grin in her direction. Evelyn suddenly realized that she had been staring this whole time. Quickly she lowered her eyes.

"That's a really nice camera you have there, looks expensive. Better not shoot it at this mug," he pointed to his irresistible smile. "I might break it!" His chuckle warmed Evelyn, releasing her from the tension she normally felt in the presence of men. There was something very different about him.

"Somehow, I don't think you would do too much damage." Evelyn blushed slightly, hoping her words didn't sound as revealing as she felt. Mentally, she kicked herself for succumbing to his good looks. She frantically searched the corners of her mind, desperate for something to change the subject. That's when she noticed the Jeep.

"So, Adam, is this your first time on the road to Hana?"

"Ha, what gave it away?"

"Oh, nothing, I didn't mean…" Evelyn felt her face redden. "I was just wondering." *What's gotten into me? C'mon Ev,* she silently coached herself, *get a grip!* She expertly buried her familiar feelings of insecurity, as she had done countless times before. She straightened her posture, feeling slightly more confident.

"I'll be perfectly honest," Evelyn turned, deciding to pack up her equipment while talking. She was much better at disguising her emotions while performing a task. Adam trailed a couple steps behind her, following the conversation while she went about dismantling the camera. She continued, "It doesn't matter if it's your first or your twenty-first time on the road to Hana. Somehow, each time, it is even more amazing than you could ever dream or remember."

Her own words instantly jolted Evelyn's mind back to when she made her first journey on the road to Hana. She was just a child at the time. Her stepfather had taken her there when she was only ten years old. If ever there was a perfect day in Evelyn's memory, it was that one. She could still feel it: the bright sun warming her skin, complimenting the comfortable, mid-seventy degree day. The sky sparkled with a perfect-shade-of-blue, punctuated by puffy-white, cumulus clouds, and the crisp air made her feel so alive that it seemed to imprint the memories of the day that much more vividly in her mind. It was as if everything was brighter that day, like reality seemed more real than ever before. Evelyn had so many wonderful memories of that day with her stepfather. If only she had known it would be their last moments together, she would have lingered a little longer when they stood at this very cliff-side, taking in the awe of the same rock formation she stood before now. She would have asked him to make one more jump with her off the rocky ledge into the turquoise pools of water. She would have asked him for one more swim under the thundering waterfall where he showed her the secret cave.

But she didn't know, so she didn't ask. And now? Her thoughts trailed off. At least she still had those life-like memories of a man who was not her father, but loved her more than anyone had ever loved her before. Evelyn felt her throat tightening and a sensation of pressure building behind her eyes. Quickly, she unzipped her camera bag and began packing the equipment. Hoping Adam hadn't noticed her little lapse, she diverted with another question.

"So, Adam, what brings you to Maui, business or pleasure?"

As she settled into the routine of packing the camera and tripod, Adam unfolded his arms, letting down his guard. His posture seemed to relax a little as Evelyn's tension subsided.

"I wish I could say pleasure," he slipped his sunglasses on top of his head, "but I'm actually supposed to be here on business. Although, I have to say I am taking full advantage of the pleasure aspect of the island today." There was a hint of suggestion in his voice. "So," he quickly redirected, seeming to skim over his last comment, "How long have you lived in Maui?"

Evelyn grinned broadly, his undertone completely forgotten by the humor of his question. "Oh, I'm actually not from the island, although, I've visited plenty of times. I'm here on business as well."

"I'm sorry," Adam stumbled, "I shouldn't have assumed."

"It's all right, really," Evelyn waved off his apology. "I don't take any offense. You are the fourth person to make that assumption, and I've only been here three days. I guess I just blend in here!" There was a sense of sincerity in her tone. Evelyn was surprised as to how easy the conversation flowed with Adam.

"I don't know that you could blend in anywhere. You're kind of hard to miss." Evelyn was shocked by his boldness. She glanced up from her task to see a genuine look of innocence in his eyes. As surprised as she was by Adam's comment, she found herself even more stunned by her own response. Evelyn was not unfamiliar to the flattery of men, but she realized in that moment, she had never before felt the warmth of an authentic, wholehearted compliment. She felt the color rising in her cheeks again. *I swear I've never blushed so much in my life!*

Changing the subject, Evelyn asked, "What kind of business are you in, Adam?"

She really was curious. In her mind she tried to imagine what kind of career would bring a guy like Adam to the island of Maui. He certainly didn't look to be the business-type, more like he just stepped out of a magazine advertisement. *Maybe that's it, a model.* He looked far too young for any sort of established career. His appearance seemed to suggest he couldn't be too far removed from college, although, she herself was here on business, and she was only twenty-four. *Certainly he can't be any older than me.* Evelyn caught herself making judgments. *There I go again.* She was always making assumptions when meeting new people. Evelyn had long ago accepted this behavior as a defense mechanism. If she always expected the least from people, she couldn't get hurt or disappointed. Though strangely, with Adam, Evelyn found herself wanting to stifle all preconceived ideas and give him an honest chance to see who he really was. Evelyn was baffled by the power this man seemed to hold over her.

"I'm actually here for the semester, teaching a course over at the university," he said nonchalantly, as if he were simply stating what he had for breakfast that morning.

Evelyn didn't even try to conceal her shock. She wasn't even close! Silently she wondered what other surprises may be hiding behind those piercing eyes.

Adam must have sensed her surprise because he continued before Evelyn even had time to respond. "I'm not really a professor, though, well... I guess I am... sort of." His expression seemed to suggest there wasn't an easy answer. "I mean, this is my first time teaching," he finally offered as an explanation.

Evelyn expressed her confusion, "Well if you aren't a professor, why are you teaching a course for the university?"

"Because, well... I'm actually a scientist."

A scientist? There really were some major surprises about this stranger. He had Evelyn's full attention now.

Just as she was about to probe further, Adam asked, "C'mon now, I'm curious. What kind of business brings you to Hawaii?"

Evelyn considered his words. *Well that sure seems like a loaded question.* There was her job and the business trip, but then there was that gnawing "unfinished business" of trying, after fourteen years, to find closure regarding her stepfather's death. Evelyn decided not to bring up that part of her past and told him about her career instead.

"Well, if you couldn't tell," Evelyn said, glancing up from her crouched position beside her equipment, "I'm a photographer."

"I would have never guessed!" Adam's smile spread across his face. Something about the way his expression lit up made Evelyn's composure take on the form of warm pudding. He knelt down beside her to offer a hand. "Okay, but seriously, what kind of photographer are you? I mean, this definitely doesn't look like your typical sight-seeing camera." Adam reached into his back pocket and produced a small digital camera. "This is more my style."

Evelyn tried to stifle a giggle.

"I know, I know, pathetic next to yours." Adam held up his camera beside Evelyn's for emphasis.

Evelyn finally gave into the laughter. *Man, it feels good to laugh!*

Adam joined in while he continued to hand Evelyn various pieces of equipment to be stowed away. Her stomach tightened as he moved closer to reach for a lens, lying on the ground next to the tripod. He was so close she could smell the woodsy cologne he was wearing. His hand brushed hers as he handed over the lens. It was only a brief second, but Evelyn could have sworn she saw a spark leap between them. Quickly, she pulled her hand away and searched his face to see if he had felt it as well. Adam averted his eyes.

"You never answered my question."

"Huh?"

"I asked what kind of photographer you are. I really am interested. It wasn't just a line." Adam looked directly into her eyes when he spoke to her. Evelyn's blood stopped cold. This guy had her pegged. Adam sensed that Evelyn already had a preconceived idea about who he was and what he wanted, but he didn't let that faze him. The funny thing was Evelyn believed him. Something about the way his eyes pierced through her soul told Evelyn that, despite them just meeting, he really did care.

Finally, Adam broke his stare, "But I'm going to warn you, I don't know the first thing about photography. I'm genuinely interested to hear about what you do, in simple terms, of course." Adam flashed that bright smile and rose to his feet, picking up one of the heavy camera bags and carrying it over to Evelyn's rental SUV.

Evelyn watched him in disbelief, partly because of the way he just stepped in to help, no questions asked. More surprisingly, this was the first time anyone had ever asked Evelyn about her career and seemed to truly care about her response.

Adam jogged back and hoisted the second equipment bag before stowing it away in the trunk with the other. He hurried back to Evelyn with a look of pure attentiveness, one that said he just couldn't wait to hear the story of her life.

Thank goodness, I won't be sharing that!

Deep down, Evelyn wondered if Adam would be a person with whom she could share something more than all the surface details of her life. She felt an odd sense of comfort when talking with this stranger, an ease she hadn't felt since her stepfather passed. All the same, Evelyn mentally promised not to cave and share her heart.

"Well, in a nutshell, I'm a freelance photographer with a focus on landscape and wildlife photography."

There, simple enough. Not even a single detour that would divulge any information about her life. *Hopefully he won't ask any questions.*

But he did.

"I don't really like nutshells." Evelyn could hear the laughter in his voice. "C'mon Ev, you've got to do better than that!"

Evelyn was just about to remind Adam of how little he offered about his own career, when his words finally hit her. *Ev.* It was the pet name her stepfather had given her as a little girl. No one else ever called her that.

"Well?" Adam interrupted her thoughts. Evelyn finally decided it would be best not to read too much into that little detail.

"All right, all right…" She rolled her eyes, pretending to be annoyed. "So, basically I work for myself. I'm either contracted out for new work, or I sell stock photos from previous assignments. Landscape and wildlife photography are definitely my niche though. I was pretty young when I determined this was my passion, but the best part," Adam raised his eyebrows with anticipation, "is that I get to travel to exotic locations all over the world, such as," Evelyn gestured around her, "Maui."

Adam's expression seemed to mirror the joyful emotions that were rising up in Evelyn. She always grew passionate when talking about her job.

"Wow, that's so awesome! What an amazing career! I have to say, you sound like a pretty fascinating person, Evelyn."

"Me? What about you? You're a scientist! Which, by the way," she pointed a playfully, accusing finger. "I want to hear more about." Evelyn reached for the water bottle she left lying on the ground. "I always liked science in school, but I'm definitely more of the artistic type. I'm a total fanatic about beauty and capturing it, whether it's on film or a canvas. But you?" she took a sip. "How cool is it that you get to study the beauty of the world in a completely different way. You get to see how all the intricacies of life fit together to make a whole. It's crazy to think that a world that has such order can also be awe inspiring and breathtakingly magnificent! When I think about it, I just can't help but wonder if there really is a God out there."

Evelyn halted abruptly. The moment the words left her mouth, she wished she could take them back. She nearly clasped her hands over her mouth, as if she might be able to reclaim her words before they reached Adam's ears. *Where did that come from?*

Adam, who had been listening intently, shifted nervously. Evelyn scrambled to regain her composure, "Although, I'm sure you will be able to tell me I'm wrong. I mean, being a scientist and all."

There that should do it, she thought. *Anything to keep us from going down that road.*

Adam didn't respond, but simply smiled and slipped his shades down over his eyes, hiding the excitement that was building inside him.

He never did acknowledge her question, but instead offered up one of his own. "So, since this isn't your first time," his eyebrows raised above the dark rims, "care to show me the road to Hana?"

{~}

I strained my eyes, trying to make out the scene. It was like peering into a pool of water, trying to see clearly the objects below. Everything looked distorted, as if someone threw a bucket of water on a painting, causing the images to run together. Still, I stood there waiting at the edge of the portal that was dividing the heavenly realm from the earthly one. Finally, when I had given up trying to make out what was unfolding below, my Master arrived. He leaned over, and with one quick swipe of His powerful hand across the surface of the portal, everything snapped into a clear, crisp picture.

There below were two humans, a man and a woman. They were riding together in some sort of open-air vehicle through one of the few remaining places that had been unstained by the humans' hands. If only they had seen their planet the way the Lord originally created it. The humans had taken something that was once perfect and lovely and destroyed it before the eyes of their very Maker. Yet God still loved them. Even in their sin, He loved them.

I watched the scene unfold. The man pulled the vehicle over on the side of the road. As soon as it came to a stop, he jumped out and rushed around to the woman's side, to open her door. The look of surprise on her face made me chuckle. The man led the woman around to the back of the vehicle where he produced a cooler full of refreshments. They stood there for a while, gazing out at the displays of my Master's handiwork. They were laughing and talking together. Even though I couldn't hear their voices, I could see the joy etched on their faces. It reminded me of how things used to be in the beginning, in a time when the humans' joy was complete.

Finally, the Lord's voice broke through my thoughts. "Michael, do you remember what My Son said on the day I redeemed Him from the depths of the Abyss?"

I glanced up from the portal, turning from the humans to stare fully into the eyes of my Master. All my focus and direction was completely lost when my eyes met His. They were so full of peace. The moment I locked my gaze with His, I couldn't turn away. His eyes were captivating. They set my heart at rest and gave life to my body. How long I stood there staring into His eyes, I cannot say.

Finally, the King's question registered in my mind. *Do I remember the words of His Son?* How could I forget the sweetest sound I'd ever heard, the first words of the Son upon His return? I played over in my mind the sound of His lyrical voice being carried up as He ascended into the heavenly realm.

Father, just as You are in Me, and I am in You, may they also be in Us so that the world may believe that You have sent Me. I have given them the glory that You gave Me, that they may be one as We are one, I in them and You in Me, so that they may be brought to complete unity. Then the world will know that you sent Me and have loved them even as You have loved Me."[1]

Father, I want those You have given Me to be with Me where I am and to see My glory, the glory You have given Me because You loved Me before the creation of the world.[2]

"Michael, it is just as He said. My people will be redeemed back to Me, just as My Son has been. It is through My Son and His sacrifice that they will be made one with Him, and just as We are one, they too shall be made one with Me. By declaring My Son as their Lord and Savior, My people are brought to life. For they were dead in their transgressions and sins when they followed the ways of this world and the ruler of the kingdom of the air, the spirit who is now at work in those who are disobedient, Satan. They all lived among him at one time, gratifying the cravings of their sinful nature and following its desires and thoughts. Like the rest, they were by nature objects of My wrath, but because of My great love for them, I, Who am rich in mercy, made them alive with Christ, even when they were dead in transgressions. It is by My grace that they have been saved."[3]

I knew of this grace of which my King spoke: it was His love. Grace is the action of the King's love. I had seen the power of His grace at work in the days following the resurrection of His Son. People all over the world who had seen Jesus believed and repented of their old ways and sins. They denounced the power of darkness, declaring the King's Son as their Lord and Savior. They began sharing this good news with others, and because of their faith, all around the world, people who had never even seen Jesus, believed. These people, who believed, those who declared their Lord as King, were released from their chains. Satan could hold their souls no longer. For the King rescued them from the dominion of darkness, and one day, He will bring them into the Kingdom of the Son He loves, in whom they have redemption, the forgiveness of sins.[4]

Even to this day, the humans continued to share the story of what their King had done. For He loved His created ones so much that He told Satan no price was too great to have them back, even the price of His one and only Son.

Throughout the earthly realm, there were thousands of humans who declared their King's name and served Him alone. These people were known to the Lord. My King knew each and every one of the humans intimately because He was their maker. He physically knit each of them together in their mother's womb. They were fearfully and wonderfully made! He knew everything about them, when they would sit and when they would rise. He perceived all their thoughts from afar. He discerned their going out and their lying down and was familiar with all their ways. Even before a word was on their tongue, the Lord knew it completely.[5]

What never ceased to amaze me was how much He cherished each and every one of them, even the ones who had not proclaimed His Kingship. He knew them all, loved them all, and cared for them all because they were His.

Although my King loved all the humans, not all loved Him in return. It was never the King's intent to force His created ones to obey and love Him, not even from the day He created the earth. That would not be true love. In order for there to be love, there must be a choice. From the beginning of creation, the King had given them that freedom to choose, and now He waited for them.

Throughout the earth, vast multitudes of humans chose not to obey the Lord and adamantly denied His Kingship. Instead, they were slaves to the wicked Satan and his demons, who roamed the earth, unseen to the human eye, searching for people to destroy and souls to claim. The humans had no knowledge of the spiritual realm that intersected their very own, but the demons were there, lying in wait, preparing for the perfect moment to attack. Those who had given into the dominion of darkness had sealed their destiny to these beasts, but the Lord did not give up on them. If only they were to see the truth, repent, and declare the Lord as King, He would come and rescue them.

Then there were the others, those who simply had no beliefs one way or the other. They were lukewarm, neither hot nor cold. Sadly, they did not realize they had been damned to the same fate as the wicked, for the Lord is King, and they must proclaim allegiance to Him in order to receive the grace He offers.[6]

The demons tempted and tormented not only the lost, but also those who belonged to the Kingdom of God. The monsters especially enjoyed terrorizing the Lord's servants, those who obeyed God's commandments and held to the testimony of Jesus. Their fates could not be changed once the King had covered His servants with His grace, but that didn't stop Satan from making valiant attempts anyway. The fact that they belonged to the King seemed to propel his fury even more; his rage caused him to strain for their demise. He knew it was in vain, for my Master's army and I were committed to serving our King. We battled daily against the powers of darkness and the ruler of evil. All the while, the humans were entirely unaware of the war being waged all around them, a battle for their souls. The Lord's army and I wrestled for their very lives! Not their lives as the humans knew it, but for the life my Master provided: eternity in His presence and in His Kingdom. They did not realize that a day of judgment was coming, a day when my Master would reclaim all who belonged to His Kingdom. The remaining souls? They belonged to Satan, and he would drag them down into the fiery furnace of the Abyss.[7]

They did not understand that in the last days, scoffers would come, scoffing and following their own evil desires. They would say, "Where is this 'coming' he promised? Ever since our fathers died, everything goes on as it has since the beginning of creation."[8]

They deliberately forgot that long ago, by God's Word, the heavens existed and the earth was formed out of the water and by the water. By these waters the world was deluged and destroyed. By the same Word, the present heavens and earth were being reserved for fire, being kept for the Day of Judgment and destruction of ungodly men.[9]

The Lord is not slow in keeping His promise, as some understand slowness, for with the Lord a day is like a thousand years, and a thousand years are like a day. He is patient with them, not wanting anyone to perish, but everyone to come to repentance.

The day of the Lord would come like a thief in the night. The heavens would disappear with a roar. The elements would be destroyed by fire, and the earth and everything in it would be laid bare. That day would bring about the destruction of the heavens by fire, and the elements would melt in the heat. But in keeping with His promise, His servants could look forward to a New Heaven and a New Earth, the home of righteousness.[10]

Yet neither I nor the Son of God Himself knew when this day would come.

"Michael, do you recognize that man?" The sweet sound of my Master's voice interrupted my thoughts, and I realized I had been staring into the Lord's eyes this entire time. I tore my gaze from His, trying not to focus on all I had seen within His eyes. It was as if they held within them the entire story, from beginning to end. I redirected my thoughts and again leaned over the portal. This time, I examined the man more closely.

Recognition set in, "Yes, my King, I know the man. He is one of Your own. I remember the day my angel warriors and I celebrated his citizenship, when he declared Your name!"

My Lord nodded his head, but His eyes prodded me to look further. I turned back to the portal.

"Who is this woman, my Lord? I don't seem to recognize her."

"She is a lost soul, Michael, one who has not yet accepted My offer into the Kingdom."

The King's words pierced through my heart, and I felt the tears welling up in my eyes. I simply could not bear the thought that some humans would never make it into the paradise that is the Lord's Kingdom.

The King didn't take His eyes away from the portal. He just continued to stare at the humans. "I need you and your army to watch over them, Michael." The Lord's knuckles went white as He clenched His fists. "It is of utmost importance that you protect these two from the warriors of darkness. They are My workmanship, created in Christ Jesus to do good works, which I prepared in advance for them to do."[11]

I bowed my head, not questioning His command. "Yes, my Lord. I will serve you with honor."

"Go quickly then, Michael, for Satan and his demons are near!"

As He said this, a dark winged figure swept past the viewing area of the portal and dove down toward the man and the woman who were laughing, completely unaware of the darkness that closed in on them.

{Chapter 10}

"THANKS, AGAIN FOR JOINING me today," Adam said to Evelyn as he pulled the Jeep alongside her own four-wheel-drive rental. It was parked in the exact spot where they left it earlier that morning.

It was late now, and they hadn't even been able to make the entire trip up the road to Hana. *Oh well, maybe there will be a next time*, Adam found himself silently hoping. He had never met a girl like Evelyn before: smart, funny, beautiful. She seemed to enjoy herself on the ride up, but at times, Adam sensed her slight unease. Then again, he couldn't blame her. It was an awfully bold move, inviting a girl he just met to take a day-long joy ride up the windy hillside of Maui. In fact, Adam was surprised she agreed to his invitation. It was strange. Even though they had just met, for Adam, it felt like he had known Evelyn a lifetime.

"It was my pleasure," Evelyn unbuckled her seatbelt and flashed Adam a look of sincerity, "I'm glad you suggested we make the trip together. I had a lot of fun."

"Well, it sure was great to have your company, not to mention you made a fantastic tour guide. How do you know so much about the history and culture of the islands?"

"Like I said, this isn't my first time making the trek." Evelyn leaned forward and reached for her jacket that was crumpled in a ball by her feet. "I used to have family on the island."

Evelyn continued gathering her things from Adam's car and searched for her keys in her backpack. Adam knew that in just a few short moments Evelyn would be out the door, but he wasn't quite ready to say goodbye. He was just getting ready to ask her about her family when he saw Evelyn's hand reach for the passenger side door. His mind started reeling, scrambling for a way to have just another moment with her. Before he could stop himself, he nearly shouted, "Hey, I was thinking..."

Evelyn stopped mid push and turned to look at Adam. *Man, she has beautiful eyes.* They seemed to be prompting him to continue.

"This was a lot of fun today, one of the best times I've had in quite a while." Adam tried not to think about how pathetic he must sound. "I guess what I'm trying to say is... I mean, if you are interested... Would you like to meet up again sometime?" *I must sound like a complete idiot!*

Evelyn gave him a warm, somewhat apologetic smile. There was hesitation in her eyes. Adam knew where this was going, *shot down.* Too late, Adam was committed now, and he wasn't willing to back down. Desperately he tried to scrape his thoughts together. *How can I convince her to see me again?* And then it hit him, as if God Himself had whispered the obvious solution. Adam would appeal to her quizzical nature!

Before Evelyn even had a chance to respond, Adam piped up, "Hey, I know. Why don't you check out my lecture this Friday? I never did get the opportunity to tell you more about my job, and it will give you a chance to see the other beautiful side of the natural world that you love so much."

Adam saw her defenses begin to melt. He could tell Evelyn was touched that he remembered what she said almost eight hours earlier. *How couldn't I? She's amazing!* The entire day, Adam clung to her every word. He latched onto them, storing them away in his memory so that later he could replay the sound of her sweet voice, but right now the only words standing out in his mind were the ones from earlier that day, the words Evelyn seemed to hopelessly utter, *I just can't help but wonder if there really is a God out there.*

Oddly enough, although Adam had spent the better part of a day with Evelyn, he never did find the right opportunity to mention that little fact about him being a Bible-believing scientist... until now. He smiled as he realized the simplicity of the matter.

There was a muffled jangling as Evelyn finally located her keys in the bottom of her bag. Fidgeting nervously, she pulled them out. Suddenly, it dawned on Adam how insane his invitation must sound. Evelyn was probably just being polite when she agreed to be his tour guide and join him for the drive. Adam had been clinging to the hope that Evelyn sensed whatever connection it was that he was feeling towards her. Now, he realized how foolish it was to think that a girl like Evelyn might possibly take interest in a guy like him. After a few brief seconds of rationalization, Adam decided the only polite thing to do would be to offer Evelyn an easy "out" if she weren't interested in him.

Despite not wanting to back down from his invitation, Adam half-heartedly offered, "I totally understand if you are busy with work and all. I mean... if you don't think you would be able to make it, I would understand."

Adam thought he saw contemplation in Evelyn's eyes, like she knew she wasn't too busy, but might take the "out" anyway. Adam had resolved her answer in his mind and was coming to terms with her expected refusal. *Time to walk her to her car.* Defeat written across his face, Adam turned from Evelyn and reached for the ignition. He was just about to shut off the Jeep when his hand was halted by a sudden jolt of energy. He glanced down to identify the source of power. Evelyn's hand was on his, pausing his action.

Adam glanced up into Evelyn's eyes where all the hesitation that had once been seemed to have faded away. She cocked her head to the side and leaned forward in her seat a little. A smile lit up her face and warmed Adam's soul.

"I'd love to."

Adam felt as if a weight had been lifted off his chest. He exhaled, not realizing he had been holding his breath. *I can't believe she said yes!* Silently, he wondered if Evelyn had any clue as to what was in store for her on Friday.

Adam returned her beaming grin. Without a word, he hopped out of the Jeep, planning to walk Evelyn to her car. As he made his way around the back of the rental, Adam lifted up an unspoken prayer that maybe, just maybe, he could impact this woman in a completely life-altering way. And perhaps, with a little help from above, she might be just the girl who would change his own world forever.

{~}

A cool breeze whipped across the hillside as the darkness of night closed in around the man and the woman. The woman shivered from the night air as the man continued giving her directions to the university where he would be speaking later that week. *Speaking, ha! More like preaching,* the demon spat in disgust as he continued watching from where he was perched in a nearby tree.

He had been sent by the boss, his mission to follow the man and do everything in his power to keep him from spreading the story of God and His Jesus. The demon shuddered at the mere thought of the Son's name.

The demon was not unfamiliar with the man. He had the pleasure of tormenting him from time to time, particularly whenever he got all "preachy." It was looking like the man's new job at the university would provide plenty of opportunities for reunion.

"How touching," the demon sputtered sarcastically. "I would have thought he'd learned his lesson by now. Yet here he is once again, making plans to save another soul." *Well not this time.*

The demon glared upward, impatiently searching the blackening sky. *Late as usual,* he fumed. The ugly beast could feel his blood boiling. He hated being made to wait. He huffed loudly, hoping his cohort was not so far off that he couldn't hear the irritation that was growing with each passing minute. Realizing his impatience was doing nothing to hurry the process, he decided to take a closer look at the man's newest interest. The demon narrowed his sulfur-colored eyes in on the woman. *Ah, of course!* He recognized her. She was the assignment of one of the other warriors of darkness, the one who was currently on his last nerve, the demon Deception. His skin crawled with frustration. Because of this wretched woman he would have to be stuck on another mission with Deception! He could have taken care of this himself.

"What a waste of time!" the demon shouted to no one in particular. *Why would Deception need reinforcement to end one miserable life?*

The monster shifted his muscled body, straining to get a better look. *So this is the woman the boss wants dead?* The demon nearly laughed. *This is pathetic!* She had no defenses. She didn't even belong to God. She was a lost soul, fair game for Satan and his minions. She sure didn't look like much of a threat. This would be an easy job for one demon to carry out, but two? *Ha, she will be dead before she ever makes it back to town!*

The demon examined the scene closer. That was when he noticed it: the look in the man's eyes as he said his goodbyes to the woman. Suddenly, it dawned on the demon why he was called in on this mission. The man was totally falling for the woman. The demon rubbed his hands together delighted at this new-found piece of information. How much easier this would make his job if the man's defenses were weakened by his flustered emotions.

A screech from above signaled the arrival of the demon Deception. The demon shook his head and snorted his disapproval as Deception swooped into view and landed on a nearby tree. The boughs bounced under his weight, and the leaves shook loudly, but for the humans it was no more than the rustling of the wind. Deception nodded at the other demon, acknowledging his presence.

Deception's partner looked him over. He was a frightful sight indeed. The demon shuddered. Deception may have been a pain, but at least he was good at his job. Between the two of them, the man and the woman didn't stand a chance! *Yes*, the demon thought, *there will be no redeeming going on during our watch.* Neither demon said a word. Now they both understood their roles on this mission.

They followed the woman with their beady, yellow eyes as she said goodbye to the man and climbed into her own vehicle. Through her open window, she gave a final wave to the man as he pulled onto the pavement and into the night. She started up the rental SUV and maneuvered onto the unlit road, leaving a small cloud of dust in her wake.

Once the man and the woman were out of sight, the heinous monsters turned toward each other. With a nod of their head, they opened their black, battered wings. Ready to take to the sky, they both lifted their hideous faces upward, and in unison, the demons leapt into the darkness. With the black of night covering them, they found their way to the road. They tracked the humans at a distance, Deception trailing the woman, while the man was followed by his own terrorizing demon, Death.

{Chapter 11}

"I AM SUCH AN IDIOT!" Evelyn slammed her fist on the steering wheel. "What was I thinking, getting into a car with a complete stranger, taking a ride up a remote jungle road?" Evelyn was practically shouting. "Oh, but he is so handsome, so nice…" she mocked herself. "He's different than the rest…" She punched the radio button with her index finger. "Oh, and then you agree to go see him speak at a lecture?" she sputtered. "Girl, where have your defenses gone? You're so weak." Evelyn shook her head in disgust, thankful no one was around to witness the verbal conflict she was having with herself.

She flipped through the radio stations, trying to find one that would come in clearly, but for one reason or another, the entire radio was static. The red glow of Adam's break lights up ahead, drew Evelyn's attention back to the road. It took a sharp turn to the left, and Evelyn slowed down, but not soon enough. She felt the weight of the SUV countering against her. Evelyn wasn't used to driving a vehicle that sat up so high. Usually on business trips, she rented something small and sporty.

It was getting darker now, and Evelyn started to have a difficult time seeing the road up ahead. There wasn't even a single street lamp to illuminate the winding path before her. She tried focusing on Adam's tail lights, but the bends and hairpin turns made it almost impossible to keep him in view. Evelyn settled in for the drive, placing both hands on the steering wheel. She tried to let the crackling of the radio soothe her frustrations like a calming white noise.

She started rationalizing with herself, "Okay, so you made a mistake. At least, nothing bad happened. You're safe. You didn't say anything you would regret, and you don't even have to go to the lecture." She smiled to herself, imagining how ridiculous her little conversation must sound if anyone were around to hear. "He won't even remember if you don't show up." Evelyn took a deep breath. Somehow she doubted that Adam would forget her promise to attend his lecture. She swallowed the lump that was building in her throat. She imagined the look that was sure to grace Adam's face when he realized Evelyn had stood him up. She felt guilty. Despite Evelyn's anger for her hasty decision to spend the day with a complete stranger, she didn't regret it. Adam was amazing. In fact, she felt completely comfortable and at ease with him. Other than that stupid little voice in her head that said, "All men are the same," Evelyn found no reason why she shouldn't trust Adam.

"Maybe I should go," she wondered aloud. She smiled, surprised to admit to herself that she actually did have fun today. Her stomach twisted a little at the thought of Adam. He really was quite the gentleman, opening doors and everything. *Good grief, make up your mind,* Evelyn silently lectured herself. *It's like there's a battle going on inside my head!* "Get a grip, Ev!"

She stopped. That was what Adam called her...Ev, the nickname her stepfather had given her. Evelyn started to consider the irony. Why would someone she had just met call her by that name, the name used by the only person with whom she had ever been close. She didn't know why, but she definitely wanted to find out. In that moment, she made up her mind. Adam hadn't given Evelyn any reason to believe he was anything but the charming, good-hearted man that he presented himself to be. She would go to the lecture. With a deep sigh, Evelyn smiled to herself, pleased that she had been able to quiet the voices of the past to pursue the intrigue of the future.

Evelyn relaxed her shoulders and leaned back into the comfort of the leather driver's seat. Now that she had finally silenced her mind, she realized just how exhausted she was from the long day. She rubbed her burning eyes and forced her heavy lids open. Evelyn knew she needed to do something to stay awake. She had at least another hour before making it back to town and then another fifteen minutes or so to the marina where she was staying. She felt along the driver's side door for the window button. The window opened to the dark night, and relief washed over her as the cool evening air glided across her face. She opened the sun roof for good measure.

Evelyn drove this way for a few minutes before deciding it was the droning static of the radio that was lulling her into such a sleepy state. With one final attempt at locating a coherent radio station, she removed her right hand from its two o'clock position on the steering wheel. She looked down at the dashboard for only a split second, but it was enough.

{~}

Gliding above the black SUV, the demon Deception had been watching closely for his moment to strike the woman. *How should I do it*, he wondered to himself. *I could toy with her mind a bit more... no, I've already tried that, and she still decided to give this man a chance.* He huffed loudly as he followed the sharp bend in the road. The SUV's tires squealed in protest. A thought came to him, *or... I could just throw her off this cliff right now!*

The demon's face broke out into a wide, evil grin, exposing his gnarled and yellow fangs. Demise was the only certain way to win her soul, and besides, the boss wanted her dead anyway. He just hadn't realized his opportunity would come so soon. He licked his lips, almost able to taste the victory.

Deception swooped lower, keeping up with the pace of the SUV and maintaining his ever-watchful eye on the woman through the open sun roof. He saw the sleepy look in her eyes. This would be too easy. He waited, knowing that sooner or later his moment would come. And it did! The woman had both hands planted firmly on the steering wheel, but only a few short minutes later, she made her fatal flaw. Deception witnessed the exact moment that her hand reached for the stereo knob. He saw his opportunity and took it!

Directly up ahead was a sharp bend in the road. It broke hard to the left, leaving the right side of the roadway fully exposed to the sudden drop, leading to whatever lay below. Beyond the cliff-side of the windy pavement, was nothing but ocean, water as far as the eye could see, and large jagged rocks breaking the waves of the angry surf.

Deception's mind raced. He knew he had mere seconds to pull off this stunt, and he would need to make use of each one if this plan was going to work. It played out in slow motion. Deception saw the woman remove her hand from the steering wheel and fix her eyes on the dashboard display. In half a second's time, Deception forced open his wings. They expanded wide, causing a parachute-like effect that slowed the beast just enough to catch the back end of the vehicle. He spread his muscled arms and locked his talon-like hands on the back corners of the SUV's roof.

There was an awful screeching sound as the demon's nails dug into the metal. Had the woman been able to hear the events taking place in the spiritual realm, she would have cringed at the horrifying noise. As Deception's claws locked in, he heaved his body sideways, throwing the vehicle off balance and causing it to spin violently out of control. The beast clung determinedly to the vehicle, allowing it to make one complete revolution before pointing the front end directly toward the edge of the cliff. It would only be a matter of seconds now, and all that stood between the woman and the Abyss was a small guardrail lining the depths to which she was doomed.

{~}

Before Evelyn could glance back up at the road, she felt the vehicle slip from her control. It spun viciously, providing only brief glimpses of the road, then the cliff, and then the rock wall opposite the cliff. Terrified, Evelyn grasped the steering wheel with both hands. She desperately tried to counter correct and pumped the brakes to no avail. The SUV screeched and whirled despite Evelyn's best attempts. She counted *one, two, three...* three complete revolutions of the vehicle as it spun like a top across the pavement.

Evelyn squeezed her eyes shut, unable to witness the sickening vision of the world dancing like a crazed ballerina before her. Silently she screamed, *help me please!*

Despite not wanting to watch the final moments of her life play out, Evelyn opened her eyes just as she felt the vehicle begin to make its fourth revolution. She was a quarter of the way into the turn and was heading straight for the edge of the cliff. *This is it.*

It was strange. Evelyn had often wondered what it would be like to live out the moments leading up to her death. She thought maybe it would be like the movies, where your entire life flashed before your eyes. Or maybe she would feel some sort of satisfaction for whatever impact she had left on the world. But this experience wasn't like that at all. Instead, it was as if time came to a screeching halt. The voices in Evelyn's mind were suddenly silenced, and she became acutely aware of her surroundings. The night wind whipping through the window sent a chill up Evelyn's spine. The orange glow of the dashboard stared back at her like haunting flames. The keys jangled noisily from the ignition, but aside from the adrenaline-induced sensory overload, Evelyn felt... empty. There was a gnawing sense of hallow regret but other than that, nothing.

Without warning, time caught up with Evelyn, or was it the other way around? Either way, it didn't matter now. It was as if her life was a film, and someone had just pressed the play button. These were the final minutes of the movie.

The vehicle continued its doom-bound journey, approaching the inevitable outcome, but Evelyn had seen enough. Knowing how this scene would end, Evelyn squeezed her eyes shut and gripped hopelessly to the wheel that she could not control.

{Chapter 12}

DECEPTION MUSTERED UP EVERY LAST bit of his strength and propelled himself and the vehicle forward, racing head first toward the edge of the cliff. This was the end of the road. The nose of the SUV peeked over the edge, followed by the left front tire. The vehicle began to tip. Deception could almost hear the approval of the boss when he delivered the news; *the woman is dead!* Deception braced himself for a final shove of the vehicle when suddenly, a force stronger than his own, counter-weighted and pushed back.

{~}

I came up from below the cliff's edge and rushed up the side of the mountain, where the vehicle was suspended precariously. It looked as if it were ready to topple. The woman was mere inches from plummeting to her death.

"Now, Michael!" Two of my angel warriors who were trailing me called out just as Deception lunged against the SUV. I reached it almost a second too late, but my hand caught the front fender right before the other front tire crossed the edge. I thrust myself against the hood of the automobile and heaved with all my might. I heard my comrades swooping in behind me, rushing to my side. I couldn't wait for them. Another second and the woman would be lost. That thought alone was enough to awaken my strength. My arms burned as I heaved once more, finally securing the vehicle back on solid ground.

My warriors were beside me now and leapt into action. One guided the front of the vehicle and the other the back. In their hands, they held the vehicle, and with their strength they carried the woman to safety. With a final turn, they brought the SUV to a stop, facing the woman away from the overhang. She was safe, *for now*.

A chilling howl pierced the night, drawing my attention away from the woman.

"Michael!" Deception growled under his breath. He began thrashing and uttering curses between snarls, tearing at his own flesh. I drew my flaming Sword of the Spirit, and my comrades rushed to my side. We didn't say a word but made our commanding presence known. All the while he snarled, sneered, and blasphemed the King.

I didn't dare bring a slanderous accusation against him, but declared in a loud voice, "The Lord rebukes you!" And with my command, he vanished into the night.[1]

I stole a final glance at the woman, ensuring she was safe before turning to my warriors. They nodded their understanding and without a word, we sheathed our weapons and took to the sky.

The battle had only begun.

{~}

A very shaky Evelyn cautiously made her way out of the vehicle that nearly tossed her to her death. She sucked in the cool night air, desperately trying to slow her racing heart and calm her labored breathing. *I'm alive!* Evelyn peered up at the nearly-full moon and traced its light back to the earth. She glanced around at the faintly illuminated scene where black tire tracks branded the pavement in a circular fashion, marking the events of the evening.

Without warning, a gut-wrenching sob erupted from deep within her soul. Evelyn lost all composure as she fell to her knees on the side of the road. Her small frame shuddered. She didn't even seem to notice the gravel scraping against her bare legs and hands as she gripped the solid ground. She frantically clung to the earth as if she might be taken from it, yet despite Evelyn's desperate hold on the physical ground, it could not stop her mind from flashing back to a memory, one she couldn't escape.

It was a night so similar to this one that Evelyn wasn't sure if she were in the past or present. She and her stepfather were traveling back late that night from spending the entire day on the road to Hana, taking in all its beauty and splendor. They were in his old, red pickup, a truck Evelyn had ridden shotgun in too many times to count. That's where she was sitting that night. If only she had been in the backseat, then maybe...

Evelyn's sobs grew louder as the oppressive and haunting reality of her past enveloped her.

{~}

When Deception was finally certain that Michael and the other angel warriors were gone, he quietly slipped out from his hiding place in the shadows. He scanned the moonlit pavement until he found the woman, crouched in the gravel on the side of the road.

"Right where I left you," he muttered under his breath. Deception was furious at the Archangel and his warriors for ruining his plan. He reared back his head and let out another howl of rage. The frightening echo of Deception's voice was interrupted by another eerie sound, wailing. Deception drew his attention back to the woman. *I guess the night isn't completely lost.* Deception couldn't destroy the woman tonight, not now that he knew Michael and his army were nearby, but he could direct all his hate and anger toward the woman. *Well, if I can't drag her there myself, I'll just make her night a living hell!* She was an absolute mess now, and the memories of her past were oh so fresh. Swooping in, Deception loomed over the woman. As her sobs continued to wrack her body, he began to whisper words over her, words that weren't true, words that were lies, words of pure deception.

{~}

In her mind's eye, Evelyn could see the dull glow of the dashboard lights in the pickup. The smell of her stepfather's aftershave mingled with the freshness of the cool night air that glided across her arm as she hung her hand out the window.

"Daddy," she gasped, "Look at all the stars! Oh, and the moon! It's beautiful. I think I can see its face!" Evelyn giggled as her stepfather leaned forward to peer up through the windshield at the nighttime display before them.

"It sure is something, Ev. Isn't it cool that God gives us amazing gifts like the night sky? And just because He loves us!" He reached over and brushed his hand softly against Evelyn's cheek, pushing back stray pieces of hair.

Evelyn's stepfather had been such a positive influence on her. Until she was five, Evelyn had never had a male role model in her life, but all that changed when her mother remarried. *Mother,* now that was a stretch. Evelyn didn't technically have a mother. She had been adopted as a baby. The woman who adopted Evelyn, the woman she would come to know as her mother figure, could not have children of her own, yet her husband desperately wanted a family. Evelyn's adoptive mother wanted nothing to do with children, but adopted Evelyn anyway to please her husband.

Evelyn never did know the man who was first married to her adoptive mother. He died of a massive heart attack when Evelyn was only seven months old, leaving Evelyn to grow up in a home with a mother, *correction,* a woman who didn't love her.

When Evelyn's adoptive mother remarried, her whole world changed with the welcoming of her stepfather. Here was a parental figure who cherished Evelyn and cared for her beyond anything she had ever known. He was a strong Christian man, a family man who had always wanted children. He told Evelyn, every night before bed, that she was a special gift to him from God.

Evelyn's adoptive mother completely changed her demeanor once her new husband, Evelyn's stepfather, came into the picture. She never let him see the resentment she had for the little girl. Instead, she played the role of the perfect, little wife, doting on her husband and hiding her secret from him.

Evelyn was almost ten when her stepfather's military job uprooted them again, this time stationing their family on the island of Hawaii. Thanks to her stepfather's career, Evelyn had been to three different schools in nearly five years. She hated moving. She was never anywhere long enough for it to feel like home, but that didn't matter. She had her stepfather, and somehow, just knowing she was with him was enough. Besides, Evelyn liked Hawaii. It was too bad they were only staying for two years. Even though the military took him away often, Evelyn's stepfather always made time with her a priority, like on Evelyn's tenth birthday when they made the drive up the road to Hana.

Evelyn's mind drifted away, and she was again sitting in the cab of the pickup, her stepfather's hand on her cheek, his words echoing softly in her ear. *It sure is something, Ev. Isn't it cool that God gives us amazing gifts like the night sky? And just because He loves us!*

Back in the present, Evelyn turned her face to that same night sky and screamed until her voice broke, "But why do You take Your gifts away!" The greatest gift Evelyn had ever received was a father who loved her, but she lost him. That night, Evelyn not only lost the only person that had ever truly loved her, but she lost all hope. She lost her faith in God.

Evelyn's mind swam with the hazy visions of that night. In her mind, she could see the small animal, illuminated by the full moon above, as it darted out across the road. The screech of the tires pierced Evelyn's ears as her stepfather willed the truck to stop. The soft notes of a ukulele drifted out of the radio, a strange contrast to the horror as the truck spun in the same top-like motion that Evelyn's SUV had done just moments before. As the vehicle danced across the pavement, Evelyn's eyes fell on the rocky, ledged wall up ahead. There was no way to avoid it. Evelyn's hand burned with the memory of her stepfather's hand squeezing her own as he whispered, "I love you, Ev."

As if playing out in slow motion, Evelyn saw the vision of her stepfather's powerful arms pulling at the steering wheel in one final and desperate attempt to protect Evelyn by redirecting the impact to the driver's side.

Memories of the hot tears rolling down her cheeks overwhelmed her. They slipped off her face and melted into her stepfather's shirt as she frantically shook him, trying to wake him from his slumber. The smell of clean linen and aftershave lulled Evelyn as she wept bitterly into his chest. She remained that way until the paramedics came and pried her away.

Evelyn clutched her chest as the familiar lump formed in her throat. Like many times before, she was overwhelmed with the sickening realization that this man died because of her.

"It's all your fault!" Deception whispered into her ear.

"It's all your fault!" her mother shouted to her at the funeral.

It's all my fault, Evelyn whispered to herself every day since the tragic loss of her stepfather.

Evelyn's mind slowly wandered back to the present. Her breathing settled, and the tears refused to fall. Just as suddenly as the memories attacked her, they began to fade away. Evelyn unfolded herself from the crumpled heap on the side of the road, realizing for the first time she was covered in dirt, blood, and tears. Slowly she stood up, rubbed her torn knees, and shook her tingling legs awake. Evelyn cautiously inhaled a deep breath to calm her shaking hands as she stumbled back to the vehicle. Once inside, she turned the key in the ignition, slowly put the SUV in reverse, and wiped her puffy eyes before looking over her shoulder. The gravel crunched softly under the tires as she maneuvered the SUV back onto the road and into the night.

For the remainder of the drive, Evelyn focused straight ahead, not taking her eyes off the road for a single second. She didn't even bother to look when, not quite a mile up ahead, she passed a familiar rock wall. Forever burned into her mind, Evelyn knew what was there, knew it from memory. She didn't need to look to know that there, planted firmly in the soil below the overhang of the cliff, stood an old wooden cross.

{Chapter 13}

A DAM DUG HIS BARE FEET into the soft sand as the surf came crashing in again, causing him to sink further with each rolling wave. The sun was just starting to hang lower in the sky, beginning its descent from the long day. Adam stuffed his hands in the front pockets of his hooded sweatshirt and whispered a soft prayer, casting to the Lord his cares and worries from the day. It had become a ritual in his daily rhythm, something Adam had picked up from watching his father when he was younger. Adam could remember his father, sitting outside on the front porch at the end of each day with a tall glass of sweet tea and talking with God. When Adam asked him what he was doing, his father told him he was throwing his worries to God so He could carry them over the horizon.

As Adam stood there on the beach, taking in the changing colors of the sunset, he could almost hear his father's deep baritone voice. "God, take this day with all its troubles and worries, tie it to the sun, and throw it over the horizon. I'll pick them back up tomorrow. And Lord," he'd call out, "somehow I know that when the sun rises, You'll make everything look a little brighter than it did the day before."

The sunset had become a visual reminder to Adam, as it was for his father, to release the stresses of the day. As Adam got older, he would often sit with his father on the front porch and join him in this little tradition. "Therefore," Adam's father's voice echoed in his mind, "do not worry about tomorrow, for tomorrow will worry about itself. Each day has enough trouble of its own."[1]

To which Adam would always reply, "Because of the Lord's great love we are not consumed, for His compassions never fail. They are new every morning. Great is Your faithfulness."[2]

The sound of laughter, coming from behind him on the beach, shook Adam from his thoughts. He turned to see a little boy running through the sand, and his father chasing after him. Not more than four years old, the little boy squealed with delight as he darted back and forth across the beach. The game continued on with the father allowing his son to outrun him for a moment or two, letting the little boy think he was the fastest thing in the world. Then, without any effort at all, the father would catch up to his son and scoop him up into his arms. He then proceeded to tackle the little boy into the sand, where a fit of tickling and laugher ensued. The child would then expertly slip out of his father's grip, and the chase would begin again.

A lump began to form in Adam's throat and a burning sensation started behind his eyes. Quickly he looked away from the happy family and turned his face upward, blinking back the tears that were sure to come. "Boy, do I miss you Dad." Adam exhaled loudly. "I thought coming here, to Maui, would help me forget and help me deal with your passing, but since I've been here…" Adam caught a tear with his sleeve, "everything reminds me of you."

Adam reached into the sand, pulled up a smooth stone, and skipped it across the surf before turning to walk in the other direction. As Adam made his way down the beach, he noticed what appeared to be a marina in the distance. It couldn't have been more than a mile past the resort where he was staying. Adam wasn't quite ready to turn in for the night. After the day he had, he wanted to watch every last color of the sunset fade away from view. *Tomorrow will be a new day*, he thought. *The weekend can't get here soon enough.*

Adam let his mind wander as his feet carried him away from the resort, shuffling through the course sand. He hoped the cool, salty air would clear his mind, but the vision of the little boy and his father kept creeping back to the forefront of his thoughts.

His father's passing had not been unexpected. When the doctors found the cancer, they didn't give him much more than a year. Adam's father shocked them all. Three years after his diagnosis, he celebrated his sixtieth birthday. He passed away almost three weeks later. That was last summer.

Although every day had been a struggle since his passing, Adam found comfort in knowing that his father had gone on to Heaven. Adam's father was a believer and devoted his life to God. In fact, he was the one who inspired Adam to pursue a career as a Bible-believing scientist. He was always encouraging Adam to follow his dreams and trust God to make them come true. For Adam, just going to work every day was a reminder of his dad. He had so much to thank him for. *How could I ever live up to a man like you?*

As Adam's stroll took him further down the beach, the sound of music danced across the breeze and greeted him with the sweet smells of barbeque. The once quiet and deserted beach was now dotted with people of all walks of life, and a growing crowd was mingling up ahead. Apparently, the marina was just a small part of the nearby attractions. An adjacent boardwalk funneled in both locals and tourists to the water's edge where sand sports and savory grilling were taking place. Couples of all ages walked hand in hand across the sandy shore, sipping their pre-dinner drinks and carrying their sandals. *Must be date night on the island*, Adam thought as he approached the marina. He shook the sand from his feet as he made his way up the boardwalk and out onto the pier, giving him a spectacular view of the amber sun melting into the honey-colored ocean. Dozens of sailboats lined the dock, and their tall masts framed the scene as the sapphire sky chased away the remaining light from the day.

Adam inhaled the cool evening air, allowing his mind to drift to the following day, Friday, which meant another open lecture for the university, and if she remembered, another chance to see Evelyn. Adam couldn't hold back his smile. Several times throughout the week, he'd found himself imagining what it would be like to see Evelyn again. On more than one occasion, he'd caught himself scanning the faces of strangers walking around town, hoping to catch a glimpse of the one who was sure to stand out.

Trying to take his mind off the beautiful Evelyn, Adam peered across the water at the sailboats lining the dock. He began reading the names bestowed upon each watercraft, loving how cleaver they sounded. The distraction seemed to be working. Adam really didn't want to get his hopes up too much. *What if she doesn't show?* He had been looking forward to their reunion all week. Adam slipped his sunglasses off and rubbed his brow. He'd never been this preoccupied with a girl before, especially one he had just met. It sure didn't seem right that a complete stranger could walk into his life and take over his thoughts so easily. "I might be in for it bad this time," Adam whispered.

The savory aromas from the restaurant grills grew heavier in the air, and Adam's stomach let out a low growl in protest. *I guess that's a sign that it's time to head back.* Adam took in one more long stare at the dipping sun before sliding his shades back down over his nose. As he did, his eye caught the glare off the back of one of the sailboats moored on the far side of the dock. Its crisp, white hull gleamed against the golden water, its stern glowing with the reflection of the sun.

Adam chuckled as he read the boat's name aloud, "Eden's Secret." It seemed fitting. With all its beauty and lushness, Maui certainly felt like a lost Eden of sorts. And secrets? It definitely seemed as if the island might have a few of those in store as well.

{Chapter 14}

"**H**AVE NO FEAR of sudden disaster or of the ruin that overtakes the wicked, for the Lord will be at your side and will keep your foot from being snared." I whispered these words in the man's ear as he stood at the podium, delivering the lecture to a crowded auditorium. He did not perceive my presence immediately to his right or the attendance of one of my angel warriors at his left.[1]

"You will be saved." I continued whispering the protecting and encouraging words of the King. "You will not fall by the sword but will escape with your life because you trust in the Lord, the Almighty King."[2]

Our flaming swords were drawn, and we stood poised, ready at a moment's notice to protect the man to the end, even to our own detriment. My comrade and I scanned the room with watchful eyes, searching for even the slightest indication that there was trouble brewing. While the man's intriguing lecture series had packed a full house, it did not compare to the crowd it had drawn in the spiritual realm. The small auditorium was at full capacity, brimming with spiritual bodies, completely unseen to the human eye. Anytime there was a gathering in the earthly realm declaring the Lord's truth, there were always spiritual forces present, both good and evil.

The space was absolutely stifling and reeked with the aroma of sulfur and decay. Demons were everywhere! They swarmed around the humans, attempting to grab hold of their minds and twist any truths that dared to enter their ears. Satan's attempt to derail the King's followers and lost souls was magnified whenever one of my Master's disciples spoke boldly the King's words.

But we were there, always present, always guarding the King's followers, protecting and waging battles for the unclaimed souls.

Again, I peered out across the room and observed the bright lights among the darkness. It was the light of the angel warriors pacing through the auditorium, watching over the humans, waiting for a demon to make its move.

As I continued to scan the perimeter, a movement in the back of the room caught the corner of my eye. I narrowed in. A large, ominous figure separated itself from the hoard of minions and leaned casually against the back wall. His thick arms were crossed in front of his chest, and his impressive wingspan was folded behind him. I followed the demon's gaze. It seemed it was focused directly on me. I gripped my hilt tighter and braced my shoulders. My comrade must have noticed the shift in my stance, for I saw his own posture go rigid as he made an advance toward me. I held up a halting hand, knowing my warrior would come to my aid without any reservations, but I had to be certain before placing one of my own in a position of danger. My fellow warrior followed my gaze, and we both waited. The man shifted at the podium and brought a bottle of water up to his lips. I saw the demon's yellow, piercing eyes follow the man's every movement. It was him. He was back once again to torment the man, the demon Death.

I stared him down, not daring to revoke my glare for even a second. I waited for him to make an advance, but Death never moved. He never looked me in the eye, but continued to observe the man. It was as if he merely wished to make his presence known, for when the lecture finally ended, and the man stepped away from the podium, Death dispersed with the other dark personalities. A sudden sense of apprehension overwhelmed me. I knew it wouldn't be the last we'd see of him.

{~}

Applause filled the auditorium as Adam stepped down from the podium, nodding his gratitude to the audience as he made his way to the side of the stage. With the conclusion of the lecture, the crowd dispersed, and individual conversations began to formulate throughout the room. Adam bit his lower lip and surveyed the crowd before taking the stairs to the auditorium floor. There, a steady line was beginning to assemble. It was a format to which Adam was becoming accustomed, as both students and faculty waited patiently to pose their burning questions.

Adam fired off answers and made small talk with his peers, all the while scanning the crowd just as he'd been doing during the delivery of his presentation. As always, there was a room filled with inquiring and inquisitive faces staring back at him, but there was only one in particular Adam hoped to see.

It didn't take him long to work his way through the line of faculty and students. He may have short-changed his answers, but only a little. He was eager to get through the crowd to see if a certain someone had made an appearance, but Adam started to get the sinking feeling he'd been stood up.

After talking briefly with a small group of students, Adam finally reached the end of the line where he was greeted by a broad, white smile. It was Evelyn.

"Hey! You made it. I'm so glad you were able to get here!" Adam extended his hand to the lovely Evelyn. She was the epitome of casual-elegance in her coral sundress and sandals. Her long, dark hair tumbled around her shoulders, and a pair of large sunglasses perched on top of her head and held the wispy pieces off her face. She accepted his handshake with little hesitation.

"So," Adam started, "How have you been? I didn't see you when I was up there talking." Adam nodded toward the stage. "I didn't think you were actually here, but I'm really glad you made it."

"I got here a few minutes late, so I sneaked in quietly and hung out by the back wall."

"Makes sense," Adam beamed, still stunned that he was standing here and actually speaking with Evelyn. All week, he envisioned what it would be like to see her again. He almost wanted to pinch himself to be certain this was not just another well-crafted product of his imagination. When Evelyn cleared her throat, Adam finally realized he had been adrift in his own little world. Still at a loss for words, he finally offered, "So what did you think?"

His question evoked a chuckle from Evelyn and brought a "you're-unbelievable" type of grin to her beautiful face. "What did I think?" Her eyebrows shot up so high Adam thought they might jump off her forehead. "I think you have some explaining to do!" Evelyn smiled, but Adam could clearly see the look of confusion and surprise in her slate-grey eyes. Adam knew he hadn't exactly prepared her for what she would be hearing in his lecture. Not once had he hinted to any sort of faith. Obviously Evelyn was baffled by Adam's line of career and more importantly, why he hadn't brought it up on their first date.

Date? Adam questioned himself, *now where did that thought come from?*

Evelyn crossed her slender arms in front of her and tapped her bronze, sandaled foot as if impatiently waiting for Adam's response.

"Okay, okay, I know I didn't exactly indulge you on all the details of my career, but in my defense, you didn't ask a lot of questions," Adam held up his hands in justification, hoping to ease any tension with humor. Evelyn rolled her eyes, still seemingly unsure of the situation. At least, she was smiling.

"Fair enough," Evelyn let her arms unfold to her sides, lowering her guard at the heart-melting smile Adam flashed in her direction. "I think you were being a little evasive, but I'll give you the benefit of the doubt. And!" she nearly shouted while pointing a jesting finger in his face, "I still say you have some explaining to do!"

A wave of relief and excitement washed over Adam. Not only was Evelyn actually standing here in front of him, but also she wasn't angry that he hadn't disclosed his faith based career until now. *A grace giving woman,* Adam thought, *just the kind I need!* The thought of having to explain himself to Evelyn was just the opportunity he had been hoping for. In order to clarify his intentions and explain his career, it would take some time, time Adam would have to spend with Evelyn. *What a shame,* he playfully thought.

"All right, all right! If you insist." He feigned reluctant submission, but his boyish grin gave it away. Evelyn leaned forward and gave him a playful punch in the arm. Adam rubbed his arm as if she had just wounded more than his pride.

Okay, so maybe it wasn't all an act. She was strong! Adam remembered a friend telling him, when he was a kid, that girls are mean to you when they like you. Silently, Adam hoped this was still true.

"Hell-o..." Adam realized he had been staring again when Evelyn waved her hand in front of his face. "I'm still waiting for my explanation." Adam could hear the impatience in her voice, but a teasing smile was still adorning her face. Adam took it as a yes and silently celebrated.

Out loud he said, "All right, I'll explain everything, but I need to know, how much time do you have?"

{~}

A few hours later, Evelyn found herself at the counter of a small, family owned café, standing beside the most fascinating man she'd ever met. Glancing at the clock behind the counter, Evelyn couldn't believe how late it was. It felt like only minutes had passed since they left the university, yet here they were already on their second cup of coffee. Adam tipped the teenage girl behind the counter, and he and Evelyn made their way back down to the sandy shore where they spent the better half of the afternoon talking.

Evelyn stole a glance at Adam as they shuffled across the beach. He had the cuffs of his grey dress pants rolled up and was carrying his shoes in his hand. He pushed up the sleeves of his white button-down shirt, revealing his strong forearms. Evelyn tried not to stare at his model-like physique and focused her attention instead on the other beach patrons. For the first time, Evelyn noticed people were staring at them. Correction, people were staring at him! Evelyn tried not to laugh. Apparently, she wasn't the only woman on the island to take notice of the man in her company.

"I'm impressed," Evelyn offered as she took a sip of her coffee.

"I know," Adam sipped his own brew, "This coffee is great. I've stopped to get a cup every morning since I've been here."

"I didn't mean the coffee." Evelyn chuckled and faced him as they reached the dry patch of sand where they had been sitting before. She lowered herself onto the soft ground.

"Oh?"

Adam took a seat across from her. As he did, Evelyn lowered her voice and leaned in like she had a secret to share. "I'm impressed because it seems as if you managed to capture the attention of every woman on the beach."

Adam leaned in closer. "You don't say?" He seemed intrigued.

"Look." Evelyn nodded her head toward the water where a woman pretended to look anywhere except directly at Adam, but she was failing miserably.

"Subtlety is not her strong suit, I see," Adam laughed before allowing his tone to take on a more serious note. "But if we are watching each other's backs..." he raised his eyebrows and lowered his voice even more, "then I have to warn you, you've drawn quite a bit of attention yourself."

Evelyn felt her face flush and her heart quicken. *Who would be staring at me?* She glanced around nervously. She didn't like the idea that someone could possibly be watching her.

"Where?" The word came out sounding a little more strained than she anticipated. Evelyn threw a quick peek over her left shoulder, and Adam let out a low chuckle. He placed a tender hand under her chin and directed her gaze back towards his.

"Right here."

Now Evelyn was really blushing, but at the same time she felt her anxiety subsiding and her pulse returning to its normal rate. She was relieved to know there wasn't some strange man lurking on the beach watching her every move, but all the same, she wasn't sure what to say to a man who had just admitted to taking some sort of interest in her.

"I can see subtlety is not your thing either?" She questioned, trying to hide her true emotions.

"Ha, no, no..." Adam started drawing with his finger in the sand. "Subtlety is definitely not my thing. I've always been one to speak my mind," his eyes shot up to meet hers, "and my heart."

"And I've always been one to sidestep awkward conversations," Evelyn interjected quickly. She liked Adam, but this was just getting a little uncomfortable.

"So," she said, not missing a beat. "Thanks for 'explaining' yourself, so to speak." She offered her warmest smile, not wanting to hurt Adam by shooting him down so fast. She just wanted to give him fair warning that those conversations were currently taboo.

"You're so knowledgeable. I never realized science and the Bible are so intertwined. I always wondered if the two fit together. I usually picture them as completely separate schools of thought, but now I can see there are definitely some other ways to look at it. It's great that you can offer such concrete support to those who share your faith."

"Well, thank you." Adam seemed to have recovered from Evelyn's candor.

"You're very welcome. And thank you," Evelyn lifted her coffee to her lips and took another sip, "for a delicious cup of coffee and great company."

Adam shifted and continued drawing shapes with his finger in the sand. He was avoiding Evelyn's eyes. "So Ev, tell me more about you. How does everything we've been talking about fit with what you believe?"

Evelyn stiffened at the shortened use of her name. *This doesn't seem like a conversation I want to have either*, she thought. She hesitated just a second too long, and Adam looked up to peer into her eyes. Evelyn realized she couldn't avoid this topic any longer. Strangely, maybe she wanted to have this conversation more than she thought.

"How does this fit with what I believe?" Evelyn repeated. She bit her lower lip, "I guess I'm not sure. I mean, I'm not a Christian, so..." she trailed off.

"Not a Christian?" Adam set his cardboard cup in the sand.

"Uh... no?" Her words came out more like a question than a statement. Adam's eyes prodded her to continue. "I guess I can't identify with the 'Christ' part," Evelyn said, realizing Adam was dredging up a discussion she'd never even had with herself, beliefs she didn't realize she had. "I suppose I feel like you have to believe that Jesus was the son of God in order to call yourself a 'Christ-ian.'" She emphasized the Christ part. "I mean, I think Jesus was probably a moral man and a good teacher, but I don't believe He was God's Son."

"Well, let me play devil's advocate for a minute. No pun intended." Adam settled into the sand with his knees propped up in front of him, leaning back on his hands for support. "Actually, I don't think Jesus was a good teacher."

Evelyn was incredulous. "Wait a minute. I thought you were a Christian?"

Adam flashed her a crooked grin. "Define Christian." Evelyn just stared back. "Most of the time that title has a negative connotation attached to it, wouldn't you agree?" Evelyn nodded. "Most people think of Christians as hypocritical, religious fanatics. I call myself a follower of Jesus. I'm not a religious person. I'm a relational person. I don't want anything to do with religion, but I want everything to do with a relationship with my King."

Evelyn was speechless. She never heard anyone talk about God in that way. It seemed disrespectful to talk about God in that manner, although she didn't think He existed. Instead, Evelyn felt a sense of peace and ease with this man and the way He talked about his King. *King?* She never heard anyone use that term when talking about God before, at least, not the way Adam did.

Evelyn leaned back in the sand and slipped off her shoes, not realizing she was mirroring the position of Adam. She cocked her head to one side, letting her long hair fall over one shoulder. "Okay, you win. You have my full attention. Go on," she prodded. The look on Adam's face said he was just waiting for her to ask him to continue.

"Okay, so a lot of people who claim they are not a Christian say the exact same thing, that Jesus was a great teacher, but they don't believe He was the Son of God. The truth is, they couldn't be any further from the truth. In Jesus' day, he was preaching against everything the law and the religion of that day taught. Jesus was a radical. The things He said, the miracles He performed, they were all highly controversial. Jesus claimed to be the Son of God. That's an incredibly bold statement for anyone to make. It's an utterly blasphemous thing to say. Unless…"

Evelyn filled in the blank, "Unless it's true."

"Exactly. So that leaves only two options. Either Jesus was Who He said He was, the Christ, the Son of God, born as a man to save us from the wages of sin, which is death, or He was the biggest liar and lunatic of all time."

Evelyn just stared back at Adam, unsure of what to say. Adam was right. *Jesus wasn't a good teacher.* Based on Evelyn's own beliefs, she would be lumping Jesus in with the crazy crowd, and the only other option was that this Man, Who walked the earth some two-thousand years ago, was the living, breathing, in-the-flesh, Son of God. Evelyn's head was spinning. Information overload was beginning to set in.

Adam must have noticed because he quickly stood up and pulled her to her feet. "Sorry, I get a little carried away when talking about this kind of stuff."

"No, don't be," Evelyn protested. "It's actually quite refreshing to see passion in someone when they talk about their faith. You don't see that very often in people professing to have a faith in God."

"You're right about that. But if people truly knew God in the way He created us to know Him, they would have that kind of passion. God's not into religion. Religion is about rituals and moral codes that pertain to a set of beliefs. God is about love, period. Religion makes people feel inadequate, like they have to strive constantly to become something they are not. But God says we are already everything we could possibly be because of Him, because He made us in His image. He doesn't want us to feel inadequate. He wants us to feel loved! And in return, He wants us to love Him and others, which quite frankly, you can't help doing when you're so filled with God's love. When you truly understand God's plan, you can't help but have passion!"

"Wow," was all Evelyn could utter. Their conversation took a detour, breezing right past the line of "uncomfortable." There was no turning back now. As Evelyn stood there with her hands still firmly held within Adam's, something was awakened inside her. She didn't know what, but one thing was for sure, she could no longer keep from spilling her heart to Adam. He was different. He was special. Although Evelyn had long ago stopped believing in a loving God, there was something so pure and raw about Adam's passion that drew her in. *I'm really in trouble now.*

As they stood there, neither one speaking, Evelyn became aware of that same warm, electrifying sensation passing between their hands. Finally, Adam's gaze met Evelyn's. His own bluish-grey eyes seemed to be searching hers, peering into her very soul. Despite all Evelyn's reservations about getting involved with another man, she couldn't help it. She was falling for Adam.

{Chapter 15}

Adam finished his afternoon run and returned to his spacious hotel suite at a quarter to six. His stomach rumbled in protest. The only thing he had offered it since breakfast that morning was an apple and a cup of coffee. He mopped his forehead with the balled up t-shirt in his hand. *By the time I get used to this heat, it will be time for me to leave the island,* he thought as he dug into his pocket for his key card.

Adam entered the room and took a quick glance at the clock on the end table. *I guess I was running longer than I thought.* He hurriedly slipped off his sand-covered gym shoes and ducked into the adjoining bathroom to turn on the shower. Not only did he have hunger pangs filling his stomach, but now he was feeling a sense of anxiety that he'd never known before. Adam never thought he'd see this day, but after a few weeks of meeting over coffee, Evelyn finally agreed to a date with him, a real date, with dinner, dessert, and the understood implication that the person extending the invitation had taken a special interest in the one being invited. Tonight was the fourth time Adam asked Evelyn out to dinner, and each time before she had promptly responded that she already had plans. Adam wasn't sure if she had been telling the truth all those times, or if he just finally wore her down. He had a hard time reading Evelyn. He didn't get it. Evelyn was amazing, yet she gave the impression that she couldn't understand why Adam, or anyone for that matter, would be interested in her. *How could anyone not be interested in her?* The past few weeks only magnified the attraction he felt. He found that the more time he spent with Evelyn, the more he wanted to be around her. Adam had crushes before, but the way he felt toward Evelyn was definitely not a crush. It was something more.

Adam threw open his suitcase to retrieve his toiletries and clean clothes. Evelyn would be meeting him in the resort lobby in fifteen minutes. It was a good thing his entire routine hardly even took him five minutes. He was still bothered by the idea that Evelyn would be picking him up for their date, instead of the other way around. Adam was insistent on picking Evelyn up from her hotel, but she was adamantly against it. He finally gave in when she pulled the, "I'm-more-familiar-with-the-island-than-you-are" card. Still, he didn't like the idea, but if it made Evelyn more comfortable, then he would just deal with it. Besides, the whole point of picking Evelyn up was to make her feel special and respected. If the idea made her uncomfortable, it was counterintuitive as far as he was concerned.

Adam dug his hand through the upper pocket of his luggage, searching for his favorite watch. *I know I packed it.* He hadn't worn it since landing on the island. It had belonged to his father. Adam only wore the watch one other time, at his father's funeral. But tonight was a special occasion, and it seemed appropriate to wear such a sentimental piece.

Finally, Adam's hand brushed against the familiar box. As he pulled it out, it caught on something. A piece of four by six photo paper slipped out of the upper pocket of Adam's luggage. It fluttered to the ground and landed face down on top of Adam's clean, folded slacks. He stopped. Adam didn't have to look. He knew what it was, but he picked it up anyway. Slowly he turned the photo over in his hand. It was a picture of Adam taken about a year ago. He was wearing a big, broad smile. Adam remembered that day. It had been awhile since he'd felt that happy, but the last few weeks with Evelyn seemed to rekindle a sense of joy that he had lost over the past year.

In the photo, Adam had his arms wrapped in an embrace around the neck of a furry, blonde retriever. The dog's tongue flopped to one side, and the corners of his mouth seemed to turn upward in a smile. His bright puppy-like eyes deceived the tell-tale signs of white around his muzzle. The dog had been Adam's closest companion for fourteen years. He was given to Adam as a puppy, a gift from someone who deeply loved him, his dad. Not wanting to be outdone in the giving of love, Adam's furry companion remained by Adam's side as his most loyal friend until he passed away just two months ago. Adam had been heart broken. He still was.

Adam lived alone in his two-bedroom ranch home, and the silence that followed the passing of first his father and then his best friend was almost unbearable at times. The wounds were still so fresh.

As Adam crouched by his luggage and stared at the photo, a burning sensation began building behind his eyes. He quickly replaced the photo to its designated pocket, scooped up his clothes and shower accessories, and crossed the floor to the bathroom. The small room was already thick with steam from when he turned on the hot water moments ago. The water rumbled loudly in the small resort bathroom and made promises to soothe Adam's pain. He stepped into the shower stall and dunked his head under the thundering flow. As he stood there allowing the shower to melt away his tension, Adam couldn't tell if it was water or tears that streamed down his face.

{~}

I stood by my Master's side, peering through the portal to the world below where Death was hovering in the man's hotel bathroom. We saw the demon whispering words in the man's ears, surfacing feelings of guilt and attempting to reopen closed wounds. It was his specialty. Death could not cause a human to kill. That was the domain of the heinous, demon Murder. What Death could do was cause uncontrollable feelings of grief and remorse that oftentimes could become even more self-destructing.

The man hung his head in his hands and pulled at his hair. He pounded his fist against the shower wall as a loud wail escaped his throat. I turned away, unable to face the painful scene. I hated seeing my King's followers tortured as if they were slaves.

The Lord recognized my anguish and stepped away from the portal. I followed His lead, making our way out across the vast field that extended over the Mountain of God. The beauty surrounding me allowed my mind a brief escape from the man's sufferings, as I took in the glory of the Almighty Creator. It was such a splendid meadow, covered with flowers so vibrant that the human mind could never conceive their brilliance. They were saturated with colors never seen by human eyes. Dragonflies and other winged creatures danced among the tall wisps of the honey-wheat field. Their grace and beauty set my heart at peace.

I kept in step with my Master as He strolled out through the tall grasses and blooms. Sapphire and amethyst colored mountains rolled into the distance, touching the sky and rising to their full splendor. The beauty of the golden land was far too majestic to take in. Even now I struggle to find human words to describe it.

"Michael," the Lord's calming voice interrupted my thoughts. "You must go with the man tonight when he meets with the woman. He will need your strength and the support of your army. This is just the beginning of the attacks on him. Summon your warriors, Michael. Their provision will be needed. This battle and each one to come carry an immense weight. With each passing day, the need for victory becomes increasingly critical. It won't be long now, Michael."

I pondered His words in my heart, not fully understanding their meaning, but nonetheless, accepting my call with honor. Long ago, when I made the vow to fight for my King, I put aside my need for understanding. The King's wisdom is complete and far deeper than my own. He is the Rock. His works are perfect, and all His ways are just. That is all the understanding I have ever required and will ever need.[1]

I brought no question before my Lord as I followed Him in silence. We continued out across the field, but as we neared its center, my King stopped. I paused, wondering what could have caught the attention of my Master. He seemed to be listening for something. After a moment, He finally turned. Looking over His shoulder, He let out a long whistle. Some distance away, the tall grasses began to rustle. They shook vigorously as something rushed wildly towards us. It was coming closer and closer, parting the field and dividing the flowers, until out bounded a vibrant, young golden retriever. He leapt for joy and cleared the distance between him and the

Lord so he could nudge His hand with his pollen covered muzzle.

The Lord patted the top of the dog's head, "Good boy," He said and continued His way across the field. In the presence of the King, the furry dog lost all interest in the delights of the field. Now he pranced along, following his Master, never leaving His side, his tail wagging joyfully behind him.

{Chapter 16}

ADAM'S HEART POUNDED LOUDLY in his chest. He could hear the sound of his pulse ringing in his ears. The thundering shower did nothing to blot out the sounds of adrenaline coursing through his veins. *Death,* he pondered the thought. He had experienced so much death in his lifetime. He had become all too familiar with the overwhelming emotions of mourning. He clung to the only hope he had left, that those he loved, those who passed, were now in the very presence of the King he called Lord. Adam knew in his heart that his loved ones were experiencing in full the Kingdom of God. He found comfort in the fact that one day he would see them again, face to face, even his beloved, loyal dog.

Adam bent his head forward, allowing the hot water to soothe the back of his neck. The shower drummed on his head, sounding like a summer thunderstorm pounding against a window pane. His mind began to drift away with the rhythmic pounding of the water.

While his hope and faith in the Kingdom and the Lord Who reigned carried Adam through these times of mourning, he still couldn't shake the sickening feeling of guilt and regret. His current feelings were nothing compared to the raw emotions he felt on the night he encountered death for the first time. Against Adam's will, his mind took him away to the place where he first tasted it.

In a matter of seconds, Adam was a young boy again, standing all alone in a cold, dark alley. He could smell the dank corridors and hear the hum of the freeway droning off in the distance. Through the window of his mind, Adam could see the back door of the art gallery, vaguely outlined in the oppressing night. He felt a surge of adrenaline and the sweat forming on his palms as fear began invading his entire body. His muscles tensed, and the hair on the back of his neck and arms stood at attention, his very being on alert.

The scene began to replay in Adam's mind as it had weeks before on the road to Hana. He had been so grateful that Evelyn interrupted his thoughts, saving him from his own nightmares. Adam thought he was beyond these feelings of remorse.

Why now? he wondered. "Why, in the midst of paradise on earth, am I being so vividly tortured by memories that I thought I had put to rest years ago?" Adam cried out to the Lord, yet still he couldn't help but walk toward the darkest corners of his past. "I thought I gave this burden over to You." He questioned the Lord, "I know You forgave me, so why does it still hurt so bad? I don't even know how You could forgive me! I'm horrible! I'm not worthy of Your grace. I'm not worthy of You! Don't You know what I've done?"

Adam's mind drifted away. He watched as a much younger version of himself lowered the gun and reached down to reclaim the crowbar, his finger still loose on the trigger. Adam began to stand up so he could make a second attempt at prying open the door, but before he even straightened from his stooped position, he heard it, a voice. It was the voice that haunted his dreams.

Hey! Who's there?

Adam replayed the memory in slow motion, as if he were watching a movie of his own childhood. In reality, it was a mere fraction of a second that altered his life forever on that fated day.

Startled, Adam jumped at the voice and turned around. He felt the cold metal bar slip through his perspiring hand, while the other clutched the gun tightly. The crowbar landed with a loud clang, and in that brief moment, time seemed to stop. A cold breeze rushed over Adam, sending chills up his spine. He became acutely aware of a putrid stench wafting from what he assumed to be the dumpsters behind him in the alley. Adam strained his eyes, willing them to make out the darkened figures of the night. The taste of blood flooded his mouth. He would later come to realize that fear caused him to bite through his lip.

Before that day, Adam had never shot a firearm of any kind, and since that day, he never so much as looked at another gun. Fear gripped him, and instinct took over. His body reacted against his will. The tough façade Adam created to impress his peers melted as he realized what was happening. Before his mind had a chance to react, his finger squeezed the trigger.

The unforgettable resonance of a single gunshot reverberated through Adam's being and echoed against the blackened city.

{~}

The tormenting demon, Death, loomed over the shower. "Murderer!" he hissed in Adam's ear, pouring waves of guilt and shame over him.

{~}

Adam clutched the side of the shower and heaved, the nightmare overwhelming him. His empty stomach churned at the physical sickness he felt in remembering the night that changed his life forever. He heaved a second time as the vision replayed in his head. A silhouette darkened against the night, a man, a human life, slumped to the ground with a deafening thud. Adam had shot and killed an innocent man.

{~}

I couldn't stand by and watch any longer. With my sword drawn, I hurled myself at the malicious demon. The man was being tortured to the point of physical illness. I slammed the demon's hideous yet strong body up against the shower wall and proceeded to drag him into the bedroom. Once he was far enough away from the man, I released him.

Death whirled around to glare at me, his sulfur colored eyes threatening me with the hate that filled him. They were the eyes of one who had seen countless acts of atrocity, eyes that had witnessed the miserable and damning Abyss where his leader had been banished. A chill swept over me, and the thought of the Lord's created ones who had not accepted the King's invitation overwhelmed my spirit. These were the souls of those who now belonged to Satan, the prince of evil, the ruler of this cursed world.

These condemned humans were alone now, each one of them. The Abyss where they resided could only be described as a place of complete and utter isolation for all eternity, a place where humans were tortured and tormented by the repercussions of their own earthly sins. Terror and horror were present, and they poured over the lost souls unrelenting. It was a place where fears were birthed, and nightmares became reality.

They were alone in that place, void of anything good or beautiful; yet they could still hear in the distance the blood curdling screams of Hell's other inhabitants. They were sinister sounds, the horror of someone being anguished to the point of death but never having the pleasure of dying. They sought out death, but never found it. They longed to die, but death eluded them. The nightmare never ended, never ceased, and never would. They would be victimized for all eternity.[1]

Above all, the most miserable element of their suffering was being able to see the truth. With their eyes now open, they realized the fullness and beauty of the King's love that had always been pursuing them. In the Abyss, the humans saw their lives in full and the way they denied the one, true King by satisfying their own earthly desires.

Even if they had not intentionally followed and served the prince of darkness, they had still denied the Lord God Almighty and withheld from Him their love. It is not worshiping Satan alone that damns them, but serving and loving anything above the one and only God, the Creator of the heavens and earth. By not giving honor to the King or reciprocating His love, they ultimately placed honor on something else, their own selfish ambitions. They loved themselves above the Lord.

Now, at the end of their earthly lives, the humans' wisdom was no longer confused. They could distinguish reality from deception. They had been deceived by Satan, the father of lies, and they deceived themselves. They paid the price of their own sin now, the sin that had already been paid with the cost of the Lord's Son. They had been offered their freedom and a way out. It was a gift, but they never accepted it.

Now the damned could see the Lord's gift in all its completeness, and they understood the mystery and awe-inspiring beauty of the King's love. They realized what He had done for them when He paid with His Own Son to have them back. They finally saw the great worth ascribed to them by their Creator, but it was too late for them. Their decisions had been made and their fate sealed. What the humans do not realize is that indecision itself is, in fact, a decision.

Now they could see the goodness and perfect will of God, yet they could not have any part of it. They longed for the Lord, longed for a savior to rescue them from the Abyss, but they were separated from Him forever. Even if God sent them a savior through the flames of Hell to rescue them, they would not accept His offer; for the Lord had done just that when He sent His Son, Jesus, to conquer death. They had made their choices, and the Lord wept over them. It was too late for them, but it wasn't too late for the Lord's created ones who still roamed the planet lost and searching.

I remembered my mission. Although the man's future in my Master's Kingdom was sealed forever, the woman's fate was still uncertain. *I have to protect them both!*

Death looked at me with an intensity that could only be born from evil and hate. He blazed at me for what seemed like an eternity before spinning on his heel and taking off in flight. He disappeared through the wall of the resort and into the night.

Relieved, I rushed back to the bathroom where the man had finished showering. He was leaning forward, hands on the bathroom vanity, his face staring down into the sink bowl. His eyes stared into nothing.

I stood in the doorway watching him. I knew the man could not physically recognize my presence, but I saw his shoulders relax and a sense of relief wash over him. Slowly the man brought his face up to peer at his reflection in the vanity mirror. "Adam," I whispered to him. Even though his ears could not hear me, I knew his heart could. "'For I know the plans I have for you,' declares the Lord, 'Plans to prosper you and not to harm you, plans to give you hope and a future. When you call on Me and come and pray to Me, I will listen to you. You will seek Me and find Me when you seek Me with all your heart. I will be found by you,' declares the Lord, 'and bring you back from captivity.'"[2]

The man turned away from the sink and crossed the few short steps to the bedroom. Now dressed, he sat on the edge of the bed and slipped on a pair of brown dress shoes. I could not read the look on his face. His eyes seemed so far away. I knew Death's words had cut deep, bringing to the surface wounds that never fully healed. I knew how crucial it was for the man to accept forgiveness for the sin he could not forget, for the Lord Himself removed his sin. As far as the east is from the west, so far had He removed the man's transgressions. The King looked upon the man as if he had never sinned, all because the man had accepted His love and been washed in the King's grace. The Lord had forgotten his sin, but the man had not.[3]

As the man finished, he grabbed his wallet from the end table and reached for the door leading to the hallway.

Before the door shut behind him, I called after the man, "Do not merely listen to the Word and so deceive yourself. Do what it says. Anyone who listens to the Word but does not do as it says is like a man who looks at his face in a mirror and, after looking at himself, goes away and immediately forgets what he looks like."[4]

{Chapter 17}

EVELYN SAT ON A PLUSH couch in the lobby of the resort where Adam was staying. At least, she hoped it was the right resort. It was already ten minutes past the time they agreed to meet for dinner. Evelyn shifted uncomfortably in her seat, wondering if maybe he had changed his mind. *I knew I should have been more careful with getting close to him.*

Evelyn grabbed the television remote off the coffee table in front of her. She clicked on the oversized screen that was provided for hotel lobby guests, hoping that maybe the mundane local news would distract her as she waited for Adam to show up… or not show up.

Evelyn settled back into the sofa as the television came to life. A red banner reading "Breaking News" flashed across the bottom of the screen and caught her attention. She leaned forward, rested her elbows on her thighs, and strained to read the tiny text as it scrolled past. Before Evelyn could make out the words, a pretty, dark-haired, anchorwoman appeared on the screen and began reporting the headlines. An earthquake had taken place mere hours ago, devastating one of the world's most densely populated cities.

Evelyn watched as images of utter catastrophe flashed across the screen, images that were hardly recognizable through the thick smoke rising from the collapsed buildings and infrastructure. Evelyn listened intently as the news anchor reported death counts estimated to be in the thousands for this once bustling metropolis. The demands of this city would be halted as the people of Shanghai, China attempted to scrape their city out from the rubble and put their lives back together.

{~}

Evelyn was so riveted by the television that she didn't notice when Adam stepped out of the elevator and crossed the hotel lobby. She stared straight ahead in a trance. From where Adam was standing, he couldn't see the television screen, only the look of complete and utter focus etched on Evelyn's face. He wondered what held her so captivated. *This must be how I look right now*, Adam thought as he caught himself staring at Evelyn. She was utterly captivating in her turquoise colored dress. It contrasted dramatically against her deep tan, revealing just enough skin to make Adam blush. He felt as if he could stand there all night, but his stomach objected with a loud growl.

Adam crossed the three steps to the couch where Evelyn was seated and placed a cautious hand on her shoulder. "Sorry I'm a little late. You ready to go eat?"

Evelyn jumped in response, clearly surprised by Adam's presence. She clutched her chest. "Adam! I didn't even hear you walk up!"

"I'm sorry. I didn't mean to scare you."

"It's okay. I guess I was a little absorbed in the news." Evelyn gestured toward the screen. Now that Adam was directly in front of the television, he could see what was holding Evelyn's attention.

He took a step back, taking in the devastating images and listening intently to the anchorwoman repeat the news of the earthquake, promising viewers more details as they were made available. "Wow," Adam whispered, "Another earthquake?"

"I know," Evelyn glanced up at him. "It seems like earthquakes and natural disasters are happening more and more frequently." Her voice was shaky.

Evelyn was right. Earthquakes, tornados, and tsunamis did seem to be occurring far more regularly than in previous decades. It seemed the earth was revolting against the vile acts its inhabitants committed.

"Are you okay?" Adam could see the questions in Evelyn's eyes and the uncertainty written across her face. Her eyes remained glued to the images on the television screen. "We can skip dinner if you're not feeling up to it now." Adam offered.

"Huh?" Evelyn turned back toward Adam. Then his question registered. "Oh... no," Evelyn attempted to regain her composure, "I mean... I'm still up for dinner if you are." Adam could tell Evelyn was trying to appear unshaken, but the slight quiver in her voice betrayed her.

He gave her a wary smile, "Well all right, let's go then. I'm starving." He offered Evelyn a hand up from the couch, which she gratefully accepted. A burst of energy passed between them as their hands connected. The jolt seemed to infuse Evelyn with the confidence she needed. She clicked off the television without so much as another glance and reached for her little white purse.

Offering a smile in return, she nodded toward the door and said, "Shall we?"

Adam linked his arm with Evelyn's, and escorted her out of the hotel lobby, but as he did, he couldn't help but notice the unmistakable look of fear in Evelyn's eyes as they stepped out into the night.

{~}

Evelyn spooned a second bite of chocolaty dessert into her mouth, "This is so good!" she gushed. "How did you say you heard about this place?"

Although Evelyn had been to the island of Maui more than a few times, she had never heard of the quaint, outdoor restaurant where she and Adam were now sharing a decadent dessert. The meal had been delicious, the wine was superb, but the dessert, *now this is truly sinful*, Evelyn thought.

"The concierge at the resort recommended it," Adam replied as he leaned in for another bite. "I told her I was looking for someplace secluded and private, away from all the tourism. I told her the food had to be the best on the island, and the music... well," Adam gestured toward the soulful singing ukulele player on the corner of the deck. "Well, I think the music speaks for itself." Adam smiled back at Evelyn. She was glowing in the midst of the candlelight.

"Sounds like the kind of place you would go if you were trying to impress someone," Evelyn offhandedly said. She didn't look up, but instead scooped up another bite of dessert, savoring the rich flavor.

After a few moments of awkward silence, Evelyn finally glanced up, realizing that Adam had been staring at her. He was wearing that devious grin. "Well, maybe I am."

"Well, maybe you are... what?" she asked from behind the spoon.

"Maybe, I am trying to impress someone."

Evelyn nearly choked on her dessert and quickly reached for her wine to wash it down. She gulped down half the glass before Adam said, "Easy, easy! I don't want you to choke, but I don't want to have to carry you out of this place either!" Adam laughed as he took the wine glass from Evelyn's hand.

Evelyn rolled her eyes, "Thanks," she half said, half coughed.

"Anytime." Adam chuckled and handed her a napkin.

Evelyn was ready to shift the direction of their conversation. "So," she cleared her throat, "excuse me." She tried again. "So, Adam, how did you get started with all this creation-science stuff? I mean, I don't remember that being a degree offered at any of the universities when I was in school. I'm guessing there's a story behind how you ended up where you are now."

Now it was Adam's turn to choke on his dessert. He coughed into his napkin then reached for his own glass of wine.

"Ah ha," Evelyn raised her eyebrows, "I must have touched on something good." She leaned forward in her chair, eager to know what nerve she had just hit. Evelyn had spent several casual afternoons with Adam over the last several weeks, but never once had she seen him flustered like this. Usually Evelyn was the one doing all the blushing and avoiding awkward conversations. Adam had not been shy about his feelings toward Evelyn, and she was definitely not blind to his advances. She just didn't understand why he would be interested in a girl like her. There was no question that Evelyn reciprocated the sentiment. Her head, however, just wasn't ready to allow her heart to surrender. Just saying yes to a date with Adam was a huge step for Evelyn. The last time she had been on a date was in college. She shivered, trying not to remember that night.

"Are you cold?" Adam broke into her thoughts, and offered her his jacket.

"Oh no, I'm fine. Sorry, I sort of spaced out there. You were just about to tell me how you ended up in your chosen career…" Evelyn's voice trailed off, waiting for Adam to pick up the conversation.

"Well," Adam hesitated.

"I'm sorry. I'm being nosey. You don't have to tell me."

"No, no, it's fine. It's just kind of a long story. I don't want to keep you out too late."

Understanding his apprehension, Evelyn smiled back at Adam. His past was not just a long story. It was uncomfortable for Adam to share. *He's nervous!* Evelyn never thought she would see the day when Mr. Confident tensed under pressure, but Evelyn knew all too well how it felt to be on the other side. Suddenly, she was overwhelmed with feelings she never felt before. Her heart melted for Adam. Maybe she wasn't the only one with insecurities. Maybe Adam and Evelyn were more alike than she realized. Before her very eyes, Adam's confident façade started to crack. If Evelyn thought she was falling hard for Adam before, she was definitely in trouble now.

Realizing how uncomfortable this must be for Adam, Evelyn finally offered, "You know what? I love stories!"

Adam raised his eyebrows, "Yeah?"

"Yeah," she smiled, "and I have all night."

{~}

Deception and Death hovered over the small, outdoor table where the man and woman were dining under the stars. Death loomed closer to the man, and Deception leaned in toward the woman.

"The boss said to do anything in our power to keep these two apart," Deception sneered.

"Yeah well, we wouldn't even be worrying about these two useless souls if you would have killed the woman in the first place!" Death was enraged that this mission had carried on so long. "This ends tonight!"

Deception fumed at his partner's rage, "You know for a fact that she would be dead if it weren't for that worthless Michael!"

"Worthless? Ha! He's at least worth enough to halt the attacks of a pathetic moron like you. And don't mention that name. You know how the boss feels about the Archangel. Satan despises him. He's still bitter about losing his position to that warrior."

Deception didn't respond, but instead asked, "Hey, do you ever wonder why the boss wants this one so desperately? I mean, the man's already a lost cause. All we can do is torment him and halt his advances for the Kingdom. But the woman? What makes this one so special?"

"She's not," Death snapped, "She's no different from the rest. She's not special. None of them are! She's just another wretched soul who, as long as we have something to do with it, will be dragged into the depths of Hell before the night is over."

{~}

Adam leaned forward in his chair, and rested his elbows on the table in front of him. He picked up a cloth napkin and began absentmindedly running his fingers over the seams.

"Where to start...?" Adam threw out the question to no one in particular as his eyes stared across the room. Finally, he turned back to Evelyn, "I guess where I start depends on what you want to know. So," he smiled, "what would you like to know?"

"Well," Evelyn relaxed back into her seat and tried to think of an unintimidating way to ease into what appeared to be an uncomfortable topic for Adam. "I guess I would like to know how you became so interested in science and its role in the Bible. I mean, were you always a…" Evelyn tried to remember the term Adam used, "a follower of Jesus? That's how you describe yourself, right?"

Adam chuckled, seeming to relax a little. "Yeah, that's usually how I describe myself. You were listening."

"Of course, I was listening. Just because I'm not a 'follower of Jesus' doesn't mean I'm not interested in what you have to say. Your faith is a part of who you are. It's part of what I enjoy about you. Besides, I've never met anyone with a faith like yours. That whole thing you said about a relationship and not a religion, I've been thinking about it ever since you mentioned it."

"Oh really?" Adam was intrigued.

"Now look, I'm not saying I'm going to start following Jesus or anything like that, but you got me thinking. If what you said about Jesus is true, that God is all about love, then it seems to me that religion is the biggest obstacle to God. That's why I'm so curious as to how you ended up where you are now. Something pretty profound must have happened in your life for you to see what God's love is really all about. Quite frankly, I have never once seen the love that you talk about in a church."

"Well, said," Adam agreed. "You're right. Oftentimes it's hard for non-believers, and even believers, to see the love of Christ in the church. Sadly, the church has become a deterrent to God when it was supposed to be the biggest advocate.

Fortunately for me, when I became a believer, I was introduced to a church that stood on the foundation of love."

"So you weren't always a believer then? How did you…?"

"My father," Adam interjected. "He was also the one who challenged me to follow my dreams of becoming a scientist."

"Yeah? Is he a scientist too?"

"No, more the artistic type… like you." Adam's smile made Evelyn blush.

"Well, tell me about him." Evelyn prodded. "Your dad, what's he like? I bet he is pretty amazing to have raised someone like you." Evelyn found the color returning to her cheeks, realizing she had just delivered another revealing statement about what she thought of Adam.

"Yeah," Adam looked away, "he was a pretty amazing guy for raising someone like me," Adam paused, "but he passed away last year."

Evelyn's stomach dropped, "Oh, Adam, I'm so sorry. I had no idea." She reached across the table and took his hand in hers.

"It's okay. You didn't know. I mean this has been a really rough year, but I am certain he is in a much better place now. My dad had cancer and was suffering quite a bit towards the end. In a way, it's a relief to know he's gone on to a place where there is no more suffering and no more pain."

Evelyn's eyes misted over, a sad smile forming on her lips. She thought of her stepfather who believed so strongly in the same God and Heaven as Adam. It was the same God and Heaven that Evelyn once believed in before her stepfather was so tragically taken. She wanted to believe everything Adam had been saying about God's love. In theory, his words made sense. Evelyn was able to wrap her mind around the concepts, but just like every other area of her life, Evelyn's mind and heart seemed to be disconnected. She didn't know how a loving God could give her a stepfather who adored her and then in the same breath snatch him right back, leaving Evelyn alone with an unloving and cruel mother.

Evelyn wanted to believe her stepfather was in a better place, but she couldn't bring herself to believe in a Heaven, if she couldn't be certain of a God.

Adam seemed to be reading her thoughts because he finally said, "I know you don't necessarily believe the Bible is true, Evelyn, but based on conversations we've had, I know you aren't completely closed to the idea of a loving God. You're searching for what is real. And it's hard to know what is real when we live in a world that is plagued with anything but the love God intended for us. There is pain in this world, but the Bible says one day, 'He will wipe every tear from our eyes. There will be no more death or mourning or crying or pain, for the old order of things will have passed away.'[1]

"I believe this with all my heart, Ev. I know that my father is in a place where beautiful doesn't even come close to describing the splendor that surrounds him. Heaven is a place where joy overwhelms the soul to the point of not even being able to recognize where one blissful moment ends and the next begins. It is a place where humans, God's creation, are reunited with their Maker. It's a gathering of all His children in the home that the King originally created for us to experience on a daily basis.

"The world was never supposed to be like this, Evelyn. Death and destruction are not what God intended for this world. Love is what He intended, but by our sin we have fallen prey to evil. The Bible says that because of our rebellion, the Lord's people were given over to their sin, and that evil prospered in everything it did, and truth was thrown to the ground.'[2]

"You were right about natural disasters. Regardless of whether or not they are actually becoming more and more frequent, it sure feels that way. The earth itself is crying out at the atrocities of mankind. It says in the Bible, 'We know that the whole creation has been groaning as in the pains of childbirth right up to the present time.' But one day, this will all come to pass when the King finally brings us into the Kingdom He originally intended to be our home. However, the Lord will not wait forever, Evelyn. He is patient, not wanting any to perish, but God will never force anyone to love Him. Rather, He loves us so much that He will give people over to their sin if that is what they truly want. He will give us the desires of our hearts, whether that desire is to be with Him or to be separated from Him. All God ever wanted was to love us and for us to love Him in return.[3]

"There is a very real battle, Evelyn. It is between good and evil, and there is a war being waged for our hearts. God wants our hearts, but Satan wants to destroy them. On the day of the final battle, the Lord will redeem His followers and bring them into His glory, while those who choose not to give their love to the King will be given over to their wickedness and live out the reality of their sin in the Abyss that is called Hell."

Adam paused and stared at Evelyn. He searched her face, desperately trying to read her thoughts.

"I just don't understand, Adam. If God is so full of love for us, why does He allow these terrible things to happen? If He is the loving God you claim Him to be, why doesn't he rescue us from all of this pain and suffering?"

"He did, Ev." Adam stated simply. "He sent us a Savior when He sent His Son, Jesus, to the earth to die on a cross for our sins. The Lord of all creation loved His people so much that He sent His perfect Son to the earth to take on the sin and blackness of humanity. God allowed His Son to die the death that we all deserve so that one day we may be reunited with our Creator in the presence of the King and His Son."

"He has saved us, Ev. His love is a gift, but it's a gift you must be willing to receive, a gift you have to want and accept. Let me tell you the rest of this passage in the Bible. Maybe it will help you understand."

"We know that the whole creation has been groaning as in the pains of childbirth right up to the present time. Not only so, but we ourselves, who have the firstfruits of the Spirit, groan inwardly as we wait eagerly for our adoption as sons, the redemption of our bodies. For it is in this hope we are saved. But hope that is seen is no hope at all. Who hopes for what he already has? But if we hope for what we do not yet have, we wait for it patiently."[4]

Evelyn took a deep breath and bit down on her bottom lip to hold back tears. She steadied her voice before she ventured to ask, "How do you have so much faith in a man and a love you have never seen? I just don't understand, Adam."

Adam looked deeply into Evelyn's eyes as if searching her soul. What he saw was hurt, a deep wound that scarred her heart. He silently wondered who could ever have hurt a woman as sweet as Evelyn. Realizing the tender state of her beliefs and a need for something to hope for, Adam leaned across the table and whispered, "I think that it's time I share with you my story."

Adam released her hands and sat back in his chair. He let out a deep sigh and began retelling the story of that cold October night.

{~}

Deception began whispering words of deceit in the woman's ear. She was completely unaware of the gnarled fangs that were mere inches from her head.

"What are you thinking, getting close to a man like this?" Deception spat. He's no different than the rest! Don't believe what he says about God and His Jesus." The demon shuddered. "You know He doesn't love you, especially after what you've done!"

Deception was unleashing every weapon in his arsenal. He had to be on the offensive as the man proclaimed the truth. *Truth, ha,* Deception spat! He despised the truth and reviled any man who dared to announce it. Deception had a job to do, and he was not about to let this man get in his way. As much as he hated to admit it, he was glad to have Death on his side, working to derail the man.

Still, there was the threat of that detested Archangel Michael and his warrior Army of God. They were protecting this man and woman at all costs. It was beginning to wreak havoc on the plans of the evil one, but Deception and Death were not given their elite status among the high ranks of the dark army for nothing. They were some of the most wretched and deranged of Satan's followers, and they did not relinquish their missions so easily.

Michael and his angel warriors have another think coming. Deception glanced over at the man where Death was hovering.

"Don't worry," Death grinned, "I had a small encounter with the man earlier. He'll never make it through the story. He will all but destroy himself as he relives the dark corners of his past!" The demon let out a low, bellowing laugh and leaned in to plant words of guilt in the man's ear.

Deception took this as his cue and moved in closer to the woman, whispering lies over her so she would not see the man for who he really was. She would not be able to discern reality from deception.

{Chapter 18}

ADAM BEGAN RECOUNTING THE STORY of the night that altered his life forever. His lips formed the words of the story, but his mind was far away.

What will she think of me now? Adam thought as he told Evelyn about the years he spent in an orphanage and the events leading up to that fateful night. In his mind, Adam recalled all the friends and individuals who had fallen away once they learned of Adam's stained past. *Will Evelyn just be one more? Maybe I shouldn't tell her.*

Evelyn was the closest Adam had come to a friend in the last several years, and after losing his faithful dog and father, he couldn't stand the thought of Evelyn walking away once she found out about his past. He couldn't risk losing her. There was something special about Evelyn. Adam had never been in love before or even in a serious relationship, but he realized the feelings erupting inside him were more than just a mere physical attraction toward Evelyn. These emotions were something much deeper. Adam silently wondered if sharing his own dark past would jeopardize his chances of getting to know Evelyn on a deeper level. Despite Adam's selfishness,

Evelyn's shaky voice echoed in his head: *how do you have so much faith in a man and a love you have never seen? I just don't understand, Adam.*

But Adam did understand that kind of love because he had seen it in a man who had given him the closest glimpse of Kingdom love he could ever possibly witness here on earth. Adam recognized Evelyn's doubts and fears. He saw something in her eyes that cried out for hope. She had secrets that, like his, seemed to haunt her and keep her from experiencing the freedom found in grace. Adam pondered the irony in that thought, *freedom found in grace*. Was he even fully experiencing the freedom of the grace extended to him? Just hours before, Adam wretched at the thought of his past. *Now, how on earth am I going to get through this story?* he wondered.

{~}

"You're a murderer!" Death hissed into the man's ear. "She's too good for you. You don't deserve her. You don't deserve anything good! Leave! Run away while you still have some dignity left. Don't you dare tell her about your past! Then she will see you for who you really are, a low-life, scum-of-the-earth, heinous, murderer! This is why everyone you've ever been close to has been torn from your life. You don't deserve them! She will leave you once she knows the truth, so you might as well spare yourself the pain." Death's talon-like hands gripped the man's shoulders as he breathed heavily on the back of his neck.

"End it now!" he demanded in a low growl.

{~}

As much as Adam wanted to cling to this moment with Evelyn, he knew he couldn't. He didn't deserve a sweet girl like Evelyn as a friend or anything more. He would only hurt her in the end. If nothing else, Evelyn had the right to know what she was getting herself into. Disclosing this information would probably bring their wonderful evening to an abrupt halt, but it would be better to end it now than to hurt Evelyn with the truth of his past later.

The story Adam originally planned to use as an illustration of grace now seemed like the end of what could have been something quite special between the two of them. Silently, Adam began to wrestle with himself. He so desperately wanted to give Evelyn a glimmer of hope, but at the same time he knew that he himself had not accepted the truth of his own forgiveness. It was as if a battle waged in his mind: *tell her, don't tell her, she will understand, she will run.*

Wishing he could erase his past, Adam swallowed the lump in his throat and took a deep breath. Somewhere in the depths of Adam's heart, a voice echoed, *I have erased it.* He couldn't take it anymore. Adam abruptly pushed back from the table. "Um... can you excuse me for a minute?"

"Uh, sure," a very startled Evelyn replied.

"I'm just going to the restroom. I'll be back in a minute." Adam lied. He had no intention of coming back.

{~}

Evelyn tried to wait patiently but couldn't stop thinking about how strangely Adam was behaving. One minute he was telling her about growing up in an orphanage and the next, he was running off to the restroom. It seemed very odd, especially for Adam. Evelyn's heart began to race, pounding loudly against her ribcage. *What would cause him to act this way? Is it something I've done?* This wasn't the Adam she knew. *What do I really know?* Evelyn silently wondered. *We've only known each other a few weeks.*

Evelyn began second guessing her decision to go on a date with Adam. It definitely went against every relational boundary she had set for herself since her last date. Evelyn cringed. *No. Adam is different. Adam is not like...* Evelyn tried not to let her mind go there, but as it always happened, Evelyn could not stop the wave of memories threatening to drown her. They were consuming.

{~}

"Well, don't just stand there!" Deception shouted. "Now is our chance! Go after the man!"

With a devious grin plastered on his face, Death willingly took off in the direction of the man. Deception turned back to the woman who was looking quite shocked at her date's abrupt exit.

"Well, well, well," Deception mocked his prey. "Looks like your date has abandoned you." Deception lowered his face to hers. He thought it was such a shame that his appearance couldn't strike fear in these wretched creatures. *That's okay,* he thought, *there are plenty of other ways I can take care of that.* The thought brought a smile to his face. "Don't you worry," Deception snarled. He grazed a scaled hand over her cheek. "I will take good care of you."

{~}

Evelyn tried to shift her mind to thoughts of work, but it was no use. A flood of memories began berating her, and before she knew it, she was back in her sophomore year of college. She attended university for photography immediately following high school, eager to move out of her mother's house and away from the woman who despised her very existence. She longed for freedom, and she longed for love.

As a young girl, who only briefly received a sense of belonging and real love from her stepfather, Evelyn began searching for her "Mr. Right" to fill the void in her heart. That's when she met Drew, the athletic and handsome football star of the university. Two months into the semester, Drew invited Evelyn to a party at his friend's house. Evelyn had an exam the next morning and really needed the extra study time, but when would she ever be given another opportunity like this? Any other girl on campus would have killed to be the one on Drew's arm for the night. After a little convincing, Evelyn finally closed up her books, put the exam out of mind, and climbed into the passenger seat of Drew's black sports car. The sound of tires peeling out of the driveway echoed in her mind.

Evelyn's memories of that night were choppy at best, yet somehow they still terrorized her dreams and moments of waking. She remembered entering the party and graciously accepting a mixed drink from one of Drew's friends. She always felt out of place at parties. A drink would help her loosen up and enjoy the night.

Beyond that, Evelyn's recollections seemed like blips on a film strip, spans of blackness punctuated by brief memories of being brutally beaten and raped. She later woke up in a hospital bed to learn that Drew, along with several of his friends, set the whole thing up. Sadly, Evelyn was not the only one invited to a party that night. Four other girls suffered the same fate. Two were not so lucky.

Evelyn felt guilty that she was alive when two others were not. She wished she were dead! She longed to die rather than suffer the images burned into her mind forever, but she hadn't died. Why was she any different from the other two girls? Why did she get to live when they could not? These questions burned in Evelyn's heart and haunted her every day of her life.

{~}

Adam splashed his face with the cold water from the bathroom sink. He was grateful there were no other restaurant patrons in the men's restroom to witness his meltdown. *What am I doing?* He questioned himself. Adam's original plan was to slip away quietly from the restaurant and out of Evelyn's life, but when he got to the parking lot, Adam realized he couldn't leave even if he wanted. Evelyn had driven.

Adam mentally kicked himself for even allowing the thought to cross his mind. *How could I even think about leaving Evelyn alone at a restaurant?* He couldn't recognize where this behavior was coming from.

{~}

Lurking in the shadows of the small restroom, Death continued to haunt the man, whispering lies and guilt, tormenting him with the memory of his sins. The man was vulnerable, and Death realized it. He crept in closer for his opportunity to strike.

{~}

Adam glanced at his flushed and now dripping-wet face in the bathroom mirror. Again, he heard Evelyn's voice in his head: *how do you have so much faith in a man and love you have never seen?*

He shook his head. "I can't do this," he uttered. "Certainly not on my own!" The sound of Adam's voice echoed in the small bathroom and bounced off the tiled walls with frightening clarity. It struck Adam odd to hear his own voice pronounce such a statement.

You're not alone, his heart whispered.

It was becoming painfully obvious to Adam that the reason he was struggling with his guilt and pain was because he was trying to conquer the shame of his past on his own. Never had he been able to rely on his own strength to do anything of value. It was always God who carried him through. A wave of emotion overwhelmed Adam. He fell to his knees, and just like all those times before, he cried out to the Lord.

{~}

"No!" Death screamed. "No! No! No!" He was losing his hold on the man. The demon began yelling at the top of his lungs, shouting obscenities and curses against the man. He lashed out desperately with every weapon in his arsenal, but to no avail. He was losing!

Howling out in defeat, Death fell to his knees and tore at his hair. The Holy Spirit was in the room. He could feel it. Its power was overwhelming, and it suffocated his own. Death grabbed at his ears, preparing for what was to come. He waited for the very sound that could split his eardrums and send a dagger through his chest. He didn't have to wait long. The divine power was building to an insufferable level. All it would take was one word… "Jesus!"

{~}

"Jesus!" Adam cried out. "Please rescue me! What is happening to me? I thought I had put all this behind me. I thought you had forgiven me."

A silent voice echoed in Adam's heart, *I have forgiven you.*

Somewhere from the deep recesses of Adam's mind, a memory came flooding back, a memory of words spoken to him long ago.

He has rescued us from the dominion of darkness and brought us into the Kingdom of the Son He loves, in Whom we have redemption, the forgiveness of sins. It is only because of this that you will be able to live a life worthy of the Lord and please Him in every way: bearing fruit in every good work and growing in the knowledge of God. You will be strengthened with all power according to His glorious might so that you may have great endurance and patience, and give joyful thanks to the Father, Who has qualified you to share in the inheritance of His holy people in the Kingdom of light.[1]

Adam took a deep breath and closed his eyes. "I'm sorry, Lord. How easy it is to allow the darkness to overwhelm me. How quickly I forget Your love. I know that You have rescued me from the darkness. Because of You, and You alone, I am forgiven. I am Yours."

As Adam continued to stand there leaning on the sink basin, time seemed to stop, and an insurmountable peace washed over him. He breathed it in, allowing it to fill his soul. How long he stayed there, he didn't know, but it was long enough to once again hear a voice calling out in his heart.

I will rescue you from your own torments, but now, I am sending you to open her eyes and turn her from darkness to light, and from the power of Satan to God, so that she may receive forgiveness for her sins and a place among those who are sanctified by faith in Me.[2]

Adam took another deep breath and slowly opened his eyes. His heart was back on track. He knew what he had to do.

{~}

"Deception!" Death's voice boomed from across the restaurant where the other beastly demon was terrorizing the woman with the pains of her own past. Deception was doing everything in his power to pull emotions from the far corners of her mind and bring her agony alive in the present.

"Deception!" Death shouted again. The demon snapped his head around and bored his piercing eyes into his counterpart.

"What?" he barked back.

"The man," Death growled, "the Spirit is strong within him. We will need to break the woman now! The success of this mission falls on her. We must destroy her!"

Deception uttered a low chuckle.

"What's so funny?" Death stormed over to his partner.

"I just don't know why you are so upset. You still have your trump card to play. You know..." Deception raised his eyebrows. "The woman..."

Finally, Death understood and grinned knowingly. He swooped across the table, where the woman was trembling from the torments of her past. He knew exactly what Deception was referring to and buzzed with a sickened delight at the thought. The woman was all but being crushed under the weight of her own agony. Deception had his fun. Now it was Death's turn, and he would finish her.

{Chapter 19}

DECEPTION GRIPPED THE WOMAN'S SHOULDERS and held her tightly as Death loomed in closer.

"Remember," Deception hissed in her ear, "it's all your fault! It's the punishment you deserve for the death of your stepfather! You will live with this pain for your entire existence because you deserve to suffer! These are the consequences of your actions."

Deception squeezed harder and dug his talons into the woman. In the earthly realm, the woman did not see the blood dripping down her shoulders from the puncture wounds of the demon's affliction, but she felt the pain as an oppressive weight on her shoulders. It was becoming harder for her to breathe as each moment of panic set in.

{~}

Evelyn slipped further and further from the present to the darkest day of her life, exactly nine weeks after the night she was brutally attacked at the party.

She smelled it before she saw it: the thick sterile smell of the clinic. Evelyn could picture the white walls and recalled the faintness overwhelming her. She stood as the nurse called her name.

The thin medical paper crinkled beneath her trembling body as she yearned for the procedure to end. A single, hot tear rolled down her cheek, slipping off her face and dissolving into the white paper as she turned her head. She was too ashamed to watch.

Evelyn had waited a couple weeks before deciding to have the abortion. She just couldn't go through with the pregnancy. She couldn't have a baby that would forever remind her of her painful past, so Evelyn did the only thing she could. She erased the evidence. What she didn't realize however, was that the memories would not go away so easily. In fact, the abortion itself left a scar so deep that nothing could cover it. The remorse she felt from the death of her stepfather was only intensified by the loss of the baby she carried.

{~}

By this point, Death and Deception were not the only demons surrounding and tormenting the woman. The high-ranking, dark winged spirits called on others from their army of wicked beasts to envelop the woman and tear through her soul. They swarmed in a dark cloud, berating her and lashing out with insults and falsehoods to force her to her knees.

Finally, Death leaned in behind the woman for the ultimate blow. He reached forward with his mangled hands and grasped a handful of hair. Closing his talons tightly around her locks, he pulled her toward him. Death's breath was hot on the back of her neck as he moved his face alongside the woman's. He breathed in her scent – fear. He could smell it all over her.

Fear mingled with guilt and sickness at the memory of her sins. Death licked his lips in delight. *This is going to taste good.*

He gripped her hair tighter and pulled back even more. Clasping his other hand around her neck, Death's evil voice penetrated the woman's mind as he sneered, "Murderer!"

{~}

I could stand to watch no longer. The dark leaders and their deranged army had crossed the line, and the woman was falling fast. I drew my flaming Sword of the Spirit and gave the battle cry, unleashing a surge of God's mightiest warriors into the night. We pierced through the darkened sky and dropped into the black world below.

{~}

As the word left the demon's mouth, a commanding force of muscle barreled into Death, forcing him off the woman and sending him into a heap on the ground. In a matter of mere seconds, the quiet, little restaurant turned into a war zone. Death grabbed his pounding head and strained to take in the scene. All around him light clashed with darkness as God's army advanced against Satan's demon warriors.

Death struggled up on his elbow, attempting to join the battle. He lifted his head only to find a figure like a man dressed in linen standing over him. He was wearing a belt of the finest gold around his waist and had a body like chrysolite. His face shone like lightning, his eyes like flaming torches, his arms and legs like the gleam of burnished bronze, and his voice like the sound of a multitude. It was Michael.[1]

{~}

I stood over Death with my sword drawn and poised, ready to strike at a moment's notice.

"So, Michael, we meet again," the demon hissed.

I gave no spoken reply, but I knew he received the message. I stared him down. Our eyes bored into one another, reaching the deepest places of the other's soul. Time froze as the deranged beast glared back up at me. I stood staring down at him.

What happened next I cannot be certain. I suppose I will never know, but for a brief moment it appeared as if his eyes changed. I recognized those eyes. They were the eyes of evil itself. I saw before me the adversary, Satan. His gaze locked with mine, and the corners of his mouth twitched in what appeared to be a sly smirk. My mind flashed back to the last time I had seen that wicked face.

"Finish Him!" Satan's voice echoed in my mind as the memory of demon warriors latching onto the Son's body erupted in my mind. I could hear the groans and cries of sheer anguish escaping from the Lord's Son as the demons tore the last ounce of life from His body.

"Father," He uttered, "Into Your hands I commit My spirit." As the words left His mouth, the demons bonded together and heaved on the Son's soul, desperately straining to rip it from His human body. With all the strength they could muster, the demons gave one final tear, and with a loud cry, Jesus breathed His last. The demon warriors tore the Son's life right out of Him and drew His soul down into the Abyss below.[2]

The sound of battle waging all around brought me back to the present. Everything played out in slow motion. Flaming swords clashed with the blackened flesh of Satan's army while talons and fangs pierced the perfect bodies of my Master's valiant warriors.

The demons were losing! Satan's greatest attempts were no match for the Army of God. One by one, they began to fall away, starting with the weakest. The demons of Satan were immortal like us. They could be wounded and maimed, but never die. They could not be killed, only injured to the point of retreat. Then they would flee and return to the depths of the Abyss where they would regain their strength for future battles.

As the Lord's army delivered blow after blow, the demons cried out in anguish. They erupted with sinister shrieks and shrill screams at each infliction of the Sword of the Spirit. My Master's army fought gallantly, overpowering each and every one until only Death and Deception remained. One of my brave warriors pinned Deception not far from where I had Death cornered and bleeding. My warrior stood poised, waiting for my command.

We lifted our Swords of the Spirit, gripping the hilt engraved with the very words of our Lord and Master. The daggers' ends were directed downward, pointing directly at the heart of the beasts. After witnessing their entire army falling by the sword, they now cowered in fear and shame. They were no match for the power of the Lord God Almighty which reigned within us. These once terrifying and bold monsters shuddered at the name of Jesus, the very name we wore, the name we carried and honored.

With our swords high, I turned my eyes toward Heaven and declared, "If we drive out demons by the Spirit of God, then the Kingdom of God has come upon you. Now have come the salvation and the power and the Kingdom of our God and the authority of His Messiah. For you are the accuser of our brothers and sisters, who accuses them before our God day and night. You will be hurled down. We will triumph over you by the blood of the Lamb and by the Word of His testimony.

"By myself I have sworn, my mouth has uttered in all integrity a word that will not be revoked. Before Him every knee will bow; by Him every tongue will swear. In the Lord alone are deliverance and strength. You and all who have raged against Him will come to Him and be put to shame!"[3]

I turned to my right and nodded to my fellow warrior before gazing back down at Death. He was covering his face, cringing at the Lord's words.

"Send our best to your leader," I jeered as I thrust my Sword of the Spirit down, piercing through the heart of Death. At the same moment, my comrade delivered a blow to Deception, and we watched as both demons vanished into thin air, disappearing into the depths below.

{Chapter 20}

Once again I found myself on the Mountain of God in the land of the Almighty. I gazed outward across the vista that stretched before me. Emerald hills, dotted with saffron colored flowers, rolled into the distance, and the sky erupted from the horizon, thrusting upward into a blanket of azure and violet. The air was still and silent.

I stood by the water's edge of the river where my Master commanded me to await His arrival. I took a step closer, peering down into the glass-like surface below. It was as clear as crystal. Gazing down at my appearance, I silently wondered why my Master would choose me for such a mission. Why had He placed me, of all His angels, of all His warriors, in a position of such honor? I was humbled at the thought and continued to gaze at my reflection, taking in my appearance, which was so very different from the Lord's. At a distance, we angels have the form of a man; yet in detail, our features are very much unlike the humans. The man and the woman were uniquely created in the image of God. It was from His very likeness that they were born!

My mind drifted back to that day of long ago, at the beginning of time and the creation of the earth. I considered the words of my Lord on that day, "Let Us make man in Our image, in Our likeness." He had spoken these words to the Trinity, to God the Holy Spirit and God the Son. *His Son*, I began to ponder the thought. It is the Son Who is the radiance of God's glory and the exact representation of His being, sustaining all things by His powerful Word. And it is His Son Whom the King appointed heir of all things, through Whom He made the universe.[1]

I fell to my knees as I humbly considered the honor bestowed upon me to serve my King and His Son. I could hardly bear the thought of being in the presence of the Lord Almighty and the great Savior, His Son, Jesus. For He, the Son, became as much superior to myself and all the angels as the name He inherited is superior to our own. For to which of us did God ever say, "You are my Son. Today I have become your Father"? Or again, "I will be His Father, and He will be my Son"? Never![2]

I dropped my head in my hands and closed my eyes, pondering the mysterious ways of the Lord.

When my Master brought His firstborn into the world, He said, "Let all God's angels worship Him." In speaking of His angels, the King said, "I make My angels winds, My servants flames of fire." But about the Son He said, "Your throne will last for ever and ever, and righteousness will be the scepter of Your Kingdom. You, My Son, have loved righteousness and hated wickedness; therefore, I, Your God and Father, have set You above Your companions by anointing You with the oil of joy." The very thought brought a smile to my face, and I inhaled deeply the sweet air surrounding me as I considered the wonders of my Master and Lord, the great mysteries of His Son and the created ones whom He loves.[3]

I continued pondering these things by the water when, suddenly, I became aware of a presence. It was my King. He didn't say a word. I didn't even hear Him approach. I just simply felt and understood that I was in the attendance of a power far greater than my own.

Without looking up from where I was kneeling at the edge of the river, I boldly called out to my King. "O Lord, my Lord, how majestic is Your name in all the earth! How great are Your signs, how mighty Your wonders! Your Kingdom is an eternal Kingdom, and Your dominion endures from generation to generation. You have set Your glory above the heavens. I consider Your heavens, the work of Your fingers, the moon and the stars, which you have set in place. In the beginning, O Lord, You laid the foundations of the earth, and the heavens are the work of Your hands. They will perish, but You remain. They will all wear out like a garment, and You will roll them up like a robe. Like a garment they will be changed, but You, my King, will remain the same, and Your years will never end."[4]

"Arise, Michael." The Lord's voice pierced through the silent air, and I rose to my feet out of respect for my Master's command. Keeping my eyes fixed low on the rushing river, I watched as a reflection appeared on the other side. It was my King, clothed in white linen, standing above the water's edge. I raised my eyes to peer across at His beauty.

He stood before me on the shore, opposite the river bank where I silently awaited instructions on my next mission. In my mind I recalled the earlier battle. Death and Deception were wounded, but they would be back. It was only a matter of time before the demons sought out the man and the woman: the man to terrorize and torment, and the woman to destroy.

"Michael, oh great prince who protects the people," my King called across to me, "the time has come for you to arise. There is going to be a time of distress that has not happened from the beginning of nations until now. At this time the people, everyone whose name is found written in the Book, will be delivered. Multitudes who sleep in the dust of the earth will awake, some to everlasting life, others to shame and everlasting contempt. Those who are wise will shine like the brightness of the heavens, and those who lead many to righteousness, like the stars for ever and ever."[5]

Again, I fell to my knees in complete and utter humility. "How long, my Lord? How long will it be before these astonishing things are fulfilled?"[6]

Silence followed, interrupted only by the soft bubbling of the river that flowed in between us. Finally, over the gentle rush of water, I heard the peaceful voice of my Master call to me. "Michael, you are wise when you say, 'they will perish, but You remain. They will all wear out like a garment, and You will roll them up like a robe. Like a garment they will be changed, but You remain the same, and Your years will never end.' Michael, this is to be the new city." He gestured to our surroundings. "This land is the new Kingdom I am creating for My Son. It will be a New Heaven and a New Earth, for one day the first Heaven and the first earth will pass away, and there will no longer be any sea, just the river of the water of life." He motioned to the gentle flowing water.[7]

I heard my King, but I did not understand, so I asked, "My Lord, what will the outcome of all this be?"[8]

He paused, waiting for me to fix my gaze on him. How handsome He was. His breathtaking eyes pierced through mine as he replied, "Go your way, Michael, because the words are closed up and sealed until the time of the end. Many will be purified, made spotless and refined, but the wicked will continue to be wicked. None of the wicked will understand, but those who are wise will understand. I will make known to them the mystery of My will according to My good pleasure, which I have purposed in My Son, to be put into effect when the time has reached its fulfillment, to bring all things in Heaven and on earth together under one head, even Christ My Son.[9]

"Michael, in Me they were chosen, having been predestined according to My plan, because I work everything out with the purpose of My will."[10]

Bowing my head, I closed my eyes before my Master. My simple mind could not conceive His wisdom, yet I declared in my heart to serve and obey, even in my own lack of understanding.

"You are all knowing and all powerful, my Lord. You are the God who was, and is, and is yet to come. All praise, glory, and honor belong to You. Your understanding, my King, no one can fathom. I will go, and I will fight valiantly in Your Great Name."[11]

{~}

"I killed him."

The words burned in Evelyn's mind as she sat there still and almost lifeless. Slowly, the tightness in her throat began to subside, and the pounding in her head faded to a dull throb.

"I killed him."

The words were softer this time, almost a whisper. Evelyn was gradually making her way back to the present, but the words still echoed in her mind. They sounded so real, as if someone were whispering them to her. That was when she realized... *those words*... they hadn't been her own. It was Adam who whispered them as he softly held Evelyn's hand, gently rubbing her trembling fingers. *When did he come back?* It was all just a blur to Evelyn. Adam had gone to the restroom and then... Evelyn tried not to think about how long she had been lost in the painful memories of her past, but instead tried focusing on what she had missed. She vaguely remembered Adam returning to the table. He apologized and asked if it were all right for him to continue with his story. Although Evelyn was not devoting her full attention to his words, the story of Adam's troubled past was beginning to come clear in her mind. Evelyn stared at their joined hands, allowing his words to sink in before looking up into Adam's piercing grey eyes.

"What did you say?" Evelyn uttered under her breath.

"I said, 'I killed him,' Ev. I killed an innocent man. And he was so young too," Adam shook his head, "only seventeen. I took the life of someone's son, someone's little boy."

That was all it took. Evelyn couldn't hold back any longer. The tears that had been threatening to spill over were unstoppable now. She buried her face in her hands. Thankful they were the only two left in the dining area, Evelyn allowed herself to pour out the gut wrenching sobs that emerged from somewhere down deep. She heard Adam shifting across from her, and before she knew what was happening, Adam swept her up in his strong arms. He didn't say a word, didn't try to calm her. He just held her as she wept. Evelyn thought she should have felt embarrassed, but she didn't. In some strange way, she felt entirely safe. Adam's arms wrapped her in a comfort she had never known, and as he stroked her long, dark hair, he whispered words of untold love. Stillness enveloped them, wrapping them together, and in that moment something changed. Evelyn's emotions overwhelmed her with a strange sense of peace as she realized things would never be the same between her and Adam ever again.

{Chapter 21}

EVELYN TOLD ADAM her entire life story as they walked along the beach. He was the one who suggested they take the after-dinner walk, but he definitely was not expecting Evelyn to open up the way she did. They must have covered miles as they strolled aimlessly down the beach, Evelyn sharing the story of her adoption, her stepfather's death, and the child she never met. Adam listened quietly, never interrupting and asking questions only where appropriate, until finally, it seemed Evelyn emptied herself of all that was left.

"Gosh, Adam," she mumbled. "What must you think of me now? I'm an absolute mess!" She gestured to her reddened face and the soaked, restaurant napkin that was balled up in her hand. "I mean, not only do I look a complete mess, but my whole life, my whole past…"

Adam stopped mid stride and turned to face Evelyn. He gently grabbed her forearms and pulled her in close. "You're right, Ev. You are a mess, a complete and utter mess. We all are. But guess what? If everything messy that's ever happened in your life is a part of who you are, then I want absolutely everything to do with your mess," Adam brushed Evelyn's hair from her face and looked down into her tear-filled eyes, "because I want everything to do with you."

Evelyn turned her eyes to their sand-covered feet as another tear slid down her face.

"Evelyn, do you remember the verse I told you at dinner?"

Shaking her head she sniffed, "No, I'm sorry, I don't remember..."

Her voice trailed off as Adam recited, "We know that the whole creation has been groaning as in the pains of childbirth right up to the present time. Not only so, but we ourselves, who have the firstfruits of the Spirit, groan inwardly as we wait eagerly for our adoption as sons, the redemption of our bodies. For in this hope, we were saved. But hope that is seen is no hope at all. Who hopes for what he already has? But if we hope for what we do not yet have, we wait for it patiently."[1]

"You asked me how I have so much faith in a man and love that I have never seen. Well, I want to tell you Evelyn, it's because I have seen a glimmer of that kind of love. And now I wait patiently for the day when I will receive that love in full." Adam could see the questions in Evelyn's eyes. "Can I tell you the rest of my story?"

Adam found a seat in the cool sand, and Evelyn silently nodded as she allowed him to draw her down next to him. Evelyn leaned against his shoulder, closing her eyes as his deep voice recounted the events following the night that changed the course of his life.

"After the shooting, I was immediately put into custody and placed on trial for murder in the first degree. I was terrified, Ev. I was all alone. I had absolutely no one in my life that I could lean on for support. No family, no friends, nothing. Not a single person from the orphanage where I was raised came to see me. I guess I burned too many bridges. I think as far as they were concerned, I was someone else's problem at that point.

"I would lay on the bed, surrounded by blank walls and stare into nothingness. I can remember thinking that it would probably be the room where I would one day die. It was the most awful feeling in the world. Then one day, while the guard was making his rounds, he stopped outside my cell.

"'Gardener,' he said, 'You have a visitor.'

"Of course, I had no idea as to who would be visiting me, but at that point, I think I was so numb that I didn't even care. The guard cuffed me, restrained my ankles like a wild animal, and led me down the corridor to the highly-secured visitor's area. He steered me into the room and stopped just inside the doorway before gesturing in the direction of a middle-aged man, sitting patiently by the window. He was waiting to speak to someone, waiting to speak to me.

"I had never seen this man before. I guessed that he was probably someone assigned to my case, or he was some sort of, I don't know... counselor. He terrified me at first. He was a hulk of a man, and he didn't look happy. He didn't look angry either though, just sort of... sad. And while his physique looked like that of a fit young man, his salt and pepper hair betrayed him. Despite his somewhat frightening stature, the thing that stood out the most about him was his eyes. Even from across the room, I could see that he had the most beautiful and peaceful eyes. They were a piercing shade of blue, striking against his ebony skin. The moment I stepped into the room, his gaze locked with mine. It was like he was staring into my soul. There was just something about him, Ev. Even though I had never seen that man before, I was captivated by him.

"As the guard led me over, the man never once took his eyes off mine. 'Hi Adam,' the man said in a deep baritone voice. I offered a short but polite reply, still trying to assess the situation.

"'My name is Abner, named after my daddy and my daddy's daddy.' He said it in such a way that revealed his southern roots. 'I came to read to you today, Adam. I heard you haven't had many visitors, so I thought I would come by and read to you.'

"He didn't phrase his words like a question. He wasn't asking if I wanted him to read to me. He said it as if it was a fact, simple and to the point. Silently I wondered who this Abner was. How did he know I didn't have any visitors, and why did he feel the need to read to me? I didn't ask him these questions though, just simply agreed to let him go on with what he came to do.

"I'll be honest, I was starving for attention. I would have taken any form of human contact at that point, so I just sat back and watched as Abner reached into his lap and pulled up a worn, leather book and placed it on the table. The golden, gilded writing on the front read 'Holy Bible.'

"Under any other circumstances, I would have wanted no part in listening to someone read the Bible, but what choice did I really have? Like I said, I was desperate just to hear the voice of another person speaking to me like I was a human being and not some rogue, wild animal.

"I listened as Abner's smooth voice recited the Scriptures. The words sounded so strange to me. I had heard passages of the Bible before in the orphanage, but never had I heard someone speak those words with such power. I was captivated. I clung to his every word as if it might be the last I would ever hear.

"Before I knew it, an hour passed, and my time with Abner came to an end. The guard came over to escort me back to my room, and Abner stood up to leave.

"'Wait!' I called after him.

"Abner turned to look back at me, his large figure looming over my small thirteen year old frame.

"'Yes,' he said as he clung tightly to that old, leather book.

"'Thank you,' I offered meekly before turning away and allowing the guard to lead me out of the room and down the dim corridor. I took one final glance over my shoulder as the door closed behind me. Tears were glistening in Abner's eyes.

"Over the course of the next three months, Abner came to visit me nearly every day. In the beginning, our time together consisted of Abner reading and me listening. That was it. Then, when the hour was up, Abner would leave and I would go back to my cell. He always left on the same note. He would give me this sad, sort of smile and say, 'See you later, kid.'

"As time went on, Abner began engaging me in conversation. He got to know me as a person, not as a criminal. Never once did he ask about why I was there or what I had done. He just wanted to know who I was. He never talked about his life, and I never thought to ask him. As far as I was concerned, it didn't matter what Abner did outside those four walls. What mattered was that he was there with me. For one hour every day, I had the company of another human being, someone who cared, someone who showed love in a way I had never before seen.

"On one particular day, Abner sat across from me with his Bible open to the Gospel of John. 'I want to tell you a story today, Adam,' He said as he glanced down at his Bible. This was the way Abner always started when he was about to read to me. He would always say that the Bible is the greatest story ever told, so people need to read it and hear it like a real story. Sometimes he would read me the Bible stories. Other times, he would recount them in his own words, sharing the stories with details and emotions that are often overlooked when reading the words within the pages of the Bible. He made them come to life, as if he had the whole book memorized.

"'Adam, once upon a time there was a father. He was a very loving father who had one child, a son, whom he adored deeply. Everything this father did, he did for his son. He longed to lavish him with gifts of his love. He even built great wealth and stored it up as a wonderful inheritance for his child, all because he loved him. The son trained under his father, and when he got older and grew in his abilities, the father gave him a part in the family business. Through the son's job, he would contribute to his father's plan and ultimately the son's inheritance. It brought the father great joy to know that the work they did together would be a blessing, not only to his son, but to others as well.

"'But something happened, Adam. The father's beloved son was murdered! Oh how the father mourned. This was his one and only son, the love of his life. And while the father's heart broke into pieces, he realized this tragedy was all a part of the plan. While most fathers would threaten revenge and destruction of the one who took their son's life, this father,' Abner shook his head in disbelief, 'this father did something very, very different. He forgave the one who murdered his son.' His voice trailed off, and Abner leaned back into his chair. His eyes seemed so far away.

"Finally, I broke the silence, 'I know that story.' I leaned forward and pointed to the open Bible on the table. 'They told us that story in the orphanage. It's the story of God's love and His Son, Jesus, Who died so that we could be with His Father someday. It's the main story of the Bible, right?'

"Abner was silent. The sound of the large clock on the wall pounded like a hammer on an anvil, counting down my remaining precious minutes with him. He was deep in thought.

Finally, he glanced down at his Bible, before turning his eyes back toward mine.

"'Well, yes,' he solemnly replied, 'you're right. God did send Jesus to earth so that we can all go to Heaven to be with Him someday, but that wasn't the story I was talking about.'

"I sat there, digging back into my memory for other Bible stories involving fathers. There was the prodigal son and Abraham…

"'Okay, Abner,' I finally said, 'I give up. Which Bible story is it?'

"Realization dawned in those piercing, blue eyes as Abner shifted uncomfortably in his seat, 'Oh, it's not a Bible story, Adam. I'm the father.'"

{Chapter 22}

EVELYN'S HEAD WAS SWIMMING as she tried to grasp what Adam was telling her. "So wait," she started, "Are you saying that Abner was the father of the seventeen year old boy you shot?"

"That's exactly what I'm saying."

Evelyn was incredulous, "I don't understand. What…" she couldn't even find the words.

"I know, I know," Adam said. "I was in shock when I finally realized what Abner was saying. I just sat there across from him with a blank stare until it all sank in. Then I broke down and started sobbing. I apologized over and over and begged for his mercy. I just remember him taking my hand as I cried. Could you imagine the scene, Evelyn? I can only think of God's love as I envision myself, a thirteen year old boy, his face buried in his arms. And this man, the father of the boy I killed, held my still-cuffed hands and patted them saying, 'There, there, it's okay, son. It's okay.'"

Evelyn's eyes filled with tears as she imagined the scene in her own mind. *What kind of love is that? How could someone forgive like Abner?*

"So what happened?" was all Evelyn could ask. She was still so dumb-founded by Adam's amazing story. "How was he able to forgive you like that, Adam?"

"I asked him the same thing, Ev. I said to him, 'How can you sit here with me after what I've done? I took the life of your son!' You know what he told me, Evelyn?" Adam shook his head, still in disbelief over the words spoken to him so many years ago. "I will never forget his words. They are written on my heart forever. Abner said to me, 'Adam, yes, you took the life of my son, but you know, my boy Joshua was God's son too, so you took the life of God's son. But who am I not to forgive you? I am guilty of the same sin. I have the blood of God's Son, Jesus, on my hands, but He forgave me. Who am I not to forgive you of the very same sin for which I am guilty?'

"His word's hit me like a ton of bricks. He was right, Evelyn. We are all guilty of the most horrific sin, the murder of God's precious Son Jesus."

Adam took Evelyn's hands in his and pulled her to her feet. "Evelyn, I know you are plagued with the guilt of taking the life of your own child…" Instinctively, Evelyn's hand clutched her stomach. Her throat tightened with grief. "But Ev, you were already stained with the sin of taking the life of God's child. All our sins are equal in the eyes of God. They are all equivalent to the most horrific depravity that we could ever commit. The amazing thing is, God will forgive us of that sin and wash us with His grace as if it never happened. Then He adopts us as His own child and lavishes upon us all the love that He has for His Own Son."

Evelyn shook her head in disbelief.

Adam squeezed her hand reassuringly, "Let me tell you what happened next."

"Abner and I sat there at the table while he explained everything. The night of the shooting, Abner's son Joshua was working late at the art gallery, the very place I was attempting to break-in. Abner owned that art gallery, and Joshua, his son, was the featured artist whose painting I had been sent to steal." Evelyn clutched her hand to her mouth.

"I know," Adam whispered as he shook his head. "Well, it didn't take long for the police to get there. Patrols that were in the neighborhood heard the gun shot. Abner was at home that night, so he rushed to the gallery as soon as he received the call from the police, but they had taken me away in a patrol car before he ever made it to the gallery.

"At first, Abner told me that his anger burned against me. He couldn't even bear the thought of sitting in the same court room as his son's murderer, let alone have a conversation with him. Abner said shortly thereafter though, God revealed to him that he was supposed to extend me his grace. Abner said he didn't know how he could ever forgive me, so he took it one day at a time, coming to visit me and getting to know me during the time I was waiting for my trial. He said it wasn't long before he realized I was just a boy like his own son, Joshua. Abner said he couldn't stand the thought of what would happen to a young, impressionable boy if I were sentenced with the kind of punishment I deserved. He wanted to give me a new start, a chance at a life I never would have been able to have.

"So he appealed to the court. Abner told them he didn't want to press charges. Instead, he pleaded for custody of me during my parole. He told the judge that he would like to adopt me so he could give me a good upbringing, discipline, and a family.

"You should have seen the way those people in the courtroom looked at him, Evelyn. They had never seen such compassion, such grace, such… love. As we were leaving the courtroom, the judge went on the record saying, 'Surely, this day, we have witnessed the grace and love of God.'

"And they were right, Evelyn. As we were walking out of the courthouse, Abner reached down and took my hand and said, 'C'mon son, let's go home. I smiled up at him, not sure of what I could say to the man who had extended the most beautiful gift I had ever received. I said the only thing I could, 'Okay, Dad,' I whispered, 'let's go home.'

"And that was it. From that day forward, Abner was my father. He loved me more than any person had ever loved me before. He taught me all about God's love, and I reasoned that if God's love was anything like Abner's, then I wanted a part in it. I became a follower of Jesus and devoted my life to Him.

"Just like God does for us, His children, Abner adopted me and gave me more life than I ever could have dreamed. He gave me so much more than I ever deserved. Because of him, not only have I been adopted by the greatest earthly father there ever was, but I have also been adopted by the greatest Father there will ever be, God."

Evelyn's eyes filled with tears, but her smile lit up the night, "It's such a beautiful story, Adam."

"I know, and guess what? You are a part of that story too. I want to share with you one of my favorite Bible verses. 'For He chose us, in Him, before the creation of the world to be holy and blameless in His sight. In love He predestined us to be adopted as His sons through Jesus Christ, in accordance with His pleasure and will, to the praise of His glorious grace, which He has freely given us in the One He loves. In Him we have redemption through His blood, the forgiveness of sins, in accordance with the riches of God's grace that He lavished on us with all wisdom and understanding.'[1]

"God loves us Evelyn, and He loves you! He loves you even more than your stepfather ever could have loved you. God wants to adopt you, Evelyn, because He created you. He wants to adopt you into His family, to love you as if you were His Own daughter."

The tears were now spilling over onto Evelyn's cheeks as she listened to Adam's words. She had never heard anyone talk about God as a loving Father. "Adam, I… I don't know what to say."

"Shhh…" Adam softly placed his fingers on her lips, "there's nothing you need to say," he whispered as he pulled Evelyn into his arms and held her as she cried.

{~}

I stood on the shore of the sea, keeping watch over the man and the woman. They were locked in an embrace, a vision that caused my mind to drift back to the day in the Garden of Eden. In my mind, I saw the Lord's first created beings as they clung to each other in desperation. Their tears spilled out and mingled so that I didn't know where one's ended and the other's began. The King had banished them from the Garden of Eden that day, and they wept for what was lost.

Now I watched as this man and this woman wept for what was being found.

I stood guard over them, for I knew it was only a matter of time before Satan's army would return. The woman, she was so close, but the time was drawing near. She didn't have much time before… My thoughts trailed off, and I began whispering a prayer over them.

"I keep asking that the God of our Lord Jesus Christ, the glorious Father, may give you both the Spirit of wisdom and revelation, so that you may know Him better. I pray also that the eyes of your heart may be enlightened in order that you both may know the hope to which He has called you, the riches of His glorious inheritance in the saints, and His incomparably great power for us who believe. That power is like the working of His mighty strength, which He exerted in Christ when He raised Him from the dead and seated Him at His right hand in the heavenly realms, far above all rule and authority, power and dominion, and every title that can be given, not only in the present age, but also in the one to come."[2]

{Chapter 23}

E VELYN SLIPPED OFF her deck shoes and tossed them from the dock to the deck of the boat. She reached down and untied the mooring rope from the large, metal cleat that secured the boat in the marina. In one swift and graceful motion, Evelyn slung her pack over her shoulder and leapt onto the swim deck of the catamaran sailboat.

It was a beautiful watercraft with pristine, white sails that stood out against the deep blues of the Pacific Ocean. It was a sailor's dream, and it was Evelyn's. The sailboat was her prized possession, the only item willed to her by her stepfather. Evelyn's mother had been furious when she found out it had been left to Evelyn. The boat was worth a pretty penny, and Evelyn's mother could not understand how her husband could leave such an expensive piece of property to, at that time, a child. Of course, Evelyn's stepfather made arrangements for the boat's safe keeping until she was old enough to take responsibility for it, but that didn't stop Evelyn's mother from complaining every opportunity she could. If it had been up to Evelyn's mother, the boat would have been sold long ago.

Evelyn never dreamed of selling the boat. She had only been out on it with her stepfather once before he passed away, but her memories of learning to sail with him were too precious to sell with the boat. There was something about knowing she was navigating the same open sea her stepfather once did that filled Evelyn with a sense of peace and completeness. In some strange way, she felt connected to him out there. It was as if her stepfather knew what kind of sanctuary this boat would be for her. Evelyn smiled at the thought of knowing that in that moment she was exactly where her stepfather wanted her to be.

Whenever an opportunity presented itself, Evelyn was on the water, and with a career that required plenty of travel, Evelyn was able to frequently use the sailboat as a means of transportation and residence. With the benefits of technology, Evelyn could conduct most of her work from anywhere in the world, as long as she had a satellite connection. Fortunately, that included the wide open sea. The nomad lifestyle didn't bother her. She didn't have a place to call home in the traditional sense, but to Evelyn, the catamaran and vistas of an endless ocean were her home.

Of course, she wouldn't mind settling down some day if the right opportunity or person presented itself. Evelyn's mind drifted to thoughts of Adam. It had been nearly a month since their first real date, and they had been inseparable ever since. Walls crumbled that night at the restaurant as they each opened up about their pasts. There was something so raw and pure about being vulnerable with someone, a risk Evelyn had never taken until now. She was still completely overwhelmed at knowing Adam accepted her just as she was. She smiled to herself, the thought of Adam warming her soul. She breathed in the crisp, salty, morning air and watched the sunrise reflecting across the cloud covered sky. It was time to prepare the sails.

In no time at all, Evelyn was gliding effortlessly across the waters, heading toward her photo destination: Molokini, a sunken crater off the island of Maui. The crater, now invaded by the inhabitants of the Pacific Ocean, had become a breathtakingly beautiful coral reef, housing over two-hundred and fifty distinct species. Many of which were endemic to the area. This photo opportunity had been the main motivation for Evelyn's return to the island.

Evelyn settled in for the ride, attempting to focus on her shot list and notes. She glanced through her reference materials and studied the identifying marks of the various fish she would be searching for amongst the reef. Her eyes scanned the waterproof reference sheets, but her mind was far away. Evelyn had been looking forward to this excursion since her arrival in Maui, but now all she could think about was having dinner with Adam later that night. He had taken her dancing the previous weekend, but Evelyn suggested the next time she should make dinner for him at her place… on the boat. Evelyn tried to hold back a smile, remembering the look on Adam's face when he finally learned where she was staying on the island.

"You never cease to amaze me," he whispered in her ear before planting a gentle kiss on her cheek. Now, Evelyn touched her fingers to the same spot, remembering the warm feeling. *How can I feel this way about someone I've only known for a few months?* Evelyn found herself asking this question more frequently as realization set in. She was falling deeply in love with Adam. She couldn't help it. The more Adam expressed his love for her, the more in-love she grew. Gone were the days of Evelyn's apprehensions about Adam. There was only one thing Adam was after: her heart. The single reason he wanted to be with Evelyn was to love her and to be loved by her. Evelyn couldn't believe the turn her life had taken. It was as if she'd fallen into a beautiful story.

Evelyn set her eyes on the horizon and reached for her thermos of hot chocolate. She pulled her sweatshirt tight around her, warding off the cool, morning breeze that came rushing over the bow of the boat. As she did, the sun broke through the clouds, casting warm rays across her skin. Its reflection created a lighted path across the sea.

Evelyn navigated the sailboat with the sun's course, following it to her destination. The white sails drifted along the golden road, illuminated by the morning sun. Its amber rays washed the entire catamaran in the sun's glow and reflected against the gilded lettering on the stern, "Eden's Secret."

{~}

Evelyn pressed her mask to her face, falling backward off the stern of the catamaran and into the cool, blue waters below. Scuba diving was an experience for all the senses: the smell of the neoprene wetsuit, the splash as her body broke the surface of the sea, the exhilarating feel of the cool water on the exposed parts of her face, the taste of salt on her lips, and the brilliant sight as a myriad of bubbles danced about in what could only be described as an underwater ballet. As the bubbles cleared from Evelyn's view, she slipped the regulator into her mouth and began the descent to the ocean floor.

Molokini was not a deep dive. In fact, Evelyn could just as easily skin dive in this situation, but when photographing, she needed the flexibility of staying underwater for extended periods of time. She glanced around, taking in the display of rainbow-colored fish dancing through the water like acrobats. *I don't think there could be anything more beautiful than this moment,*

Evelyn thought as she set her dive watch. She wanted to allow as much time as possible before she would need to resurface and switch tanks. *If I even need to.* It was shaping up to be a perfect day, and she was thrilled to discover that she had made it out early enough to beat the snorkel and scuba tours that made daily visits to the reef. Molokini was a very popular tourist attraction for the islands, bringing in boat loads of inexperienced divers. Fortunately, much of the marine life had become accustomed to the invasion, but still, Evelyn set about her work quickly, hoping to finish before any other visitors arrived.

Evelyn spent most of her time drifting along the ocean floor, snapping photographs of some of the more friendly fish while slowly making her way to the crater's rim where she would search for the more elusive species. Evelyn learned long ago that to see the ocean floor in its natural state, you must blend in as much as possible when you're a human in a fish's world. She slowed her breathing and body movements, allowing the current to carry her along the rocky ledge. She began pondering the mysteries of this foreign place, and her mind wandered to previous conversations with Adam. *Could there really be a God of the universe Who created all this?* Evelyn was contemplating the thought when a small Yellow Tang darted past her face, drawing her attention to a large crevice in the rock-wall up ahead. It looked like the perfect hiding place for a camera-shy creature. Evelyn readied her equipment, swimming closer to discover what was hiding inside.

Now, hovering in front of the crevice, Evelyn could see it was not so much a cleft in the rock-wall as it was a tunnel. It was large, big enough for a grown man to fit inside. Evelyn knew the risks of entering any type of underwater cave, whether it was a large cavern or a small tunnel like this one. There was no way she was going to attempt swimming into the passageway, but peeking her head inside with her camera didn't seem out of the question.

Evelyn checked her gauges and dive watch. She had a small amount of time before she would need to resurface, not a lot of time, but the surface was not far. It wouldn't take long for her to reach the boat that was anchored above. Normally, she would plan for a safety decompression stop, *but it's not absolutely necessary*, Evelyn reasoned with herself. *I could skip it and be just fine.* Mentally, Evelyn went through the shots she already captured on her camera. The memory card was nearly full, and she had most of the shots she planned to capture on this trip. She could call it a day now, and it would be a success. *What if the best shot of the day is hiding just inside this rock?* Evelyn glanced at her gauges again. *I'll just take a quick peek. I can always come back down with another tank.* Evelyn knew that would not be the case. If she were to take the time to resurface, switch tanks, and make it back to this crevice, whatever creature that might be hiding inside could be long gone. She also knew that entering the tunnel was against her better judgment, but her curiosity was getting the best of her. She brought her camera into position, ready to capture any timid creatures that might be lurking in the darkness.

The entry point of the opening was even wider than the tunnel that led inside the wall, but it was still dark and hard for Evelyn to see, for the morning sun was at such an angle that no light could reach the inside. Evelyn slowly drifted in, allowing only the front half of her body to enter the tunnel. She was careful not to touch the sides of the opening, not wanting to damage the natural reef. Slowly, she reached for her dive light to illuminate the tunnel up ahead. She turned it on. For a brief second, it flooded the tunnel, but she couldn't see anything. She had underestimated the brightness of the light in such a small space. Her eyes would need to adjust, but just as the thought crossed her mind, the light vanished. Darkness surrounded Evelyn. In contrast to the brightness of the dive light, the absence seemed even darker than before. *I just checked this light before my dive,* Evelyn thought, wondering how her equipment could have failed. *Good thing I have a backup.* Evelyn was reaching for her second dive light when she sensed a movement in the water in front of her. She had just barely noticed it, but in the stillness of the opening, it was easily discerned. *I need to get out of here.* Evelyn started slowly backing up while still grasping for her second dive light, but it was too late. Whatever creature was hiding in the darkness was clearly disturbed by her intrusion. Before Evelyn had time to react, something lunged and struck her. It all happened so fast. Evelyn heard a crack and felt a warm sensation on the back of her head as it slammed into the jagged edges of the rock overhang. Before the pain had a chance to register, the darkness around her flooded with bursts of color. It was the last thing Evelyn remembered before everything faded to black.

{~}

The lack of oxygen woke her from a state of unconsciousness. Evelyn tried to inhale from her regulator, but nothing came out. She was out of air! Her eyes flew open to find the darkness still surrounding her. Panic set in! *What happened? Where am I?* These questions raced through Evelyn's mind as she tried to get her bearings straight. As she looked around, an oval of light blue caught her attention. That's when she remembered that she was just inside the entrance to the rock-wall. The open water was right behind her. Evelyn made a conscious effort to hold her breath and slow her heart rate. She wasn't sure how long she had been unconscious or how long she'd been without air. She would need to be mindful of how much oxygen her body was burning. Evelyn was trained to hold her breath for extended periods of time, and the surface wasn't far away. *I'll be fine*, she coached herself.

She managed to reach her spare dive light. Switching it on, she glanced down at her gauges and dive watch. She was shocked when she realized how long she had been unconscious. Fear gripped her as she imagined what could have happened in that span of time: *I could have died!* Evelyn pushed the thought from her mind, knowing it would only increase her heart rate and need for oxygen.

Her throbbing head reminded her to move slowly and to be mindful of any injuries she may have sustained as she attempted to maneuver out of the crevice. Finally, she was able to back up a few feet, just enough for her body to be completely removed from the overhang, but then she stopped. She couldn't move. She was caught on something. Evelyn turned, straining to see which piece of equipment was lodged, but as she did, a searing pain burned across the back of her head. Evelyn became suddenly aware of a reddish tint forming in the water around her, blood! Now she was panicking. Most of the sharks in the waters off Maui were harmless, but any shark could become dangerous when it smelled blood in the water. A gushing wound could attract sharks from miles away.

Evelyn's lungs were beginning to burn, and her head felt cloudy. She wasn't sure if it was from the impact, the lack of oxygen, or both. *I need to get to the surface!* The voice in Evelyn's head was screaming. She was having trouble concentrating. *Think, Evelyn, think!* Crystals of light from the surface poured through the water and danced across Evelyn's skin. She could see the hull of the catamaran up above. She was so close! Evelyn tried to calm her whirling mind. She couldn't focus on anything with her throbbing head.

Please, please help me! Evelyn called out in her head. She realized she was praying, praying to a God she wasn't even sure existed, but what other hope did she have? *God, if You are really there, please save me!*

As if in response, Evelyn was instantly washed in an overwhelming sense of peace. Her racing mind slowed, her heart rate decelerated, and she was able to focus. Her mind began thinking properly, and she was able to assess the situation. One piece at a time, Evelyn began stripping off her gear, hoping to unchain herself from whatever was holding her in bondage. Finally, she felt the release. She was free! Not caring anymore about burning oxygen, Evelyn made a mad dash for the surface, kicking with all her strength. Her lungs were on fire, and she was fighting her body's natural instinct to inhale. She had lost her fins somewhere along the way, so ascending fast was a struggle. Even though Evelyn was out in the light now, darkness was beginning to fill her peripheral vision. She was going to pass out if she didn't get air. *Almost there!* Evelyn pushed while visions of color burst before her eyes. Her chest felt like it would explode, and the darkness was taking over her full vision. It would only be a matter of seconds before...

Evelyn burst through the surface, gasping as the cool air filled her lungs. It hurt to breathe, but at the same time, nothing had ever felt so good. She was crying now, unable to believe that she was alive. She wanted to roll over on her back and float to catch her breath, but at the same time knew that she needed to get out of the water. She was still bleeding, and at this point, any blood she had lost would have been dispersed through the water, attracting predators from the deep. She needed to get somewhere safe and assess her injuries. Mustering up the last of her strength, Evelyn forced her arms and legs to propel her through the water and cover the last few yards between her and the boat. Finally, her hand landed on the cold, metal rung of the ladder.

Evelyn fell to the floor of the catamaran, unable to move. Her whole body ached with exhaustion. She knew she needed to examine her wound, but she couldn't find the strength to pick up her body. She reached a cautious hand to the back of her head. There was a huge lump, but as far as she could tell, the gash was long but not deep. She didn't even think stitches would be required. Evelyn pulled her hand away and saw only a small amount of blood on it. She breathed a sigh of relief and reached for a towel. She balled it up and pressed it against her wound while rolling over to her side. She closed her eyes, allowing the sun to warm her skin. She felt as though she were fading in and out of a dream. She was so tired. *I can't fall asleep*, Evelyn whispered to herself. *I've got to stay awake*. She wasn't sure if she faced the possibility of a concussion, but with being all alone on the open water, Evelyn couldn't risk falling asleep. She might never wake up.

She tried focusing on something other than her exhaustion, like the fact that she was alive. She remembered her desperate plea to God when she thought she would never see the light of day again. *Did God really answer me? Did He really save me?*

Evelyn felt the hot tears rolling down her cheeks as Adam's words came flooding back to her, *"For it is in this hope we are saved. But hope that is seen is no hope at all. Who hopes for what he already has? But if we hope for what we do not yet have, we wait for it patiently."*[1]

"I want something to hope for," she whispered quietly.

As the words left her lips, a cool breeze began to blow, drifting across her skin and leaving goose bumps. As the rhythmic waves lapped the sides of the boat, the gentle rocking eased her tired mind. Just before giving into the inevitable sleep, Evelyn thought she heard a soft reply in the wind. *I will give you hope. I am good to those whose hope is in Me, to the one who seeks Me. For you have this hope as an anchor for the soul, firm and secure.*[2]

{~}

I stood by my King and peered down through the portal at the woman lying on the boat. Her lips moved silently. I glanced over at my Master. He was gripping the sides of the portal and staring intently at His created one. Even though the woman spoke with the faintest whisper, my Lord heard her every word. I watched my Master's lips move in response to the woman. It was the language of prayer, the private and intimate conversation that took place between the humans and the Lord. The angel warriors and I could lift up prayers to the King as well, but it was somehow different between the Lord and His created ones. He heard their desperate cries and searched the depths of their hearts. He knew every intimate thought. He heard their gentle whispers.

The King tilted His head to one side, listening for the voice of His beloved, the one He longed for, the one He so desperately wanted to turn to Him and come running into His arms, but no reply came. The woman was asleep. Without taking His eyes off the portal, the King said to me, "Michael, it is I Who made the earth and created mankind upon it. My Own hands stretched out the heavens; it was I Who marshaled their starry hosts."[3]

I listened in silence as my Master declared what I already knew to be true, for I was there! That which was from the beginning, not only had I heard, but also I had seen with my own eyes and touched with my hands. I was there when He set the heavens in place and witnessed Him marking out the horizon on the face of the deep. With my own eyes, I saw Him

235

establish the clouds above and fix securely the fountains of the deep and give the sea its boundary so the waters would not overstep His command. That was when He marked out the foundations of the earth. Then I was constantly at His side. I was filled with delight day after day, rejoicing always in His presence, rejoicing in His whole world, and delighting in mankind.[4]

I smiled in remembrance as my King continued to speak. "Michael, in the beginning was the Word, and the Word was with Me, and the Word was Me. He was with Me in the beginning. Through Him all things were made; without Him nothing was made that has been made."[5]

Humbly I bowed my head before the Lord, not comprehending the deepness of what He spoke to me, His wisdom and understanding far exceeding my own. I listened intently, clinging to His every word as if it may be the last sound my ears would ever hear.

"In Him, Michael, was life, and that life was the light of men. The light shines in the darkness, but the darkness has not understood it, for the fear of the Lord is the beginning of wisdom, and knowledge of the Holy One is understanding. Therefore, listen closely to My words, and then you will be able to understand My insight into the mystery of Christ, which was not made known in other generations as I am now revealing it to you. Michael, my Son, Jesus, is the way, the truth, and the life. No one can come to Me except through My Son by faith. It is by this same faith that the humans understand that the universe was formed at My command, because what is seen was not made out of what was visible. By their faith they are sure of what they hope for and certain of what they do not see. Blessed are those who have not seen My Son and yet believe.[6]

"You see, Michael, in the past I spoke to my created ones through prophets at many times and in various ways, but in the last days I spoke to them through My Son, Whom I appointed heir of all things, and through Whom I have made the universe. My Son is the radiance of My glory and the exact representation of My being, sustaining all things by My powerful Word. One day, I will present to you the Word in its fullness, the mystery that has been kept hidden for ages and generations, only then will I disclose it. I have selected them, Michael. I have chosen to make known to them the glorious riches of this mystery, which is Christ, in them, the hope of glory."[7]

I grasped at the King's words, trying desperately to make sense of all He said. His wisdom washed over me like a wave. The King's understanding is so great, so vast and immeasurable, that no one but the One can understand His power and plan. My head was swimming. I was drowning in the Lord's wisdom. In His compassion, my Master reached down and placed a strong hand under my chin and lifted my face toward His. He stared deeply into my eyes. He searched my spirit, my inmost being, looking for a glimmer of understanding, the slightest hint that I recognized His deep vision.[8]

"My Lord," I said as I gently folded my wings, "This mystery you speak of, I ..."

My Master paused for a moment, as if waiting for me to finish. When I did not continue, He gently drew back His hand and placed it on top of my head. As He did, a sweet smell began to emanate from the Lord. It pierced my nostrils and a warm sensation washed over me. I became aware of a soft rumbling in the distance, and without warning, a bolt of lightning blazed across the sky, shaking the ground with an ensuing clap of thunder. At that moment, a flash of purest light enveloped us, stealing my sight.

Immediately we were transported to a different location in the heavenly realm. The light subsided, my vision returned, and I glanced around, taking in my surroundings. We were standing side by side in a spacious field. The air was still and silent, and the sky surrounded us like a dome, illuminated with colors my eyes had never seen.

I looked, and there before me stood a tree in the middle of the land. Its height was enormous! It grew large and strong, and its top touched the sky; it was visible to the ends of the earth. Its leaves were beautiful, its fruit abundant, and on it was food for all. Under the tree flowed a magnificent river. It was clear as crystal and stretched as far as the eye could see in either direction, to the east and to the west. It was the river of the water of life. The tree and river were illuminated by the light of the land, the light of the King and His Son. For in this land, there was no more night. There was no need for the light of the lamp or the light of the sun, for the Lord God was its light![9]

Then I remembered. I had seen this place before. This was the city, the Kingdom the Lord was preparing. The Kingdom for His Son! It was from the very throne of God and the Lamb that the River of Life flowed down through the middle of the great street and through the Holy City. I turned to my Lord, searching His face for answers, but He did not take His eyes from the place where He was staring – the tree.[10]

"Michael, the mystery is this, My Son, Jesus is the final piece. It was I Who made the two of them one and destroyed the barrier, the dividing wall of hostility by abolishing the law with its commandments and regulations through My Son's flesh. My purpose was to create in Him one new man out of the two of them, thus making peace. And in this one body to reconcile both of them to Me through the cross, the tree on which I put to death their hostility. Behold, Michael, for I am coming soon! My reward will be with Me, and I will give to everyone according to what he has done. I am the Alpha and the Omega, the First and the Last, the Beginning and the End. Blessed are those who wash their robes, that they may have the right to the Tree of Life and may go through the gates into the city.[11]

"Michael, the time is drawing near."

Suddenly, there was another flash, and just as quickly as we had arrived, we were instantly back at the edge of the portal. I peered down below where the woman was still fast asleep. *How long have we been gone?* It felt like ages, but it could have only been mere minutes.

"You must go to her, Michael. You must go to them both. Death and Deception have already broken loose from the depths of the Abyss. They are already in pursuit of the man and the woman, and this time they are not alone. Though they plot evil against you and devise wicked schemes, they cannot succeed; for you will make them turn their backs when you aim at them with sword or drawn bow. You must protect them, Michael, for much is at stake. The woman's very life is hanging by a thread. This very day I call Heaven and earth as witnesses that I have set before her life and death, blessings and curses. She must choose life, so that she may live. And she must love Me, the Lord God. She must listen to My voice and hold fast to Me, for I, the Lord, am life. Michael, there is no other way, and time is running out.[12]

"The time is coming for you to arise, and at that time the people, everyone whose name is found written in the Book, will be delivered. Then death and hades will be thrown into the lake of fire, which is the second death. And Michael, if anyone's name is not found written in the Book..." the Lord paused and glanced down at the woman. His face grew solemn, and the air became quiet. "If anyone's name is not found written in the book, they too will be thrown into the lake of fire."[13]

The King's words pierced through my heart: *the lake of fire, the second death*. I thought back to the day in the Garden of Eden, that fateful day when the Lord's created ones brought upon the world the first death, but my Master had bought them back at the greatest cost. The King had won. His love always wins. But the second death? It was up to the Lord's created ones to accept the gift of grace to be saved from the second death, eternal separation from their Maker, their King, their Lord and God. For it is by grace that they are saved, through faith and not by themselves, for it is a gift from God.[14]

No words passed between us. We both understood. There was nothing to be said. The seconds passed like days as my Master and I watched over His beautiful created one. Eventually she began to stir, rubbing the back of her head and slowly getting up from where she had been lying. As she hoisted the sails, I tore my gaze from her to look upon the face of her Maker beside me. He didn't take His eyes away from her. As I gazed at Him, I noticed a single tear escape, sliding slowly down His cheek. It rolled down His face and slipped off the curve of His chin, dropping in slow motion through the portal, descending to the earthly realm below.

{~}

Evelyn stirred, realizing she had fallen asleep. Surprisingly, she felt a bit better. She rubbed her throbbing head and glanced at her watch. Slowly she climbed to her feet and prepared for her journey back. She hoisted the sails and glanced up at the afternoon sky, still wondering if maybe, just maybe, someone had heard her whispers. As she lifted her face upward, searching the sky, a single droplet of water fell and landed on her cheek. Then, without warning, it began to rain.

{Chapter 24}

IN THE DARKNESS of the Abyss, Satan paced back and forth, his mangled hands clasped behind his back. The thousands of years that he remained locked away had done nothing in the way of aiding his already-horrific appearance. In fact, he and his demonic warriors no longer bore even the slightest resemblance to their once angelic forms. Their own sin and rebellion had led to their slow demise. These, who were once angels, did not keep their positions of authority and abandoned their own home. At the command of the eternal God, they had been kept in darkness, bound with everlasting chains for judgment on the great day. Since the day they were cast from Heaven, their large forms had taken on an ominous appearance. Their mere shadows evoked a sense of fear. Their presence was always made known by their putrid, sulfurous stench and the chill they brought with them. They were a terrifying sight indeed, strong, chiseled bodies as big as a horse, fangs like a lion, and a face which once resembled that of a human, now grotesque beyond recognition. They were filled with every kind of wickedness, evil, greed, and depravity, full of envy, murder, strife, deceit, and malice. These were the beasts, the demons of Hell.[1]

They went about the murky corridors, torturing the inhabitants of Hell while the sound of their wings filled the dark Abyss like the thundering of many horses and chariots rushing into battle. They had tails that stung like a scorpion's and with them the power to torment those who had denied the one true God. As ghastly and terrifying as the demons were, they were no comparison in fright to their leader himself, Satan. Once a beautiful guardian cherub, he was a murderer from the beginning, not holding to the truth, for there was no truth in him. When he lied, he spoke his native language, for he was a liar and the father of lies. While being the master of disguise and deceit, Satan could take on any form he chose. Because of his cunning and convincing nature, he could make himself appear beautiful under the cover of deceit and darkness. It was the truth, however, that exposed him for who he really was. No words could describe his horror. His very presence exuded pure evil, his appearance portraying something that could only be described as a vile beast. Being the most devious of all created beings, he could change his appearance, making himself more appealing, even tempting to the humans. They saw him as he chose: a seductive and alluring affair, a profitable yet unethical job, a smooth talking man whose true desires were to lure, conquer, and kill. Even still, Satan's evil presence was not always easy to recognize, for more often than not, he used his power to take things that were true and twist them ever so slightly so they still seemed credible. *Like making a young girl believe she was responsible for the death of her stepfather.* Satan chuckled at the memory.[2]

Somewhere in the shadows of the surrounding Abyss, he heard an echo of laughter from Death and Deception. "What are you laughing about?" Satan barked at them. "Show yourselves!" The two demons instantly silenced their mouths as they stepped out from the shadows that shrouded them. "I don't think the two of you have any room for laughter given the mistakes you've made." Satan was glaring down at them. Even though Death and Deception were two of the largest demons, they were dwarfed in comparison to their leader. "How hard is it to separate one man and one woman? You were supposed to have killed the woman by now!"

Satan's anger burned. He continued to pace, wringing his hands in frustration as Death and Deception lowered their heads, knowing full well their inadequacy. They cast sidelong glances at each other, throwing darts with their accusatory glares, each believing the other was to blame.

"Don't you two realize the importance of this situation?" Satan glared at them as if they were idiots. Death's and Deception's hatred lessened as the demons looked to each other for answers. Finally, they turned back to their fuming leader with nothing to offer in response. Satan threw up his hands in exasperation and turned to storm away. "Pathetic!" he mumbled under his breath. "If you want something done right, you have to do it yourself."

Satan made it only a few paces further when an idea dawned on him. He stopped, turning back to glower at his wretched minions as a cunning grin spread across his face. Death and Deception had already turned to leave. "Not so fast!" Satan called after them. The two demons halted. "Assemble my army! You two may be useless imps, but I am not walking away from this mission without a fight!"

{~}

I dove down through the portal and into the earthly realm just as the woman pulled the catamaran into the dock slip. I watched closely as she secured the large watercraft, all the while, keeping my Master's warning in the back of my mind. I scanned the horizon. The sun was already hanging lower in the sky. It wouldn't be long before the man arrived. Then the two of them would be together as the Lord wanted, but Satan would be enraged if he found out. That is, if he weren't already aware. Their reunion went against every grain of the enemy's plan. I knew I had to be alert and on guard against Death and Deception, for I could almost guarantee they would make an appearance that night.

I moved in closer to have a better view of the woman. She seemed to be doing okay given the injuries she sustained earlier. Once the man arrived, he could care for her physical well-being. But me? No. I was there for a far greater purpose, her spiritual well-being. The woman was completely oblivious to the waves she was causing in the spiritual realm. Battles were being waged for her very soul! They had been small encounters up until that point, but I wasn't sure how much longer Satan would wait before realizing the Lord's Army was not going to back down. I was certain that before long, we could anticipate a collision with his army of evil and wrath.

Knowing all this, I began scanning the surroundings, searching for any indication of an approaching invasion. Everything was clear. It seemed as if it might be a calm evening after all. I was just about to secure the area when I heard it, a rumbling behind me off towards the open sea.

I turned to face the horizon, shielding my eyes against the descending sun. Some distance off the shoreline, I noticed the waters of the deeper sea begin to ripple and bubble. I watched for a few moments as the undulations continued to swell, growing in intensity until there were large geysers of water shooting skyward. The fountains of water caused white caps to form and race inland, crashing violently against the rocky shoreline. To the earthly realm, this scene appeared to be merely inclement weather, an approaching storm causing a disturbance in the sea, but to the eye of the one in the spiritual realm, it was a foreshadowing of the night to come. I drew my sword and braced myself, preparing to take on any power that would challenge my mission or my King's.

I readied myself for the attacks of Death and Deception. If they were who the Abyss dared to spew forth, I was ready. As the storming waters continued to brew, I felt my heart begin to race. A wave of apprehension enveloped me as the scene unfolded. There in the distance I saw a beast coming out of the sea, a red dragon-like creature with ten horns and seven heads. It was enormous in stature, yet slender and stealthy like a leopard. It had the strength and power of a bear in its feet and its seven mouths, full of glistening fangs, threatened like a lion. My breath caught in my throat as realization set in. I recognized the monster that rose from those dark waters, from a place far below in the depths of the Abyss. It was Satan.[3]

He did not see me suspended in the air over the shoreline near the marina and the woman. Instead, the beast's attention was drawn to something under the water. Its seven heads attached to seven long necks craned, examining something below the surface. The sea launched itself at the dragon, releasing two dark forms that shot up through the surf and stopped to hover in front of him, Death and Deception. Four of the beast's seven heads lashed forward at the two demons as if to devour them. At the same time, its three other heads reared back and let out a piercing, blood-curdling howl. In response to the beast's call, the surrounding waters began to churn with even more ferocity, preparing to spew forth Hell's inhabitants. Finally, the ocean erupted, unleashing with it a legion of demon warriors prepared for battle.

The dragon barked its orders to the army before diving down through the dark waters and disappearing into the depths below. The hoard of demon warriors congregated out over the deeper waters of the ocean, aligning themselves according to the commands of Death and Deception. They formed a massive wall of dark, winged bodies as far as I could see in either direction. They lined the horizon in a dense mass, their sheer numbers blanketing the sky as an ominous storm cloud suspended over the ocean. I waited, but they did not advance.

I glanced down at the woman. They knew she was there, but she remained completely unaware of the battle forming around her. She had just finished showering in the cabin below deck and was beginning to prepare the meal she would be sharing with the man. Without hesitation, I sheathed my sword, bolting upward into the heavenly realm. My mission was to protect the man and the woman, especially the woman. In order to do so, I was going to need an army.

{~}

"I still can't believe you own a sailboat," Adam said as he tore off another piece of bread. He leaned back onto the makeshift picnic blanket Evelyn had spread out on the bow of the boat. "This is incredible, Evelyn. Thanks for inviting me to dinner tonight."

Evelyn smiled back, "You're very welcome," she said before taking another bite of her salad. "Wait until you see the view from out here! The stars should be out soon, as long as the weather holds out." Evelyn gestured toward the open water where a thick thundercloud lined the horizon.

Adam glanced over his shoulder. "I know. I noticed the storm clouds earlier. It looks like they're threatening rain."

"Well, that's the best part about having the cabin below. We can always move dinner inside. Speaking of dinner," Evelyn stood up from where she had been reclining on the blanket. "I should probably go get the main course."

As she stood and turned toward the cabin, Adam again noticed the matted spot in the back of Evelyn's hair where the blood had dried. "How's your head feeling?" he asked.

Evelyn paused and touched a cautious hand to her wound. "Better," she offered, "the shower and aspirin definitely helped. It's still throbbing, but I think the bleeding stopped."

"You sure you don't want to have it looked at by a doctor?"

"I'm fine," she smiled. "I promise. I probably hurt my pride more than anything."

"Well, I'm really glad you're safe. I don't know what I would do if something happened to you, Ev." Adam stood up and took Evelyn's hands into his own. "Now that I have you in my life, I don't want to ever live without you."

Evelyn's heart raced with the emotion and energy that surged through their joined hands. "I don't want to have to live without you either," Evelyn replied, looking up into Adam's eyes. "I can't even think about the school semester ending. Then you will be leaving..." her voice trailed off as she turned her eyes toward the horizon, trying not to think about the tears that were sure to come.

Adam squeezed her hands, "Let's not worry about that right now. I don't want to be sad about leaving when all I can think about is how happy I am to be here with you. Let's just enjoy our evening togeth..." he was interrupted by a crash of thunder in the distance. Evelyn jumped, and the thick cloud-cover lit up in response.

"Speaking of enjoying our evening, we'd better get started before it gets rained out." Adam gestured toward the cabin. "Why don't you get the food? We can talk after dinner." Evelyn nodded her silent agreement. Forcing a smile, she ducked into the cabin just as another clap of thunder rolled in the distance.

{~}

"Tonight is the night!" Death shouted above the roar of the demon army before him. "You heard the boss. He doesn't care what happens to the man, but the woman? Tonight she dies!" The crowd erupted with shrieks of delight and the howling of their restlessness. These beasts had a thirst for blood. "Remember, if anything or anyone so much as tries to get in your way... destroy them!"

{~}

My army and I encircled the watercraft and the man and woman who were upon it. The angelic warriors and I stood shoulder to shoulder with blazing swords drawn and shields raised high. We were poised and ready to strike down anything that dared to penetrate the barrier we created with our bodies. We knew what was at stake. The woman's eternal life was hanging in the balance. She was so close. We had to give the man one more opportunity to reach her.

In the distance, the legion of demon warriors began their advance. Like an approaching storm, they rolled in toward the shore, and a cold chill came rushing in from the sea. My comrade who was beside me shivered. He was a brave warrior. They all were. It was not the beasts advancing towards us or the monster of the deep that we feared, for even though their numbers were thick and many, those who were with us were more than those who were with them. No, we did not fear Satan. For it was the Lord who split open the sea by His power, and it was He who would break the heads of the monster in the waters. On that day, the Lord would punish with His sword, by His fierce, great, and powerful sword, the gliding and coiling serpent would fall. He would slay the monster of the sea. Because of the Lord's great love, we knew we would not be consumed, for His compassions never fail. We knew He would strengthen and help us. He alone, would uphold us with His righteous right hand. No, it was not the fear of the enemy that caused my comrades to tremble. It was the fear of what would happen to the woman, should she fall prey to him.[4]

Like a fiery ring of protection, my army of brave angelic warriors and I crowded tighter, forming an impenetrable wall around the Lord's created ones. Nothing was going to get in, and no one was going to get out. We braced ourselves as the demonic warriors continued their advance.

"Ready yourselves!" I shouted over the thundering of the approaching army. "Be strong and courageous! Do not be afraid or terrified because of them, for the Lord your God goes with you. He will never leave you or forsake you. The Lord your God and King, Who is going before you, He will fight for you!"[5]

{~}

Evelyn returned within minutes, carrying the main course in a glass baking pan. "Smells amazing, Evelyn!" Adam said as he stood to take the warm dish from her hands.

"Oh wow, look at the storm!" Evelyn nodded with her head in the direction of the sea as she handed over the pan to Adam. "I was only gone a couple minutes, but it already looks closer than before."

"Do you think we should move dinner indoors?"

"Well..." Evelyn paused, examining the sky. "It might pass us by. Rainstorms never last very long in Hawaii. They usually move pretty fast. We'll just keep an eye on it."

"Sounds like a plan." Adam smiled and took Evelyn's hand, leading her down to the picnic blanket. "May I?" Adam asked as he reached for her other hand.

"Huh? Oh." Evelyn quickly realized what was happening as Adam closed his eyes and lowered his head.

"God, thank You so much for this amazing meal that You have provided. And thank You even more for the amazing woman who prepared it."

Evelyn couldn't hold back her grin. She loved listening to Adam pray. The way he spoke to God was refreshing and unique, just like Adam. Evelyn stole a quick glance. His eyes were still closed, but he was smiling too.

"God thank You for Your beautiful creation and the fact that we get to enjoy it from such a unique location this evening. Even though the weather looks stormy, I ask that the only thing that would rain on us would be Your love. Oh, and God, thank You for this life changing trip. Amen."

"Amen." Evelyn echoed. "Let's eat!" No sooner had the words left her mouth, when an earth-shattering crack of thunder boomed throughout the land, rocking the boat upon the waves.

{~}

A loud clash rang throughout the spiritual realm as demon bodies collided with the wall of angelic warriors surrounding the catamaran sailboat. "Steady yourselves!" I called out to the army. Each warrior braced himself with a shield, creating an armored barrier that no man or beast could pierce. The battle had begun.

The demonic beasts struck again, charging us with broad shoulders as if we were a door to be broken down. Yet no weapon forged against us could prevail, not even the gates of Hell![6]

We braced ourselves, preparing for the next blow, but nothing happened. I peered over my shield where I had been crouching, firmly planted and ready to receive the full force of the attack. I held up a halting hand to my army as I surveyed the scene. They were retreating. The entire hoard of demons was withdrawing, receding to the open waters. Or were they? The angel warriors and I watched as the evil spirits of the Abyss pulled back, farther and father over the open ocean. They weren't retracting. They were creating distance between us, more ground for building up momentum! They continued out until they were nearly specks on the horizon. The warriors of my army and I rose to our feet, watching the dark army fade into the distance, but just before the enemy disappeared from sight, they halted. Abruptly, they turned on their heels in hatred and rage, and like a heard of wild beasts, they began to charge.

"Take hold of your Sword of the Spirit!" I turned and shouted to my valiant soldiers. "This time, we strike!" Each angelic warrior drew his sword, preparing to penetrate the flesh of evil. We took the stance not of a barricade, but of an impenetrable wall of muscle ready to attack.

The demons continued their advance, stampeding toward us as one unit, like one enormous monster prepared to devour its prey. Their eyes blazed yellow against the darkened sky, and the beating of their wings shook our very core. I glanced to my left and to my right, embracing the feeling of warmth and power that surged through my being as I witnessed the look of pure trust and confidence on the faces of my army. For it was in Him that they trusted; it was in their King that they placed their confidence.

I gripped the hilt of my flaming sword and ran my thumb over the engravings, the very words of my Master and King, inlaid on the weapon that was always at my side, the Word of God. I inhaled deeply, reining in every ounce of courage and strength before thrusting my sword high and calling out to the Lord. "Oh Lord, how many are our foes! How many rise up against us! They do not believe that our God will deliver us, but You are a shield around us, O Lord. You bestow glory on us and lift up our heads. To the Lord we cry aloud, and You will answer us from Your holy hill, the Mountain of God."[7]

The thundering grew louder as the demons drew near. My warriors stood taller, empowered by the Word of God! We tightened ourselves, strengthening the hedge of protection surrounding the man and woman.

"We will not fear the tens of thousands drawn up against us on every side," I continued. "Arise O Lord, deliver us, O God! Strike all our enemies on the jaw. Break the teeth of the wicked. For from the Lord comes deliverance!" As the final words departed my lips, the demons came hurling into the barricade we created. A deafening battle cry rose from the Lord's Army as each warrior wielded his fiery Sword of the Spirit and tore through the flesh of the black, winged creatures. Flashes of light and sparks flew as good collided with evil. We drew back slightly, tightening the ring of protection as the back row of angels leapt forth, swords aimed, and ready to strike down the enemy.[8]

My soldiers dropped down into the thick of the combat, going head to head with Hell's worst. The battle waged on around us as the demons advanced relentlessly. The reality of time ceased to exist. It felt as though we had been fighting for centuries. While the duration of this battle was uncertain, I knew that the war we were fighting against evil had gone on far longer.

My men were brave and noble warriors, but as the fight continued I could see their bodies tiring despite their will. I knew they would not give in, but they needed renewed strength. They needed the strength of their Lord. Almost silently I began to whisper, "I pray to You, O Lord, in the time of Your favor, in Your great love, O God, answer us with Your sure salvation!" I sensed my King's presence as I murmured the words. He was listening. With just the mere utterance of a prayer, our King heard my call to Him. "Hear me, Lord," I urged, "my plea is just. Listen to my cry. Hear my prayer!"[9]

As the words still clung to my lips, I received my response. The battle cries surrounding me began to fade even while the war continued to wage. It was as if someone covered my ears to blot out all distractions, and in the stillness of my soul I felt an enveloping peace. All around me destruction ensued, but in my heart, I felt the presence of my King. I heard His still, small voice whisper to me, "I have heard the prayer and plea you made before Me. I will sustain you."[10]

Then, just as quickly, the sounds of battle resumed around me. Cries of pain mixed with shrieks of rage rang out, deafening me to the soft whispering of my Lord. I lifted my sword and burst into the crowd, knowing that it was only a matter of time before my comrades, too, felt the sustaining power of the Lord and the peace He brings in spite of the storm. I waited for the gentle wind to fill their sails, yet the annihilation continued. We were holding off the enemy, but they were gaining ground. I clung to the words of my King, for He is quick to keep His promises. *I will sustain you*, I repeated in my mind as I lashed out with my sword, bringing down the nearest demon. A blood-curdling scream erupted from its being as the demon fell to its back. It cried out in agony and hurled curses upon me. The nearest demons joined in, sputtering obscenities with their vulgar lips. They began to advance toward me, surrounding me on all sides, all the while chanting their demonic praise. Despite their outnumbering me, I was ready. I gripped the hilt of my sword tighter as I felt the comforting engravings of the Word of God. I lifted my shield to block the advancing of one demon to my left just as another launched itself to my right, but instantly they were halted. They abruptly ceased their attack and instead began to look around, listening for something.

That's when I noticed it... a soft wind beginning to blow. Recognizing the presence of my King, I became empowered. I scanned the crowd, watching as all around the battle halted. Angelic warriors soaked up the power of their Lord while the demons fell to their knees. The wind picked up pace, becoming stronger and whipping through the crowd in forceful gusts. It pressed itself upon us, nearly knocking us over with its force and might, and then suddenly, it stopped. The wind died, and the air became still. Silence enveloped us all except for one sound, the voice of the Lord.

Piercing through the silence, His mighty voice boomed "Pursue your enemies, My great warriors, and they will fall by the sword before you. Five of you will chase a hundred, and a hundred of you will chase ten thousand, and your enemies will fall!" The King's powerful words shook the land. The demons groped at their ears; the sound of the Lord's voice deafening them, they cried out in agony, their terror filling the land. They cringed, trembling and shuddering at the very words of God.[11]

"Be strengthened!" the King's voice rang out, "for I will go before you!"

Immediately, I began to call back the angel warriors, reining them into formation. "Into your positions!" I bellowed over the shrieks and cries of Satan's army. Without haste, my warriors reverted to their places in the wall of fortification. With swords drawn and shields held high we hunkered down, a multitude becoming one in strength and power. "Be still!" I shouted, "The Lord will fight for us. We need only to be still!"[12]

It was at this time that a hush fell over the armies. Again, we were wrapped in the thick silence while a radiating light from above caused all who were present, both angels and demons, to look to the sky. We watched in awe as the clouds parted. The heavens were opening up! The demons' jaws went slack, and their eyes widened in terror at the power before them. With a command from the eternal God who reigns forever and ever, a blinding flash appeared in the sky, hurling down torrents of fire on Satan's Army.

{Chapter 25}

Flashes of lightning blinded the sky as an earth-shattering crash of thunder rocked the sailboat upon the waves. A chill rushed off the ocean, sweeping over the bow of the boat and blowing napkins into a white frenzy. Before Adam and Evelyn had a chance to snatch them from the air, the sky burst forth with a torrential downpour.

"Quick!" Evelyn shouted over another earsplitting crash, "Get below deck!" Adam and Evelyn frantically grabbed everything within reach in a desperate attempt to salvage what was left of their romantic dinner. Adam held open the door as a sopping wet Evelyn dashed into the cabin. He followed right behind her, his shoes sloshing beneath him.

"I have never seen it rain like this in all my life!" Adam shouted over the downpour. "I'm glad were on a boat. This storm kind of has a Noah's Ark feel to it." He could hear Evelyn's muffled laughter coming from the room in the back of the cabin. Finally, she appeared.

"Me either!" Evelyn tossed Adam a bath towel and began drying her own hair. "Look at you!" she shook her head, "you're soaking wet!"

"Speak for yourself!" Adam gestured to Evelyn's bright colored sundress which was now clinging to her bare legs.

"I know, I know, so much for our nice dinner." Evelyn stooped to mop up the puddles on the floor before one of them slipped. Then she proceeded to examine what was left of their meal. "Looks like we might be going straight to dessert," she extended the pan for Adam to have a look.

He grimaced, "Yeah, the bread looks a little soggy too. But hey," He took Evelyn's face in his hands, recognizing the defeat in her eyes. "This just means that you will have to cook for me on another date, and spending more time with you is all I care about." He planted a soft kiss on her forehead.

Evelyn peered up into Adam's grey eyes as he wrapped his strong arms around her. He always knew the right thing to say. "So is that a yes to dessert?" she questioned as she wriggled out of his embrace.

"Tempting me with food again, I see."

"Whatever works," Evelyn winked at Adam and motioned for him to have a seat at the table. She brought over a covered tray and slid into the bench seat across from him. Adam waited expectantly as she unveiled the dessert with mock flair. "Brownies! And not soggy, I might add."

"I'm impressed," Adam selected one and took a cautious bite. "I must say," he said slowly, "if your plan for this evening was to win over my heart, then you've succeeded. I have a confession to make though." Adam paused. "You didn't even have to try. You've had my heart from the first day I met you."

Evelyn could feel the color rising in her cheeks. No one had ever treated her with such love. *Well... almost no one.* "My stepfather would have loved you, Adam," she whispered.

Adam pushed away his brownie and folded his hands in front of him. He studied her for a few moments before finally saying, "I would have loved to meet him, especially if he was anything like his little girl." Evelyn tore her gaze away and stared down at the table. She feared the tears would spill over if she kept looking into Adam's deep, kind eyes.

He sensed her emotions. "Evelyn," She glanced up. "Your stepfather's death was an accident. You can't hold yourself accountable for it. You can't harbor all this guilt from something that wasn't your fault."

"I know that deep down, but it's just…" Evelyn paused and peered out the small porthole window. The storm outside raged on, but inside, in the presence of Adam, she felt a calming peace. She brought her focus back on the man who was sitting across from her. *What is it about him that makes me want to tell him everything? How does he cut to my heart like this?* "The thing is, if I wouldn't have been in the truck with my stepfather, he would still be alive." Adam shook his head, signaling he didn't understand.

"All my life, I've been an accident waiting to happen. Do you know how many times I've nearly died? Or had something traumatic happen to me? Even today… out there." Evelyn gestured toward the open sea. "I could have died but…" Evelyn's mind flashed back to the terror of nearly drowning. She could feel the fear coursing through her veins just as vividly as before. She shook the thought from her head, but couldn't as easily dismiss the question that had been gnawing at her since earlier that day. *Did God really save me?*

Adam reached for her hand, bringing her back to the present. "Adam, if I wouldn't have been in that truck, my stepfather wouldn't have died. When the truck started spinning out of control, and he realized it was going to crash, he directed the impact to the driver's side instead of where I was sitting. He saved my life, but he died."

Slowly, Adam leaned back in his seat. He was silent for a few moments as the words sunk in. Finally, he slid forward, reaching across the table and taking both of Evelyn's hands into his own. He stared down at their clasped fingers. Without looking up he whispered, "Greater love has no one than this… that he lay down his life for his friends."[1]

Evelyn shook her head, "What?"

"Evelyn, your stepfather lived out Jesus' command to love others as Christ loved us. Your stepfather gave his life so that you could live. What your stepfather did…" Adam shook his head, "is the picture of perfect love."

Evelyn was speechless. She could feel the tears welling in her eyes.

"Evelyn, you've experienced the love of God through your stepfather. He wanted you to live because he knew he was already alive."

Evelyn wiped her eyes, "What do you mean?"

"You told me shortly after we met that your stepfather was a follower of Jesus. That means your stepfather committed his life to serving God, his King, just like I have. Evelyn, the God I serve and the God your stepfather served is a living God. God gave the life of His Son, Jesus, to conquer death, but His plan didn't end there. He rose from the dead, Ev, and through the payment God made, we are bought back. We can choose to accept the incomprehensible forgiveness and love of God and be made alive in Him because Jesus died so that we may live.

"Life, Evelyn, is not what we see here," Adam gestured toward everything surrounding them. "True life is being in the presence of the one and only God. Your stepfather is in Heaven. He is alive!" Adam paused, "There is a verse in the Bible that says, 'We were dead in our transgressions,' and that's exactly what we are. Here on earth, we are dead when we are separated from God before we surrender to Him. We are dead in our sins, but when we accept the grace of God, we are given the gift of life, which we receive in full when we finally leave this world and go to be with our Maker in Heaven."[2]

Evelyn bit her lower lip and glanced out the window. She turned Adam's words over in her mind while bolts of lightning continued to dance outside. A deafening crack of thunder made her jump. Evelyn turned back toward Adam. "You make believing sound so wonderful."

"It is wonderful, Ev. Nothing compares to the assurance of knowing that you are forgiven from everything horrible you've ever done in your life and to the peace of being confident in going to Heaven to be reunited with the Creator of the Universe. Evelyn, if your stepfather loved you enough to die for you, just imagine how much God loves you."

Tears streamed down Evelyn's cheeks as she tried to comprehend that kind of love. Her small view through the boat's porthole began to blur. Through her tear-filled eyes, it seemed as if the sky and sea were merging together; it looked like Heaven itself was colliding with the earth. She couldn't tell where one ended and the other began.

Adam rubbed his thumb across the back of her hand. "Evelyn, your stepfather did not die so that you could live in the sense that we live here on the earth. He gave his earthly life so that you could have eternal life."

Evelyn's small frame shook as she began to sob. They were not tears of grief and pain like before, but tears of being overwhelmed by love. She tried to grasp the meaning of what Adam was saying, but she couldn't. Evelyn couldn't even begin to imagine what kind of love it would take to see past everything she had done. Every time her mind tried to wrap itself around the idea, she was overcome with humility. It broke her. It wrecked her to her core.

Evelyn buried her face in her hands. A vision began to form in her mind, a quiet moment on a sailboat docked by the sea, lost on an endless ocean that spanned across a great big world... a mere speck in the vast universe. And there sat Evelyn. One girl loved by one amazing God. Warmth flooded her body. A sense of peace like she had never known washed over her; it overwhelmed her. Finally, Evelyn lifted her face to peer up at Adam. Through her tears she whispered, "I want what you have, Adam. I want to be loved like you are loved. I want to be forgiven... for everything."

"You can have it, Evelyn. God makes it so easy." Adam squeezed her hands. "All you have to do is confess with your mouth that Jesus is Lord and believe in your heart that God raised Him from the dead. Then you will be saved from death and made alive in Him. For it is with your heart that you believe and are justified, and it is with your mouth that you confess and are saved. The Bible says, 'Anyone who trusts in Him will never be put to shame. For there is no difference between Jew and Gentile, the same Lord is Lord of all and richly blesses all who call on Him,'" Adam paused, "Evelyn, everyone who calls on the name of the Lord will be saved.'"[3]

{~}

Flames continued to rain down from the heavens, blinding the demons with flashes of piercing white light. They cowered and covered their eyes, trying to hide from the presence of the Almighty, but they could not. They cried out in agony, shrieking in pain as their eyes were blinded and their skin singed.

Finally, with a bold command from the Lord, the torrents of fire retreated from the demon army. The flames merged together into a wave-like inferno, turning from Satan's demons and rushing wildly in the direction of the army of angelic warriors. Before we could even take in what was happening, the blaze leapt over the wall of protection that our army was creating, and it took up position behind us, forming a ring, a barricade of fire where we had been standing. The King was relieving us of our position!

We charged forward courageously with strident battle cries and swords lifted high. Boldly we fought, and bravely my warriors stood their ground, striking down the enemy. One by one they fell by our sword, just as the Lord had promised. We were strengthened by the words of our God. We fought harder and stronger, knowing we were in the presence of our King. He was fighting by our side.

The ring of flames continued to burn, consuming any demon who dared to pass it. It reduced them to piles of ash in front of all who were present and cast down wrathful bursts of lightning with each monster it claimed. Sparks flew as our swords collided with the flesh of the evil beasts, and thunderous rumbles shook the land with the sounds of the battle that ensued. In the spiritual realm it seemed as if time stopped. The battle waged on for what felt like years, growing in intensity and strength. The savage nature of the beasts grew in ferocity. They burned with a vengeance, knowing what was at stake. They were here to destroy the very thing we had been sent to protect, the woman. The demons knew there wasn't much time, and right now she was alone with the man who was speaking to her the very words of the King!

Suddenly, all went silent.

Every one present, both angels and demons, abruptly halted their attacks. The only sound to be heard was the soft hissing and popping of the ring of fire surrounding the boat. My angelic warriors and I peered down in awe at the raging sea below us. We listened intently, straining our ears to hear… *voices*, the voices of the man and the woman. At the sound of their conversation, even the flames fell into a hush; they too were listening.

We heard the voice of the woman whisper, "I want what you have." At the sound of her softly spoken words, the muscle fibers of every angel and demon tensed: the angels in anticipation, the demons in fear and utter outrage.

"You can have it, all you need to do is confess with your mouth that Jesus is Lord and believe in your heart that God raised Him from the dead. Then you will be saved from death and made alive in Him." The man's voice echoed through the land, causing the demons to howl and grasp their ears. They fell to their knees and cried out in pain. They knew they were losing![4]

"For it is with your heart that you believe and are justified, and it is with your mouth that you confess and are saved. Anyone who trusts in Him will never be put to shame. For there is no difference between Jew and Gentile, the same Lord is Lord of all and richly blesses all who call on Him, for everyone who calls on the name of the Lord will be saved."[5]

The angel warriors waited with bated breath. We strained our ears to hear her reply. Would the Lord's army celebrate the victory of one more saved soul?

The woman opened her mouth, but just as she was about to speak there was a thunderous explosion behind us. We whirled around just in time to witness an eruption from the depths of the sea. It was the dragon. Satan knew he was running out of time. He realized his army was fighting a losing battle, but he was not ready to back down, not yet.

The dragon sprang forth with a force of violence and terror, leaping over, first its own hoard of demons and then lunging wildly over the Lord's Army. The dragon was heading directly toward the ring of fire. It was going straight for the man and the woman. All seven of its heads were aimed directly toward its target, and all seven mouths were open wide, fangs bared, ready to devour their victim.

We should have been terrified. The outcome should have appeared bleak, but we knew our hope was secure in the Lord. The King was fighting on our side.

Just as the dragon reached the edge of the ring, the Lord gave His thundering command. The flames obeyed, leaping forth in a blazing waterfall of fire. They shot up, overtaking the dragon. They continued to pour forth as a rushing wave, sweeping over and consuming the demon army. The inferno was drowning Satan and his wretched followers. The Lord Himself was rescuing the woman from the enemy!

An earsplitting howl erupted from the seven heads of the dragon, echoed by the shrieks of pain from the demon monsters as they were overtaken by the flourish of flames. The pouring fire continued its course, rushing out past the shore of the sea into the deeper waters of the ocean. The King was fighting our battle. He would win. The angelic army and I watched in astonishment as the power of the Almighty was displayed with a final word from the King, hurling the enemy down into a whirlpool of fire and throwing them back into the murky depths of the Abyss.

As the final cry faded, a chill swept over the sea and darkness enveloped us. Silence filled the land except for the still, small voice of the Lord as He whispered, "Woe to the earth and the sea. The devil has gone down to you. He is filled with fury because he knows that his time is short."[6]

{Chapter 26}

WE STOOD THERE IN SILENCE and reverence, trying to grasp what we just witnessed, the mighty power of the King. The demons, the dragon, they were gone. The Lord himself fought for the protection of His created ones, the ones He loves.

The King's fire was gone now, but His presence was still made known in the soft, sea breeze. It drifted out across the waters and lifted the storm from the ocean to reveal a breathtaking sunset. The glowing white of the sun was surrounded by deep hues of crimson, fading into liquid violet. The sapphire night beyond was punctuated with the dazzling white diamonds of the sky.

The quiet breeze rushed over the sea and gently rocked the sailboat in the marina. My angel warriors and I slowly advanced toward the boat. We surrounded it from all sides, again forming a ring of protection, but this time was different. Instead of lifting our swords to fight, the mighty warriors of the King and I fell to our knees. We lifted our hands high and called out the name of our Lord. We prayed. We prayed for the man and the woman.

Our interceding became more fervent, and with tears streaming down our faces, we prayed for the woman, for strength, for clarity, and for faith. For faith is being sure of what you hope for and certain of what you do not see.[1]

This decision was the woman's, not God's, for He loved her enough to wait. He loved her enough to wait for her to come running to Him so He could scoop her up in His arms and call her His beloved. What is love if it is forced? It is not love at all.

The wall of angels moved in tighter, closing in around the man and the woman, surrounding them in prayer.

{~}

For it is with your heart that you believe and are justified, and it is with your mouth that you confess and are saved. Evelyn replayed Adam's words in her mind. She closed her eyes. "I do believe," she whispered softly. After all that happened over the past few months, and especially after the experience she had earlier that day, Evelyn could no longer convince herself of the lies she once believed. She knew it was God who rescued her. She felt Adam squeeze her hands; she heard his voice in her mind, *and it is with your mouth that you confess and are saved.* Evelyn knew what she needed to do.[2]

She closed her eyes and softly began to whisper. In the stillness of the night, Evelyn whispered a prayer that only she, Adam, and the King for Whom it was intended could hear. "God…?" Evelyn paused, "I uh… I'm not entirely sure what to say…"

Adam stared in disbelief. Just moments before he had been silently praying for Evelyn, *now she is praying*? He shook his head in amazement. He felt a smile forming in the corners of his mouth and a tightness constricting his throat. Was this really happening? Adam closed his eyes and lowered his head, giving Evelyn's hands another encouraging squeeze, but this time he didn't let go. He clung tightly to the woman he never wanted to lose.

Evelyn continued, "God, I do believe that You hear me right now, and I do believe that You are the One Who created the earth and everything in it, even me. Thank You for sending Adam to show me that everything in all of creation points to You. Your eternal power and divine nature are clearly seen in all that You have made. I don't have any excuse to not believe."[3]

Tears welled up in Evelyn's eyes, spilling onto her cheeks as she continued. "God, I don't know how You could even begin to forgive me for all the horrible things I've done. I am so sorry for taking the life of my child before it was even born." She was sobbing, breaking down and releasing guilt and emotions that had been stored up for years. "It was Your child too."

Evelyn wiped her eyes and took a deep breath, trying to settle her breathing. "But God, most of all, I am so, so sorry for running from You all these years. Deep down, I think I've always known. I think we all do, but I tried so hard to shut You out because I couldn't face a God Who would allow me to be raped, Who would place me in a family with a hateful mother, and Who would take from me the only man who ever loved me, my stepfather." Evelyn's tears turned to rage as she poured out the hurt and pain from her past.

"Now I realize, after all these years, You weren't taking away the love of my stepfather. You were showing me, through him, the great and immeasurable love of You, my real Father. Please, please!" Evelyn pounded her fist on the table. "Please forgive me! I do believe! I believe with all my heart that not only have You shown me Your great love through the death of my stepfather, but also through the death of Your Son, Jesus."

"Jesus," she repeated, "such a sweet word to hear in the darkness of all my sin. God, I ask that you would cover me with Your grace and erase forever the sin and blackness that stains my hands, the blood of Your Own Son..." her voice trailed off. "I don't want to be without You any longer. I want to be alive with You. Thank You. Thank You for what You have done for me. And thank You for bringing Adam into my life to show me just how much I need You and just how much You love me."

The sound of Evelyn's voice slowly faded and silence filled the cabin. After waiting a few moments, Adam finally opened his eyes. He was met with a piercing, slate-grey stare from Evelyn. They were the eyes of the women he fell in love with, but now even more beautiful. He recognized something different in them. He saw everything in her eyes. He saw hope. He saw his future. Adam smiled as tears filled his own eyes. He gave her hands another squeeze.

"Amen," Evelyn whispered.

"Amen," Adam echoed.

{Chapter 27}

THUNDERING APPLAUSE AND JOYFUL CRIES erupted from the multitude of angel warriors surrounding the man and the woman. We jumped and cheered, clapping each other on the back. The battle had been won!

"Give thanks to the Lord, call on His name. Make known among the nations what He has done, and proclaim that His name is exalted!" I shouted to the army over their rejoicing. "Sing to the Lord for He has done glorious things; let this be known to all the world. For He has rescued her from the dominion of darkness and brought her into the Kingdom of the Son He loves, in Whom she now has redemption, the forgiveness of sins! Shout aloud and sing for joy, warriors of Zion, for great is the Holy One among us!"[1]

In unison, the throng of angel warriors bellowed back their reply. With the voice of a thundering multitude, the great and mighty army of the Lord shouted, "Now to the King eternal, immortal, and invisible, the only God! To Him be honor and glory for ever and ever. Amen."[2]

"Amen!"

{Chapter 28}

ADAM HELD EVELYN'S HAND tightly within his own as they walked down the shoreline of the picturesque Maui beach. Adam was still in complete and utter awe of the transformation that had taken place in Evelyn since weeks before when she accepted the grace and love of the King. If he thought he loved Evelyn before, he was hopelessly head over heels now. He always knew that the woman he would one day love and marry would have to be someone who shared his faith and honored the same God he did. He was overwhelmed with joy at the thought that maybe, just maybe, Evelyn could be the one.

And Evelyn? She showed more exuberance now than Adam had ever seen in all their times together. She overflowed with excitement about her new-found future and life in Jesus. She behaved as though a weight had been lifted from her. And it had. All the weight of Evelyn's past, her sins, shames, and secrets, had all been completely erased by the grace of the Creator Who loved her. And the transformation showed. Evelyn could not stop talking about God's love and asking Adam questions about the Bible. She was a different person, the same person, but better. When Adam looked at Evelyn, he saw someone who had spent her entire life living in a world of darkness and now, for the first time, saw the light; she was beautiful. He saw himself in Evelyn. He saw the young boy he once was and the joy that he experienced when he was adopted by a father who loved him, an earthly father but also a heavenly Father.

As they continued along the shore, Adam was again reminded of the very first Bible verse his father taught him. He repeated it silently in his mind, *for you were once darkness, but now you are light in the Lord. Live as children of the light.* Adam looked to the setting sun, fighting back tears as he thought of his father. He was overwhelmed.

When Adam first arrived in Hawaii, he was in a very different place than he was today. The recent death of his father poured salt into wounds that had never quite healed, forcing him to wrestle with guilt for things that God had long ago forgiven. He was still holding on to those things that God chose to forget. He was living as if he were in the darkness when God had already called him a child of the light.

Now Adam smiled as he thought of the love of God. He knew deep down the Lord had brought him on this trip for a reason. How easy it could be to forget that right here, right now, in that very moment, he was caught up in the immenseness of God's love!

As Adam pondered all that happened over the past several months, a thought dawned on him. *Love is the reason You brought me here!* Adam prayed silently. His mind started spinning as he began to see the big picture. *It takes love to understand love. This is why You call us to love!* Adam continued his unspoken prayer. *How can anyone comprehend the love of God if we, those who are created in Your image, do not reflect Your love? It was the love of my earthly father that revealed the love of You, my heavenly Father. And it was my love for Evelyn that helped her to see how the love of her stepfather reflected the love of Jesus.*

Adam felt like he was going to burst. He was overcome with emotion and gratitude. *Thank You for bringing me here! Thank You for reminding me of Your unfathomable, unconditional, amazing love!*[1]

Adam stopped in the sand and spun Evelyn around to face him. He pulled her into his arms and held her in a tight embrace. "I just can't believe how wonderful this trip has been," he whispered. "Meeting you has been one of the best things that's happened to me. And you have no idea how thrilled I am that you have chosen to make Jesus your King." Adam placed a tender kiss on her forehead and pulled back, taking her hands into his own. "It feels like it was just yesterday that we met on the road to Hana. I can't believe there is only one week left in the semester." Adam felt a twinge of longing as he took in her beautiful smile. He didn't want to ever have to miss that smile. Adam's own joy began to fade as he looked into the face of the most incredible person he had ever met. "I don't want to have to say good bye, Ev." Adam released his hands from Evelyn's and shoved them into his pockets.

"Me either," Evelyn reached out and touched his arm. "Adam, I can't explain the way I feel around you. It's so … surreal. I've never met anyone like you. You've changed my life in more ways than one." She moved in closer.

"Evelyn, can I talk to you about something?" Adam questioned.

Evelyn cocked her head to the side giving him a quizzical look. She paused for a second and examined Adam's tense posture. "Yes," she finally replied, "but I have something that I need to ask you first."

Adam looked around at the empty beach. The sun was hanging lower in the sky, preparing to make its decent into the ocean. What Adam wanted to say to Evelyn was important. He didn't want to leave Monday with things unsaid, but nothing was more important right now than this moment here with Evelyn. "Ask me anything, Ev," he whispered. "There is nothing you could ask for that would be too great for me to grant you."

Evelyn smiled and Adam saw tears filling her eyes. "Baptize me, Adam."

Adam took a step back, stunned at what her sweet lips just whispered. "What?"

"Adam, you mentioned once before that after you decided to follow Jesus, your dad baptized you on your vacation at the lake. Look," Evelyn gestured out toward the crashing surf, "here is water. Why shouldn't I be baptized? There is no other person in the world that I'd rather have by my side as I make a physical declaration of dying to my past and being raised in life. I would be honored if the very man who led me to life would be the one to baptize me. Please?" she whispered.[2]

Adam was grinning ear to ear, and tears were welling up in his eyes. He couldn't believe the words he was hearing. They only confirmed in his mind the decision he already made. Adam slowly removed his hands from his pockets and reached for Evelyn's. "I would be honored," he whispered as he stared into those piercing eyes. "But Ev, before I baptize you, there's something I need to do. There's something I need to say." His heart was pounding out of his chest. Adam pulled Evelyn back into his arms. She peered up into his pleading eyes and placed one hand over his pulsing heart. With the other, she reached up and placed a tender finger over Adam's lips, silencing his words. Adam's pulse slowed, and a sense of peace enveloped him as he looked down into the face of the woman who he knew, deep down, was made for him.

Evelyn kept her finger over his lips and softly said, "Adam, I already know. I love you too."

Adam and Evelyn waded out into the surf, jumping over the waves as they came rolling into the shore. They laughed as they struggled to walk through the ocean tide in their soaked, and now very heavy, clothes. Adam reached back with one hand, steadying Evelyn and leading her out into the deeper waters. They kept walking until they were a little over waist deep in the tide. Even though it was late spring, the water was still cool and sent chills up Evelyn's spine.

Finally, Adam came to a stop and turned to face Evelyn, taking her by the hands and pulling her in close. Evelyn looked up at Adam and saw the fading colors of the sunset reflecting in his tear-filled eyes. He drew Evelyn to him and held her tightly, resting his head on top of hers. She heard Adam whispering something, but couldn't quite make out the words over the sound of the crashing waves around them. Finally, Adam lifted his head from hers and planted a gentle kiss on the top of her head.

Adam turned them both to face the horizon; it couldn't have been a more perfect night. He placed a cautious hand on the small of Evelyn's back and offered his other arm for support. Evelyn looked up into Adam's face and instantly felt all her fears and worries melt away. She felt so safe in his arms, and in that moment, Evelyn knew that God was giving her more than just His love. He was giving her Adam's love too.

Adam drew Evelyn into him, so close that she could feel the steady, rhythmic beating of his heart against her shoulder. She heard him inhale nervously and clear his throat. Then he began to speak. "Evelyn, because you have believed in your heart that the living God is the Creator of the heavens and the earth, and that because of His immeasurable love for you, He covered your sins with the cost of His one and only Son. Because you believe that it is by His blood that you are saved from your sin and that it is through Jesus you are redeemed to His Father, and because you have confessed this with your mouth, I now baptize you in the name of the Father, and the Son, and the Holy Spirit. Amen."

Evelyn reached up to hold her nose, and Adam held tightly to her arms while he lowered her beneath the cool waters of the Pacific. Evelyn felt the waters envelop and cover her. She was wrapped up in the water as if it were the very love of God. She knew she was only under the water for mere seconds, but it felt as if an eternity of peace was washing over her, undulating with the waves. She opened her eyes and saw the crimson red of the setting sun, melting into the waters around her. It was as if the very blood of Jesus was washing her in that moment. Through the blur of red water, Evelyn saw Adam's solid figure silhouetted against the setting sun. The next thing she knew, his strong arms were lifting her from the crashing waves. She broke through the surface, inhaling deeply the cool, crisp night air. Without a second's hesitation, Adam pulled her into his arms and wrapped her in an overwhelming embrace.

A sudden realization occurred to Evelyn. She had thought when her stepfather passed away that she lost the only person who ever loved her, but right here, right now, God was giving her the love of another man. Evelyn felt herself melting into Adam's embrace. She never wanted this moment to end.

"Evelyn?" She felt Adam's heart pounding against her own chest.

"Yes?"

"Remember how I said I wanted to talk to you about something?"

In the excitement of getting baptized, Evelyn had completely forgotten. She nodded her response.

A broad grin spread across Adam's face, the same warm smile that she fell in love with the day she first met him. It warmed her soul. Before Evelyn realized what was happening, Adam pulled away from her. He thrust his hand into his pocket and pulled out a, now wet, black velvet box. He opened it slowly, revealing a sparkling white, trillion-cut diamond, placed in a setting of the purest sapphires. Adam glanced down at the ring and then up into the tear-filled eyes of the woman with whom he wanted to spend all of eternity.

"Evelyn, will you marry me?"

{Chapter 29}

I GAZED OUT at the vast countryside, taking in the beauty of my Master's Kingdom. It was nearly complete. Many times before, my King had brought me to this very hillside to show me the progress of the Kingdom as it was being built. Now, as it reached its fullness, it sparkled with radiance and splendor, the glory of the Lord filling every peak and valley. How amazing are the works of the Lord's hands, and how great this realm He was preparing for His Son. Courtyards dotted the hillside, and brilliant colored vegetation sprang from the fertile land. Creatures of every kind and others not known to man roamed across the vast fields, delighting in the Lord's creation. There were soaring vistas that surrounded the Kingdom, places where one could gaze up into an endless sky of untold sunsets and others where turquoise seas stretched upward, containing the melodic songs of watery beasts. It was a land so magnificent; words could not begin to describe it. It seemed as though this land defied the earthly laws of physics. It was simply beautiful beyond explanation.

I closed my eyes, pondering the many wonders of the Lord and the greatness of His love that surpasses knowledge and fills His created ones to the measure of all the fullness of God. It was in them that His joy was made complete, by them being like-minded and having the same love, being one in spirit and of one mind with Christ, the Son. It was because of the King's amazing love for His Son that the Kingdom was being created. How great are His signs, how mighty His wonders! His Kingdom would be an eternal Kingdom and His dominion would endure from generation to generation![1]

Again, I gazed out across the mighty land, silently praising my King as a warm breeze swept up over the hillside. It sang a sweet tune, like a quiet hallelujah. I whispered the words, feeling the warm peace of the Lord enveloping me. Everything surrounding me faded away until all that remained was a soft voice calling my name.

"Michael," it uttered.

"Yes, my Lord?"

"Michael," it whispered again.

"Speak, my King, for Your servant is listening."[2]

My Master's soft voice came from behind me, "Michael, the Kingdom I am creating is nearly complete." The Lord was standing beside me now. He gestured out toward the fruitful lands and regal palaces and then turned to look at me. "But Michael, I have much more to say to you."

"Anything, my Lord," I whispered, respectfully bowing my head.

My Master lifted my chin so He could look me in the eye. His face had become somber. "Michael, it is more than you can now bear, but My Holy Spirit will come to you, and when the Spirit of truth comes, He will guide you into all truth. He will speak to you not on His own, for I am the Father, the Son, and the Spirit. We will speak to you together, only what We hear from each other, and We will tell you what is yet to come."[3]

I fell facedown to the ground in reverence, ready to receive the words of truth. "What message does my Lord have for His servant?" I waited for His words but no response came. I listened for His voice but heard nothing.[4]

After a few moments of complete silence, I heard a sound like a whispering multitude, like the sound of the wind dancing through a thousand trees. It called to me, "Michael, look!"

Slowly, I lifted my forehead from the ground. I looked, and there before me was a door standing open in Heaven. And the voice I had first heard speaking to me sounded like a trumpet and said, "Come up here, and I will show you what must take place after this."[5]

{~}

After passing through the doorway, I was taken away by the Spirit to a realm that was far and wide, a place where land ceased to exist. Sky and sea collided, stretching out into eternity to the east and west. Stone bridges pierced the surface of the sea. They rose upward toward the misty sky then turned downward, falling like dancing arches in the water. The bridges were many, and they were connected by round platforms surrounded by columns, like little gazebos floating out amongst the endless sea. It was when we reached one of these platforms that the Holy Spirit finally stopped. He was glowing with the radiant colors of precious emeralds and sapphires, and light poured out of Him as if He had turned the ocean's waves to light. He did not speak but gestured for me to follow Him into the colonnade. I obeyed, trailing Him in silence, knowing my Master would speak when He was ready.

Upon entering the open room, I was overcome by a strange emotion, I could not place it, but I sensed the attendance of a power far greater than my own, or even that of the Holy Spirit. Then I realized. I was in the presence of the Holy Trinity.

Immediately I fell to the ground, lowering myself before them as the Holy Spirit took His place to the left of God the Father. The columns seemed to close in around me. Everything became dwarfed in comparison to the magnitude of God the Trinity. My heart pounded in my chest, thumping against the cool marble floors of the portico. A sweet aroma engulfed me, and emotions of untold greatness filled my soul.

"Rise, Michael." It was God the Holy Spirit Who spoke. Slowly, I rose to my feet, standing before the Holy Trinity. God the Father, my Master, stood beside the Holy Spirit Who spoke. Directly to the right of the Father was the Son, beaming with perfection and holiness. He radiated with hues of deepest crimson, the color of His blood that was shed. His beauty stole my breath away.

"Come!" the Spirit said, motioning for me to follow the Trinity out onto the stone walkway. I lowered my head and silently followed, realizing the King was about to tell me something of utmost importance. When we reached the center of the bridge, the pinnacle of the arch, the Trinity finally stopped. I waited patiently, anticipating the voice of the Holy Spirit and His mighty words of wisdom.

"Michael, look!" The Holy Spirit urged, gesturing out toward the open sea. I turned to watch as the sky became like a giant projector, and a vision played out before my very eyes. The vision revealed a picture of the earthly realm. In that world, there was a great earthquake! The sun turned black like sackcloth made of goat hair, the whole moon turned blood red, and the stars in the sky fell to earth, as figs drop from a fig tree when shaken by a strong wind. The heavens receded like a scroll being rolled up, and every mountain and island was removed from its place. Then the kings of the earth, the princes, the generals, the rich, the mighty, and everyone else, both slave and free, hid in caves and among the rocks of the mountains. They called to the mountains and the rocks, "Fall on us and hide us from the face of Him who sits on the throne and from the wrath of the Lamb! For the great day of Their wrath has come, and who can withstand it?"[6]

I gripped my chest, appalled by the vision, for it was beyond my understanding. The Spirit advanced toward me, and as He came near the place where I was standing, I was terrified and fell prostrate. Gently He spoke to me, "Michael, understand that the vision concerns the time of the end. I have seen how great the wickedness of the human race has become on the earth, and that every inclination of the thoughts of the human heart is evil all the time. I am grieved by them, and My heart is filled with pain. Are they ashamed of their loathsome conduct? No, they have no shame at all! They do not even know how to blush, so they will fall among the fallen. They will be brought down when I punish them. For I have said to them, 'Stand at the crossroads and look. Ask for the ancient paths, ask where the good way is, and walk in it, and you will find rest for your souls.' but they said, 'We will not walk in it.' I appointed watchmen, the angel warriors of Heaven, over them and said, 'Listen to the sound of the trumpet!' but they said, 'We will not listen.' Therefore, Michael, hear my words. Hear, O nations; observe, O witnesses, what will happen to them. Hear, O earth: I am bringing disaster on this people, the fruit of their schemes, because they have not listened to My words and have rejected My law."[7]

As God the Spirit spoke to me, I was overwhelmed with emotion and my strength was stolen from me. I bowed with my face toward the ground and was speechless. I was overcome with grief for those who denied the love of the King. Then He, the One Who looked like the very man He created, the Son, touched my lips. I opened my mouth and began to speak. I said to my Master standing before me, "I am overcome with anguish because of the vision, my Lord, and I am helpless. How can I, Your servant, talk with You, my Lord? My strength is gone, and I can hardly breathe."[8]

Again, the Son, touched me and gave me strength. "Do not be afraid, you who are highly esteemed," He said. "Peace! Be strong now; be strong."

It was only when my Master spoke to me that I was strengthened. Finally, I was able to say, "Speak, my Lord, for You have given me strength." My King, God the Father, gestured for me to rise to my feet, and the Trinity continued to lead me across the bridge.[9]

"Come, Michael," the Spirit spoke, "I will show you the bride, the wife of the Lamb." Again, He pointed out across the water, this time to one of the nearby colonnades. "Michael, in the heavens God has pitched a tent for the sun. It is like a bridegroom coming out of his chamber, like a champion rejoicing to run his course. It rises at one end of the heavens and makes its circuit to the other. Nothing is deprived of its warmth." At the Spirit's words, a flash of light blazed across the eastern sky, disappearing under the western horizon. It lit up the heavens and illuminated the floating gazebo in the distance. Standing in the center of the portico was one who looked like a man, yet His face shone with the radiance of joy. He had the face of God. It was the Son! He was dressed as a groom on His wedding day, but the bride was nowhere to be found.[10]

"Make the price for the bride and the gift I am to bring as great as you like." The groom's voice carried across the water. "I will pay whatever you ask me. Only give Me the young woman as my wife."[11]

When the Groom finished speaking, the Spirit declared in a mighty voice, "Let Us rejoice and be glad and give Him glory! For the wedding of the Lamb has come, and His bride has made herself ready!"[12]

I watched in awe as the Groom turned to His right, and out from the shadows stepped the most beautiful woman I had ever seen. She was dressed as a lovely bride, ready to be given over to her new husband. The Groom gathered her into His arms. He caressed her cheek and planted a tender kiss on her forehead before speaking these words over her. "You have stolen My heart, My sister, My bride. You have stolen My heart with one glance of your eyes, with one jewel of your necklace. How delightful is your love! How much more pleasing is your love than wine, and the fragrance of your perfume more than any spice! Your lips drop sweetness as the honeycomb; milk and honey are under your tongue. The fragrance of your garments is like the fragrance of Lebanon. You are a garden locked up, My sister, My bride. You are a spring enclosed, a sealed fountain. You are a garden fountain, a well of flowing water streaming down from Lebanon."[13]

I pondered the words the Groom spoke. They sounded so... familiar. Suddenly, I was overwhelmed by a memory. I began recalling words that my King spoke to me so long ago, at the creation of the world. *Michael, whoever drinks the water I give them will never thirst. Indeed, the water I give them will become in them a spring of water welling up to eternal life. I am life, Michael. I am the Alpha and the Omega, the Beginning and the End. To the thirsty, I will give water without cost from the Spring of the Water of Life.*[14]

The voice of the Spirit called to me, interrupting my thoughts, "Michael, once more there will be heard the sounds of joy and gladness, the voices of bride and bridegroom, and the voices of those who bring thank offerings to the house of the Lord. They will say, 'Give thanks to the Lord Almighty, for the Lord is good. His love endures forever!'" The Holy Spirit lifted His arms out to the side and His voice carried across the water. He looked directly at me as He spoke. He peered into my soul, and His eyes sparkled with wisdom. "Michael," he nearly whispered, "I will restore the fortunes of the land as they were before, but I declare to you, flesh and blood cannot inherit the Kingdom of God, nor does the perishable inherit the imperishable. Listen, Michael," He uttered, "and I will tell you a mystery."[15]

With the spoken words of the Spirit, the bride and Groom vanished, leaving only the Trinity standing before me. I remained humbled in my place on the cool, stone floor of the bridge. As I watched, a piercing light began to blaze in front of me, and a song filled the land with purity as the Holy Trinity merged together as One. Never had I seen such beauty! Where before stood God the Father, God the Son, and God the Holy Spirit, now in Their place stood God the Trinity in One! He had the appearance of a man, dressed in a robe reaching down to His feet, and He had a golden sash around His chest. His head and hair were white as wool, as white as snow, and His eyes were like blazing fire. His feet were like bronze glowing in a furnace, and His voice was like the sound of rushing waters. Yet the most beautiful thing about Him was the change that took place in His light. Before, the Father blazed brightly with the purest, whitest light, while the Spirit beamed with shades of azure and the Son with deepest crimson. Now, there before me, their colors combined! Together, the Holy Trinity cast rays of the most regal shade of violet throughout the land. It stole my breath away.[16]

God the Trinity motioned for me to stand and come toward Him. Slowly, I rose to me feet. "Come," He whispered. I moved in toward my Master, falling into stride with Him. He put His strong arm around me and drew me into Him as we walked together, the bond between us being indescribable in earthly relationships. It was a uniting cord of trust and honor, flowing with ease between the Master and His servant. I felt the warmth of His approval and His love for me as He began to tell me the great mysteries of His untold wisdom.

"They will not all sleep, Michael," He whispered, "but they will all be changed, in a flash, in the twinkling of an eye, at the last trumpet. For the trumpet will sound, the dead will be raised imperishable, and they will be changed. For the perishable must clothe itself with the imperishable, and the mortal with immortality. When the perishable has been clothed with the imperishable, and the mortal with immortality, then the saying that is written will come true: 'Death has been swallowed up in victory.' And then all will say, 'Where, O death, is your victory? Where, O death, is your sting?'" [17]

"Michael, you have loved righteousness and hated wickedness; therefore, I have set you above your companions by anointing you with the oil of joy. It is as I told you before. The time is coming for you to arise, and at that time the people, everyone whose name is found written in the Book, will be delivered. Then death and hades will be thrown into the lake of fire, which is the second death. But if anyone's name is not found written in the Book, they too will be thrown into the lake of fire. Yet, if they obeyed My Word, the love of God has been truly made complete in them, and that is how they know that they are in Me. My love is life! For the world and its desires will pass away, but whoever does the will of God lives forever. For if I did not spare angels when they sinned, but sent them to Hell, putting them into gloomy dungeons to be held for judgment; if I did not spare the ancient world when I brought the flood on its ungodly people, but protected Noah, a preacher of righteousness, and seven others; if this is so, then I, the Lord, know how to rescue godly men from trials and to hold the unrighteous for the day of judgment while continuing their punishment. This fate is especially true of those who follow the corrupt desire of their sinful nature and despise authority. Bold and arrogant they are. These men are not afraid to slander celestial beings; yet even My angels, such as you, although you are stronger and more powerful, do not bring slanderous accusations against such beings in my presence. But these men blaspheme in matters they do not understand. They are like brute beasts, creatures of instinct, born only to be caught and destroyed, and like beasts, they too will perish."[18]

My Master's words hung in the air as He stopped and turned to face me. He looked deep into my eyes, searching for my understanding as He had time and time before, but today there was something different in His eyes. He said to me, "Michael, do you know why I have come to you?" I did not respond, but humbly fell to one knee and bowed my head before my King, sensing the fullness of my promise of service descending upon me. "Michael, soon I will return to fight against the prince of darkness, and when I go, the Prince of Peace will come, but first," He paused, "first, I will tell you what is written in the Book."[19]

The Lord placed His mighty hand on my shoulder and said, "These things I testify to you, Michael, O Archangel Warrior. Yes, Michael, I am coming soon."[20]

{Chapter 30}

THE WEEKEND HAD COME and gone, and Adam found himself reminiscing what seemed to be such a brief trip to Hawaii. In reality, it was a small blip on the timeline of his existence, yet somehow it seemed as if he had been there a lifetime. Adam pondered all that had taken place during that one semester while he patiently waited to board the plane back home. What a life changing trip it had been for him. He was finally able to find closure from his father's death, his faith was stronger than ever, and he met a woman who changed his world: *Evelyn*. He just couldn't stop thinking about her. Adam was surprised how his heart already ached in her absence. As he stood there, he found himself longing for her presence at his side, to feel her soft, warm hand in his. Adam's gaze landed on the window that overlooked the tarmac where the plane he would soon be boarding awaited its final inspection before taking its passengers home. Adam's eyes glazed over as he stared out the window lost in thoughts of Evelyn.

Adam imagined the look on her beautiful face and the last smile she directed at him. He played the sound of her sweet voice over and over in his mind. He didn't think he could ever tire of it. The physical world surrounding Adam faded away, completely removing him from the present, so far removed that he almost didn't hear his name being called behind him. "Adam?" There was a soft tug on his shirt sleeve.

"Look, I got us coffee to go with the snacks since it's such a long flight." Evelyn smiled up at Adam. "Are you okay? Is something wrong?"

Adam chuckled. "No, no, I'm fine. Coffee sounds great, thank you." Adam took the cardboard mug from Evelyn's hand and wrapped his arm around his beautiful bride.

"You looked very deep in thought. What were you thinking about?" Evelyn nestled up to Adam's chest and took a sip of her own coffee.

"Honestly?" Adam kissed the top of Evelyn's head, brushing her chocolate brown hair from her face. "I was missing you!"

Evelyn grinned, "Missing me? I was gone five minutes! I told you I was just going to grab some snacks."

"I know, I know. It just felt like you were gone so much longer. Now that I have you in my life, I don't want to spend a single moment without you."

Evelyn smiled broadly at her amazing husband and turned to lean back against his chest. She wrapped his arms around her and squeezed tightly, "Well, you don't ever have to worry about that, Adam. I'm yours now. For all eternity."

{~}

Just a few moments later, the flight attendant announced over the intercom that they were now boarding the last section of the plane. Adam and Evelyn moved forward with the line.

"I still can't believe were married now!" Evelyn exclaimed as she dug through her purse searching for her boarding pass.

"I know," Adam reached into his back pocket for his wallet. "Every once in a while, I pinch myself just to make sure it's real. It seems too wonderful to be true."

"You know," Evelyn continued, "I was never one of those girls who dreamed of being engaged or getting married, but I certainly never considered that I would meet a man, fall in love, and be married in less than a year! I'm so glad we decided not to wait. Who needs a long engagement to plan a wedding when you can have a private ceremony on the beaches of Maui? I can't imagine anything more perfect."

Adam took his bride's hand in his as they made their way toward the front of the line, "I know," he smiled. "I wouldn't have had it any other way."

{~}

Finally, Adam and Evelyn were next in line to hand over their boarding passes. Adam was holding Evelyn against him, mindlessly watching the television in the terminal when an earsplitting crack of thunder broke through the airport chatter. All the televisions flickered at once and everyone stopped to look up. It seemed that for one brief second, the thunder silenced the whole world. And then, everything continued on as before.

Adam peeked around the people ahead of them to get a better view out the terminal window. "That's odd," he said.

"What's odd?" Evelyn tiptoed, craning her neck to see for herself.

Adam turned back to his wife as the line moved forward. He and Evelyn stepped up to the flight attendant. "It's just odd because the skies are completely clear. It doesn't look like it's going to storm at all."

Adam placed Evelyn's boarding pass with his and handed them both over to the smiling flight attendant. "Thank you for visiting the island," she said as she scanned their tickets. "Aloha, and have a wonderful flight home!"

Adam reached for his wife's hand, leading her toward the entrance of the passenger boarding tunnel where a steady line formed. Because they were the last section to board, they would still have to wait for everyone else to find their seats. Adam was eager to get home with his new bride, but all the same, he didn't mind. *As long as I have Evelyn by my side, I have no reason to be in a hurry*, he thought. "You know Ev," Adam said aloud as the line inched further into the tunnel. "I have never been so happy to go back home. I just know it will seem more like home than it's ever felt before because now I have you with me."

When the passengers in front of them shuffled forward, Adam and Evelyn moved with them. Adam shifted the luggage to his other hand so he could pull Evelyn in closer. "It's like there has been something missing all along. I couldn't quite put my finger on it, but now I know. It was you, Ev. You were the one missing from my life."

There was another rumble of thunder as Evelyn wrapped her arm around Adam's waist, "I agree Adam. It's such a strange and wonderful feeling. It feels as though we've been reunited, like I was always meant to share my life with you. It just seems... natural." Evelyn reached up and planted a gentle kiss on Adam's cheek.

"I really can't wait to get back home," Adam said as they continued to move forward.

Evelyn smiled up at him, "I just can't wait to finally have a place to call home."

{~}

It was almost Adam and Evelyn's turn to board the plane. They could see the smiling faces of the flight attendants as they helped passengers with their luggage. *It won't be long before we're heading home,* Adam thought as he reached down for his bag. *I can't wait to start our new life together.* He secured Evelyn's hand in his own and stepped forward.

"What's that sound?" Evelyn whispered.

Adam paused and listened. "What sound? I don't hear..." And then he did hear it, a low rumbling coming from outside.

"Probably just more thunder," Adam gave his bride's hand a reassuring squeeze.

"It doesn't sound like a storm." Evelyn's face revealed her concern as the noise grew louder and became more intense. Evelyn was right. Was it a plane taking off from the tarmac? No, that didn't seem right either. It was a continuous sound, and it seemed to be getting closer.

Adam and Evelyn were no longer the only two aware of the strange noise. As they looked around, they noticed questioning faces on the other passengers as well. Adam turned toward the flight crew, hoping for an explanation. If they were at all concerned, they hid it well. They just kept waving people onto the plane and moving the line forward.

Adam began whispering a silent prayer for their safe return home. *God, I'm not sure what is going on with the plane, but I just ask that you get us home safely.* He barely finished the prayer when the floor of the boarding tunnel began to shake. It started as a small vibration under their feet, but began growing with rapid intensity.

"What's happening?" Adam could hear the fear in Evelyn's voice as she clung to his arm.

"I'm not sure." Adam focused on remaining calm for the sake of Evelyn, but when the tunnel lights began to flicker, he knew it was no use. The electrical connection was being disrupted with the increasing magnitude of the vibrations. The tunnel began to sway. The ground was becoming so unstable that people started losing their footing and were thrown to the floor. Adam's luggage bounced out of his hand and knocked over the person in front of him. He shouted an apology over the deafening roar and strained to help the man up. As he did, the tunnel lurched again, and Evelyn was thrown up against the flimsy, tunnel wall. Adam quickly pulled her back to him and coaxed her down to the floor, where others were already crouching. The lights continued to flicker, and somewhere in the tunnel, another passenger cried out in agony. The floor pitched again, this time, disconnecting all power. Everything went black. An instinct of protection was awakened in Adam, and he covered Evelyn's body with his own, shielding her from any falling objects. Cries of fear echoed through the tunnel as it heaved to the right. Adam heard the frantic voices of the flight crew. *Something is very wrong!* He wrapped his body tighter around Evelyn, suddenly realizing what was taking place, an earthquake.

The gyrations of the tunnel became more and more violent as the earthquake's magnitude increased. It tossed the tunnel around until it took its final heave. This time, the shift was strong enough to dislodge the entire walkway from the plane, flooding the tunnel with daylight and allowing everyone to witness the trauma as it unfolded.

Adam wished for the darkness to envelop them. The scene was just too horrible to view. The tunnel rolled and pulled away from the plane, providing the perfect vantage point to watch as the runway pavement cracked under the plane's tires. The earth split wide open, and the plane was swallowed whole.

Fear gripped Adam as he held tighter to his bride. He placed his lips next to Evelyn's ears, hoping she could hear him above the chaos. Softly he whispered, "I love you." A loud metallic groan echoed through the tunnel as the floor gave way beneath them. They were falling!

He wasn't sure if she heard him, but as the tunnel plummeted toward the ground, her reply came. "I love you too." It was the last thing Adam heard as the walkway collapsed, and the walls closed in around them. Then all went black.

{Chapter 31}

Adam's eyes fluttered as he struggled to open them. The darkness was so thick and enveloping. He wasn't sure if he was awake or unconscious. "Evelyn!" his voice sounded strange as he desperately called to his wife. "Evelyn! Where are you? Can you hear me?"

There was no response.

"Evelyn!"

Finally, he heard a soft reply, "Adam, I'm right here." The voice was that of his wife, but unusual. It was her voice but different; it was... sweeter? It was odd. She sounded strangely calm.

"Where are you, Evelyn? I can't see you. I can't see anything!" Adam groped in the darkness, frantically searching for his wife with his hands.

"Adam, it's okay. I'm right here." Her soft hand slipped into his. Warmth flooded his body at the thought of knowing Evelyn was here with him and alive.

"Are you hurt, Ev? Are you okay?" Adam was surprised to find that he felt perfectly fine given the trauma they sustained. It was strange that nothing on his body ached. In fact, he felt fantastic. His body seemed vibrant in a way it never had before. *Probably the adrenaline,* he thought. *But Evelyn? Is she hurt?* It was too dark to tell.

"Shhh..." Evelyn whispered. "Adam, look!"

For a split second, Adam wondered where he could possibly look in the darkness that surrounded them, but then he saw it... Far in the distance, was a small pinprick of light. It looked like a lone star contrasted against a dark night sky. It was at that moment that it occurred to Adam; he and Evelyn were not buried among the rubble and devastation left by the earthquake. In fact, the only thing surrounding them was the overwhelming obscurity of pitch black. As Adam tried to make sense of their situation he also became increasingly aware of the fact that gravity seemed to have abandoned them. It was as if they were floating weightless through the universe. The only thing grounding Adam was the sensation of his wife's hand held tightly within his own. *Where are we,* he wondered?

"Adam, the light... Look!" Evelyn's voice broke through his thoughts. "It's growing!" Indeed it was, and it seemed to be getting closer. Or were they getting closer to the light? He couldn't tell.

Before Adam had time to even consider what was happening, a strange emotion swept over him. The light continued to swell, piercing through the darkness and chasing away the night; it completely engulfed them. Suddenly, everything surrounding them began to change. The air became thick, warm, and sweet, *almost delicious,* Adam thought. And as the light expanded to its fullness, it transformed into a brilliant sky. It was so clear, clearer than the clearest sky Adam and Evelyn had ever seen. It was a color that could only be described as a harmonious blend of all the hues in a rainbow. It sparkled as if it were made with some precious stone, reflecting light and color in a splendid display of illumination. A gentle breeze began to blow, and in the whisper of the wind, they heard a soft melody, a sound so sweet and pure it gave life to their bodies. In the distance they could hear a chorus of voices, a humming tune they couldn't quite pick out, but knew it was the most striking song their ears could ever taste. It was a tune that reverberated in their very core and moved them in ways beyond understanding. It was the most beautiful experience they had ever known.

{~}

It was a beautiful day like no other, like no day that had ever occurred before. More beautiful than the day before, yet somehow not as beautiful as tomorrow promised. It reminded me of a time long ago. I pondered this thought in my heart as my King and I traveled along the hillside, no words passing between us. Over the ages, I'd grown accustomed to these daily walks with my Lord. I'd come to yearn for them and anticipate them each and every day. These walks became a representation of our unique bond, a beautiful illustration, Master and servant walking side by side, the servant overjoyed at the opportunity to be in the mere presence of his Master. No words needed to pass between us, just a flow of love. To say I enjoyed these moments would not even begin to describe the emotions that flooded my soul.

Oftentimes, our walks would lead us to the site of the New Kingdom, the place my King had been diligently preparing since the day His Son was called back up to Him. My Lord loved to show me the place He was creating. He swelled with joy knowing this land would one day be the Kingdom of His Son. It was His inheritance. I was anticipating the progress that day. It seemed as though it had been ages since I last walked with my Master through the Kingdom. As we walked along, I tried to imagine the changes that could have taken place since I last gazed upon the regal land, yet I knew my simple mind could not even begin to conceive what the Lord's hands could create. For the Lord's works are wonderful; I know that full well.[1]

As we continued along in silence, I became suddenly aware of our surroundings. They were unfamiliar. *Where are we?* I wondered. It was then it occurred to me that my Master was not planning to lead me through the Kingdom streets as He'd done in the past. Today he was taking me on a very different path. I followed my King closely as He continued guiding me to a place on the Mountain of God that I had never seen before. I looked around in awe and wonder, for His ways never ceased to amaze me. I had been with the Lord on His Mountain longer than any of the other warriors. I was the King's closest confidant, the leader and commander of the Army of God. It was only He who could reveal to me a place in this land that I had never seen.

Finally, He stopped. "Michael, look out and tell me what you see." My King beckoned me to stand next to Him on the edge of the hilltop. I moved in closer to Him, taking in the view He longed to reveal to me. My Master wrapped His strong arm around my shoulder and drew me in to Him. "Look!" He extended His other hand toward the horizon and gestured to the valley below. I did look. And when I did, my heart stopped. With a sharp intake of breath, I fell to my knees and clutched my chest. Tears streamed down my face. Never had I seen something so… alive.

Below me, as far as the eye could see and beyond, stretched the finished Kingdom of my Lord and King. It shone with the glory of God, and its brilliance was like that of a very precious jewel, like a jasper, clear as crystal. The city was laid out like a square, as long as it was wide, and it had a great, high wall with twelve gates with twelve angels, one at each gate. The wall was made of jasper, and the city of pure gold, as pure as glass. The foundations of the city walls were decorated with every kind of precious stone, and the twelve gates were twelve pearls, each gate made of a single pearl, and the great street of the city was of pure gold, like transparent glass. As I looked out across the majestic land, I noticed that I did not see a temple in the city, and I realized it is because the Lord God Almighty and the Lamb, His Son, are its temple. The city did not need the sun or the moon to shine on it, for the glory of God gave it light, and the Lamb was its lamp.[2]

I tried to take it all in, but the beauty of the Kingdom overwhelmed me. I strained to catch a glimpse of every corner of the city, but its pleasure was too great for me to experience. I began to turn back to my Lord, longing to sing my praises to Him, when something caught my eye. There, in the middle of the city, in the very center of the Kingdom, was a garden, and in the middle of the garden stood a tree. Its height was enormous! It grew large and strong and its top touched the sky; it was visible to the ends of the land. Its leaves were beautiful, its fruit abundant, and on it was food for all! Under the tree flowed a magnificent river. It was clear as crystal and stretched as far as the eye could see in either direction, to the east and to the west.[3]

It was then that I realized where my King had brought me. It was a place of which I was given tiny glimpses in the past. I did not understand then, but now I knew. My Master carried me away in the Spirit to a mountain great and high. He was showing me the Kingdom, the Holy City, the New Jerusalem. We were standing on the apex of the Mountain of God. We were on Zion. I buried my face in my hands, finally grasping what was taking place.[4]

My Master's voice came softly from behind me. "It is finished, Michael. I am the Alpha and the Omega, the Beginning and the End. To him who is thirsty I will give to drink without cost from the Spring of the Water of Life. He who overcomes will inherit all this, and I will be his God and he will be My son." I say to them, 'Come!' Whoever is thirsty, let him come, and whoever wishes, let him take the free gift of the water of life. Blessed are those who have washed their robes, that they may have the right to the Tree of Life and may go through the gates into the city.[5]

"Michael, the time is drawing near. Prepare the armies. Inform every warrior to make ready for battle, dressing himself with the armor of God. For you will all be like mighty men trampling the muddy streets in battle, but because I, the Lord, will be with you, you will fight and overthrow the horsemen of the army of Satan. But mark this, Michael, there will be terrible times in the last days."[6]

With these words, the King handed me a scroll, "In reading this, Michael, then you will be able to understand My insight into the mystery of Christ, which was not made known to you or the people of other generations as it is now being revealed to you by Me. This mystery is that through the gospel, the Gentiles are heirs together with Israel, members together of one body and sharers together in the promise in Christ Jesus. I have written these things so that they, those who believe in the name of My Son, may know that they have eternal life. Look, I am coming soon! My reward is with Me, and I will give to each person according to what they have done. My coming will be announced by messengers. Holy ones will declare the verdict, so that the living may know that the Most High is sovereign over all kingdoms on earth, and gives them to anyone He wishes, and sets over them the lowliest of people.[7]

"Now is the appointed time, Michael. You will go to them, and you will say to them, 'Now, dear children, continue in Him, so that when He appears you may be confident and unashamed before Him at His coming. If you know that He is righteous, you know that everyone who does what is right has been born of Him.' Because, you have been raised with Christ, set your hearts on things above, where Christ is seated at the right hand of God. Set your minds on things above, not on earthly things. For you died, and your life is now hidden with Christ in God. He has saved you and called you to a holy life, not because of anything you have done but because of His own purpose and grace. This grace was given to you in Christ Jesus before the beginning of time, but it has now been revealed through the appearing of the Savior, Christ Jesus, Who has destroyed death and has brought life and immortality to light.' You will say to them, 'Look, He is coming soon! Blessed is the one who keeps the words of the prophecy written in this scroll.'"[8]

My hands trembled as I struggled to wrap my mind around the enormity of what my Lord was proclaiming. "Please my Lord... what is written in the scroll?" I watched a soft smile dance on the corner of my Masters lips as I prepared myself for what He would say next.

"This, Michael, is 'The Book of Life.' It is My final Word, the last piece to the puzzle. With this book, My Word is complete."

"Your final Word, My Lord?"

"Yes, Michael. This is My Last Will and Testament, and within it are the names of My heirs. Every single one of My children who have declared Me, and in turn, My Son as the Lord of their life. They will receive My inheritance, the gift of life. My inheritance belongs to all of them, for they are all My children, and now their Kingdom is ready.

"See what great love I have lavished on them, that they should be called children of God! And that is what they are! The reason the world did not know them is that it did not know My Son. Michael, now they are children of God, and what they will be has not yet been made known to them. But when Christ appears, they shall be like Him, for they shall see Him as He is!"[9]

"You see, Michael, everyone who loves, has been born of Me and knows Me. Whoever does not love, does not know Me, because I am love. This is how I showed My love among them: I sent My one and only Son into the world that they might live through Him. I bought them back. And that is love! Not that they loved Me, but that I loved them and sent My Son as an atoning sacrifice for their sins. I am love! Whoever lives in love, lives in Me, and I in them. This is how love is made complete among them so that they may have confidence, today, on the Day of Judgment. In this world they are like Jesus."[10]

"Michael, I am the One Who has built a house for Him, and I will establish My Son's throne forever. I will be His Father, and He will be My Son. I will never take My love away from Him as I took it away from the predecessors. I will set Him over My house and My Kingdom, and His throne will be established forever. He will be given all authority, glory and sovereign power. All nations and peoples of every language will worship Him. His dominion will not pass away, and His Kingdom is one that will never be destroyed. No longer will there be any curse! The throne of God and of the Lamb will be in the city, and His servants will serve him. They will see His face, and His name will be on their foreheads. There will be no more night. They will not need the light of a lamp or the light of the sun, for I, the Lord God, will give them light. And they will reign for ever and ever!"[11]

I stood silenced before my Lord, my lips unable to utter a word.

"Blessed is the one who reads the words of this prophecy, and blessed are those who hear it and take to heart what is written in it, because the time is near. Come, Michael. It is time to call My heirs home. They have been held captive long enough. Their estate is ready."[12]

{~}

As I stood for the final time before the mighty Army of the Lord, my mind flashed back to the day the Great War began. A warm tear slid down my cheek as I relished in the revelation of my Master's wisdom. Today the war would end. This would be the greatest battle ever fought.

"Praise be to the name of God for ever and ever!" I shouted to my warriors. "Wisdom and power are His. He gives wisdom to the wise and knowledge to the discerning. He reveals deep and hidden things; He knows what lies in darkness, and light dwells with Him. This is the message of Jesus Christ, the mystery hidden for long ages past. This mystery has been revealed to me and made known through the final writings of the eternal God.[13]

"Warriors," I continued, "the Lord your God sends these words for your strengthening and encouragement. Heed His words. You will not have to fight this battle; take up your positions, stand firm, and you will see the deliverance the Lord will give you. Do not be afraid; do not be discouraged. Go out to face them; be strong and courageous. Do not be afraid or terrified because of them, for the Lord your God will go with you. He will never leave you or forsake you.

"Though you fight this battle in the world, do not wage war as the world does. The weapons you fight with are not the weapons of the world, for your struggle is not against flesh and blood, but against the rulers, against the authorities, against the powers of this dark world and against the spiritual forces of evil in the heavenly realms. You will demolish every pretension that sets itself up against the knowledge of God. And you will be ready to punish every act of disobedience, once obedience is complete.[14]

"Take up your Sword of the Spirit," I commanded them, "the very Word of God! For the Word of the Lord is living and active. Sharper than any double-edged sword, it penetrates even to dividing soul and spirit, joints and marrow; it judges the thoughts and attitudes of the heart. Today, my warriors, you fight against the knowledge of evil! And it will be defeated so wisdom can reign! Today soldiers, every knee shall bow and every tongue confess, 'In the Lord, alone, are deliverance and strength. All who have raged against Him will come to Him and be put to shame, but the King's descendants, the Lord's heirs will find deliverance in Him!'"[15]

A cheer erupted, and joy spread through the crowd of warriors as they lifted their swords high, shaking the Mountain of God like a great torrent of thunder. "The time has come, great warriors! The Kingdom of God is near," I shouted, "The Lord's created ones are arriving now."[16]

{~}

Evelyn awoke with a start. *How long have I been asleep? And what a strange dream,* she thought as she sat up, taking in her surroundings. Evelyn's hand flew to her mouth as she gasped in surprise. *It wasn't a dream!* Evelyn could scarcely believe what she was seeing. She was lying in the middle of a garden, but not just any garden. It was the most beautiful garden she had ever seen. The foliage was lush and brilliant. Large emerald-colored vines with leaves climbed the great walls enclosing the garden. Even the walls themselves sparkled with color, for they were made of jasper and decorated with every precious stone. Evelyn was surprised to find she could actually taste the air that filled the land. It was thick with notes of floral and citrus. Of all the beauty that filled the garden, it was the flowers that were the most striking. Their hues reflected in the prisms on the garden walls, and luminous flecks of color danced across every surface, including her bare skin. *Bare skin? Where had her clothes gone?* It was at that moment Evelyn realized she was naked, but not bare in the human sense she once knew.

"Evelyn!" Adam's voice came from behind her. "Look at this place! And look at you! You are different yet familiar at the same time. You are more beautiful than ever!"

Evelyn was shocked when she turned around to see her husband. He too was naked, yet neither of them was ashamed. Their bodies had taken on a new form, a form so lovely it was beyond description. Their bodies were perfect and unflawed, brilliant and vibrant. Each of them reflected beams of colored light and the purest emotions ever known. They were not human in a worldly sense but human as God originally created them.

Evelyn was still trying to wrap her mind around what was happening when Adam's voice interrupted her thoughts. "Evelyn! Here, come with me." Adam pulled her to her feet. "Look!" he exclaimed, pointing straight ahead at a golden path that cut through the foliage. It was as pure and transparent as glass, reflecting a light that warmed their hearts and called out to their souls. "Come," it seemed to whisper. Without another thought or question, Adam slipped his hand into Evelyn's, and they made their way down the path to the center of the garden.

{~}

Along the path, Adam and Evelyn were greeted with sights of amazing splendor, each more stunning than the one before but not as beautiful as the one to follow. It stole their breath away.

As they continued toward the center of the garden, Adam became increasingly aware of the fact that time was passing, yet how long he was not sure. It seemed that time was ambiguous in this land. He couldn't tell if they had been wandering for mere minutes, hours, or even days. Adam was used to time being a measure that varied by how you spent it. When performing mundane tasks, time seemed to creep by slowly, but when working on things he enjoyed, time seemed to move faster than desired. But here? Everything was so wonderful. This experience was more delightful than any before, yet time seemed neither too slow nor too quick. It was just... constant. Eventually, the concept of time was completely forgotten when Adam and Evelyn reached the center of the garden. It was absolutely unmistakable because it seemed as if everything surrounding built up to this moment, like the whole world centered upon this very place. *The world*, Adam thought. *What world is this?*

They stepped forward into the clearing, but before Adam and Evelyn even had a chance to take in its beauty, their attention was drawn to a rustling sound in the garden. *Is it the wind*, Adam wondered? *Or perhaps, we are not alone...* The sound seemed to be getting closer, approaching from behind them. Adam gave his wife's hand a reassuring squeeze as they turned to see what, or who, was coming, but never could they have anticipated the awe-inspiring vision they would see.

A man-like figure moved toward them. Slowly He walked, neither rushing nor delaying. Everything about Him seemed purposed and poised. He was the most handsome being they ever laid eyes upon. His stature was noble and strong. His very presence was overwhelming with pure, raw emotion, and His face shone like the sun. Adam and Evelyn were completely drawn to Him. They couldn't help it. They could not will their feet to stop proceeding in His direction. Without thought or purpose, their bodies led them into the center of the garden where the Man stopped. He was standing beside a tree.

It was a magnificent, towering tree, full and vibrant, covered with lush greenery, succulent fruit, and beautiful branches that overshadowed the garden. It towered on high, its top above the thick foliage, higher than any tree in the land. Below it flowed a river, a crystal-clear stream that sparkled in the light that was radiating from the Man before them. The waters of the river nourished the tree, the deep spring made it grow tall, flowing all around its base and sending smaller channels to all the other trees of the field.[17]

Adam and Evelyn watched as the man-like figure selected a single piece of fruit from the tree. He began to examine it in His hands, rolling the fruit back and forth, looking it over closely from every angle. It was the most delicious looking piece of fruit Adam and Evelyn had ever seen. Its color was a deep, luscious red, and dew clung to its soft edible skin. Evelyn thought she could smell its fragrance from where she was standing. It made her mouth water. She craved it like no food ever before.

The man-like figure continued examining the fruit. It seemed He was trying to draw their attention to it, but He didn't even have to try. They could fix their eyes nowhere else. It was only when Adam and Evelyn looked closer that they noticed it. On this flawless figure, on each of His perfect, masculine hands, there was a scar, one on each hand, directly in the center of His palms. When they looked to His feet, realization set in. They fell to their knees, their faces to the ground. On His feet were two scars, ugly marks that didn't belong on this beautiful being. They were a remembrance of a wager, a memory of a war, and the promise of a Lord and God Who would redeem His people.

"Please stand, My created ones," His mighty voice echoed throughout the garden. Adam and Evelyn were too humbled to face their Lord but even more humbled not to obey. Slowly, they rose to their feet to look upon the face of God Himself.

Evelyn gasped. "His eyes!" she whispered. They were mesmerizing, so full of joy, so full of... love. It was in those eyes that Adam and Evelyn saw all that had ever been, all that was, and all that is yet to come. This was the Alpha and the Omega, the Beginning and the End, the Father, the Spirit, the Son.

"Look, My created ones," He gestured toward the garden. "Take in all that is around you. This is your home. Does it feel familiar to you?" In a strange way, yes, the garden did feel like home to Adam and Evelyn. Something was indeed familiar about this place, but neither could place their finger on it.

The Lord smiled and laughed at the confusion on their faces, "Do you not yet realize who you are?" Upon seeing the questioning look in their eyes, the Lord continued. "You are My created ones, the ones that I love, the ones I have chosen. I created you. Adam, it was I who formed you from the dust of the ground. I made you and breathed life into your nostrils. And you Evelyn... My precious Eve, I created you from a rib that I took from your husband. You are both my workmanship, created in Me. I chose to give you birth through the Word of Truth, that you might be a kind of firstfruits of all I created. You were made by Me and for Me to do good works which I prepared in advance for you to do. Do you not know that your body is a temple of My Spirit? My essence, My very Being is in you. You are not your own; you were bought at a price. I paid it all to have you back. The day you walked out of the garden, the day I banished you, My heart broke, and I wept bitterly. That day, I made a wager with Satan. No price was too great to have you back with Me again because I made you, and I loved you.

"On the day I created you, Adam, forming you from the dust of the earth, I already knew. And Eve, when I took you from the place in your husband's side, creating you as a piece of him, I already knew. As I breathed My very life into you, making you a part of Me, I already knew you would abandon Me. I also knew that I would never abandon you because love believes all things and hopes all things. I set before you life and death, blessings and curses, believing and hoping you would choose life and live, praying you would choose Me. Yet, at the same time, I already knew that I loved you enough to die for you. While I created you, forming you to look just like Me, and placing Myself inside you, I already knew I would give My very life for you.[18]

"I paid Satan the greatest price, the only value that would cover the sin that was on you. I gave him My Son, My only Son, so that you could return to Me as My heirs, receive My inheritance, and be able to live the life I originally created for you. Now, through this, I am able to give you My very great and precious promises, so that through them you may participate in the divine nature. The world knew you as Adam and Evelyn, but I know you as Adam and Eve. Your spirit is their spirit, My Spirit, and now you are being redeemed to Me."[19]

At His words, the Great Army of the Lord appeared and surrounded the garden. I stood at the lead, presenting the readied warriors before their King. Never has such a powerful sight existed. The stature of each warrior created a gallant and bold presence.

"Adam and Eve, this is My army," the Lord declared. "They are waiting on My Word to descend into the world below and fight the final and greatest battle of the war. There is great trouble in the world where you once lived, but take heart, for today I will overcome the world. You too, My dear children, have overcome them because the One Who is in you is greater than the one who is in the world. Therefore, fix your eyes, My created ones, not on what is seen, but on what is unseen. For what is seen is temporary, but what is unseen... is eternal."[20]

My Master glanced over at me, and I knew the time had come. As I stood before the Great Army, I raised my right hand to the heavens and swore, "By Him Who lives for ever and ever, Who created the heavens and all that is in them, the earth and all that is in it, and the sea and all that is in it. There will be no more delay!"[21]

The warriors drew their swords and lifted their shields high, ready for the signal to charge down into the earthly realm below and destroy the enemy for good. Today, the shaft of the Abyss would be sealed with Satan and all of Hell's inhabitants locked inside. They would be thrown into the lake of fire.

The Lord beamed proudly at His valiant warriors and called out to them, "On this day, when the seventh angel is about to sound his trumpet, the mystery of God will be accomplished just as I announced to My servants the prophets." At the Lord's commanding voice, the garden trembled and peals of thunder rolled through the land. "Look!" His voice boomed as He gestured toward the heavens. Awestruck we watched as the clouds peeled back. They were rolled up like a scroll, and the sky burst open. It was the portal to the earthly world below. Not the portal to the spiritual realm where angels and demons fought unseen to the human eye, but for the first time in history, Heaven's angelic warriors and Satan's beasts would battle in the realm of the earth. All people would see the spectacle that was before them, and they would be terrified. Only those who knew the promise of their Lord would be able to withstand the terror, for they would know their time had come.[22]

My angelic warriors and I prepared for flight, placing our helmets on our heads and affixing our breastplates to our chests. We knew full well that the moment the King's command was uttered, it would be a declaration of a war that would end in the purest peace.

"One thing remains My created ones, you must unlock the Kingdom. Your actions at this moment will usher in My inheritance, making it a reality for all My heirs. Everything is ready. This is the last thing that must take place."

After speaking these words, the Lord God extended His nail scarred hand, offering the fruit to Adam and Eve. It overwhelmed them with a flood of memories, transporting them to a time of long ago. They saw in their mind's eye the Garden of Eden, and there in the center stood two trees. But now, one did not look as appealing as it had long ago. It was a dark tree with gnarled branches, dying leaves, and rotting fruit. Beside it stood the Tree of Life, the same tree that now lay before them, the same tree from which their Creator now offered them the fruit of life. The Lord's hand reached toward His created ones, and they leaned forward into His offer. My warriors and I tensed. This was the moment.

"Ready yourselves, warriors!" I shouted, "On the Almighty's Word." With this I lifted my trumpet to my lips, and I, the seventh angel, blasted the trumpet call. It was the trumpet that we knew was heard around the world. I lifted my voice and shouted, "The Kingdom of the world has become the

Kingdom of our Lord and of His Son, Jesus Christ, and He will reign for ever and ever."[23]

My warriors chanted their reply in unison. "For the Lord Himself will come down from Heaven. He will come with a loud command, with the voice of the Archangel Michael, and with the trumpet call of God, and the dead in Christ will rise first."[24]

"And after that," I shouted back, "they who are still alive and are left will be caught up together with them in the clouds to meet the Lord in the air. And so will they be with the Lord forever." A cheer erupted through the sea of angelic warriors. We celebrated our impending victory, yet we knew there was still one thing to be done, one final command to be given.[25]

Adam and Eve moved in closer to the Lord and slowly extended their hands to meet His. The tension was thick and enveloped all who were present. Silence covered the garden. The only sound to be heard was the steady beating of the King's heart.

Eve took the fruit first and ate of it, and then offered it to her husband. It was the sweetest, most delicious flavor they ever experienced. Warmth and pleasure flooded their bodies with the explosion of the taste in their mouths.

God smiled and looked up at me where I waited anxiously for my Master's command. And in that moment, I knew exactly what He was thinking. *Michael, this is good, very good.*

With a smile dancing upon His lips, the Lord raised His mighty hands to the sky and lifted His voice for all to hear as He gave His final command.

And God said, "Let there be Life!"

{About the Writer}

Heather lives with her husband in Northern Kentucky where they enjoy spending time outdoors, working in their yard or garden, and playing with their beloved dog. They both have a love for photography and enjoy traveling. Heather's creativity and passion are not limited to writing and photography. She's also an artist whose first loves were drawing and painting. Now she happily adds "painting pictures with words" to her creative repertoire.

Heather has many more literary projects in the works. For more information about upcoming projects, or if you'd like to contact her, please visit HeatherRaeHutzel.com.

You can also follow Heather Rae Hutzel on Facebook and Twitter: @HeatherRHutzel.

{Endnotes}

Prologue

1. Proverbs 8:22-31
2. Revelation 4:8
3. Revelation 4:11
4. Revelation 4:6-8
5. Psalm 35:10; Isaiah 40:28
6. Revelation 4:3
7. Psalm 143:8
8. Ezekiel 28:12; Ezekiel 28:16-17
9. Isaiah 14:13-14; Isaiah 46:9
10. Ezekiel 28:15-16
11. Ephesians 6:12-17
12. Revelation 12:7-8
13. 1 Samuel 17:47
14. Ezekiel 28:12-17
15. Isaiah 14:11, 15
16. Genesis 1:3

Chapter 1

1. Genesis 1:3
2. Isaiah 55:8
3. Genesis 1:1-2
4. Genesis 1:3
5. Genesis 1:4-5
6. Genesis 1:6
7. Matthew 8:27
8. Genesis 1:7-8
9. Matthew 19:26
10. Genesis 1:9
11. Isaiah 46:9
12. 2 Corinthians 5:17
13. 1 Corinthians 13:12-13
14. Genesis 1:11
15. Genesis 1:12
16. Genesis 2:6
17. Genesis 1:13
18. Genesis 1:14-15
19. Genesis 1:16-18
20. Genesis 1:19
21. John 4:13-14
22. Revelation 21:6; John 8:12
23. Genesis 1:20
24. Genesis 1:20
25. Genesis 1:22
26. Psalm 19:1-4
27. Genesis 1:23
28. Genesis 1:24
29. Job 40:16-18

Chapter 2

1. Genesis 2:8
2. Genesis 1:26
3. Genesis 2:7
4. Song of Solomon 5:10-15
5. Genesis 2:9
6. Genesis 2:19
7. Genesis: 2:20; Genesis 2:19
8. Genesis 2:18
9. John 8:12
10. Song of Solomon 4:1,3,7,11; Song of Solomon 2:1; Song of Solomon 7:1
11. Genesis 2:23; Song of Solomon 4:9-10
12. Genesis 2:24; Ephesians 5:22, 28; Genesis 2:22
13. Genesis 1:28-30
14. Genesis 2:25
15. 1 Corinthians 13:12-13; John 15:13
16. Genesis 1:27
17. Genesis 1:31

Chapter 3

1. Genesis 2:1-3

Chapter 4

1. Ezekiel 28:16-17
2. Revelation 9:1-2; Isaiah 14:15

3. Isaiah 14:11, 15
4. Revelation 12:1-6

Chapter 5

1. Luke 12:22-26
2. Luke 12:22; Genesis 2:25; Genesis 1:27; 1 Samuel 16:7
3. Genesis 2:3
4. Revelation 21:3
5. 1 Corinthians 2:9
6. Matthew 11:30; Mark 12:30
7. Genesis 1:28
8. Job 1:7
9. Job 1:7
10. Hebrews 4:13
11. John 18:11
12. Job 1:9-11
13. James 1:13-14; Matthew 4:7
14. Isaiah 40:28; Job 1:12; Matthew 4:10
15. Job 1:12
16. Ezekiel 31:3-9
17. Genesis 1:29
18. Genesis 2:17; Matthew 26:41
19. John 21:15-17

Chapter 6

1. Genesis 3:1
2. Ezekiel 31:3-5
3. Genesis 3:1

4. Genesis 3:2-3
5. Genesis 3:4-5
6. Ezekiel 31:3-5
7. Genesis 3:4-5
8. Ezekiel 31:5-8
9. Genesis 3:4-5
10. Genesis 3:6
11. Genesis 3:7
12. Genesis 3:7
13. 1 Samuel 3:8
14. Genesis 3:10
15. Genesis 3:11
16. Genesis 3:12
17. Genesis 3:13
18. Genesis 3:13
19. Genesis 3:14-15
20. Genesis 3:16
21. Genesis 3:17-19
22. Genesis 3:21
23. Genesis 3:22
24. Genesis 3:23-24

Chapter 7

1. John 18:11
2. 2 Chronicles 20:17
3. Exodus 14:14
4. 2 Corinthians 4:18; John 16:33
5. Matthew 4:6
6. Romans 6:23; John 10:10; Colossians 1:13-14
7. Malachi 3:6

8. 1 Corinthians 2:8; Matthew 27:39
9. Matthew 27:40
10. Matthew 27:41-42
11. Hebrews 10:36 (AMP); Psalm 71:20 (GOD'S WORD)
12. Jeremiah 29:11; Luke 22:42
13. Isaiah 40:28
14. Proverbs 3:5-6; Isaiah 55:9
15. Isaiah 40:28
16. 1 Corinthians 13:12-13
17. Matthew 27:46
18. Luke 23:46
19. 2 Corinthians 4:6
20. 1 Corinthians 15:45-49
21. Philippians 2:6-11
22. Romans 5:18-19
23. Psalm 16:11
24. Revelation 1:7
25. John 17:20-23
26. John 17:24

Chapter 8

1. Romans 5:8-14

Chapter 9

1. John 17:21-23
2. John 17:24
3. Ephesians 2:1-6
4. Colossians 1:13-14

5. Psalm 139:13-14; Psalm 139:2-4
6. Revelation 3:16
7. Revelation 12:17
8. 2 Peter 3:3-4
9. 2 Peter 3:5-7
10. 2 Peter 3:8-10; 2 Peter 3:12-13
11. Ephesians 2:10

Chapter 12

1. Jude 1:9

Chapter 13

1. Matthew 6:34
2 Lamentations 3:22-23

Chapter 14

1. Proverbs 3:25-26
2. Jeremiah 39:18

Chapter 15

1. Deuteronomy 32:4

Chapter 16

1. Revelation 9:6
2. Jeremiah 29:11-14
3. Psalm 103:12
4. James 1:22-24

Chapter 17

1. Revelation 21:4
2. Daniel 8:12
3. Romans 8:22
4. Romans 8:22-25

Chapter 18

1. Colossians 1:13-14; Colossians 1:10-12
2. Acts 26:17-18

Chapter 19

1. Daniel 10:5-6
2. Luke 23:46
3. Mathew 12:28; Revelation 12:10-11; Isaiah 45:23-24

Chapter 20

1. Genesis 1:26; Hebrews 1:2-3
2. Hebrews 1:4-5
3. Hebrews 1:6-9
4. Daniel 4:3; Psalm 8:1,3; Hebrews 1:10-12
5. Daniel 12:1-3
6. Daniel 12:6
7. Hebrews 1:11-12; Revelation 21:1
8. Daniel 12:8
9. Daniel 12:9-10; Ephesians 1:9-10
10. Ephesians 1:11
11. Isaiah 40:28

Chapter 21

1. Romans 8:22-25

Chapter 22

1. Ephesians 1:4-8
2. Ephesians 1:17-21

Chapter 23

1. Romans 8:24-25
2. Lamentations 3:25; Hebrews 6:19

3. Isaiah 45:12
4. 1 John 1:1; Proverbs 8:27-31
5. John 1:1-3
6. John 1:4-5; Proverbs 9:10; Ephesians 3:4-5; John 14:6; Hebrews 11:1-3; John 20:29
7. Hebrews 1:1-3; Colossians 1:25-27
8. Proverbs 20:27
9. Daniel 4:10-12; Revelation 22:1; Revelation 22:5
10. Revelation 22:1-2
11. Ephesians 2:14-16; Revelation 22:12-14
12. Psalm 21:11-12; Deuteronomy 30:19-20
13. Daniel 12:1; Revelation 20:14-15
14. Ephesians 2:8

Chapter 24

1. Jude 1:6; Revelation 9:7-8; Romans 1:29
2. Revelation 9:9-10; John 8:44
3. Revelation 13:1-2
4. 2 Kings 6:16; Psalm 74:13; Isaiah 27:1; Lamentations 3:22; Isaiah 41:10
5. Deuteronomy 31:6; Deuteronomy 1:30
6. Isaiah 54:17; Matthew 16:18 (ESV)
7. Psalm 3:1-4
8. Psalm 3:6-8
9. Psalm 69:13; Psalm 17:1
10. 1 Kings 9:3
11. Leviticus 26:7-8
12. Exodus 14:14

Chapter 25

1. John 15:13
2. Ephesians 2:1
2. Romans 10:9-13
3. Romans 10:9
4. Romans 10:10-13
5. Revelation 12:12

Chapter 26

1. Hebrews 11:1
2. Romans 10:10
3. Romans 1:20

Chapter 27

1. Isaiah 12:4; Isaiah 12:5-6; Colossians 1:13-14
2. 1 Timothy 1:17

Chapter 28

1. Ephesians 5:8
2. Acts 8:36

Chapter 29

1. Ephesians 3:19; Philippians 2:2; Daniel 4:3
2. 1 Samuel 3:10
3. John 16:12-13
4. Joshua 5:14
5. Revelation 4:1
6. Revelation 6:12-17
7. Daniel 8:27; Daniel 8:17; Genesis 6:5 (TNIV); Genesis 6:6; Jeremiah 6:15-19
8. Daniel 10:15-17
9. Daniel 10:18-19
10. Revelation 21:9; Psalm 19:4-6
11. Genesis 34:12
12. Revelation 19:7
13. Song of Solomon 4:9-12,15
14. John 4:14; Revelation 21:6
15. Jeremiah 33:10-11; 1 Corinthians 15:50-51
16. Revelation 1:13-15
17. 1 Corinthians 15:51-55
18. Hebrews 1:9; Daniel 12:1; Revelation 20:14-15; 1 John 2:5; 1 John 2:17; 2 Peter 2:4-5, 9-12
19. Daniel 10:20; Daniel 10:20-21
20. Revelation 22:20

Chapter 31

1. Psalm 139:14
2. Revelation 21:11-12, 16, 18-19, 21; Revelation 21:22-23
3. Daniel 4:10-12; Revelation 22:1
4. Revelation 21:10

5. Revelation 21:6-7; Revelation 22:17; Revelation 22:14
6. Zechariah 10:5; 2 Timothy 3:1
7. Ephesians 3:4-6; 1 John 5:13; Revelation 22:12; Daniel 4:17
8. 1 John 2:28-29; Colossians 3:1-3; 2 Timothy 1:9-10; Revelation 22:7
9. 1 John 3:1-2
10. 1 John 4:7-10; 1 John 4:16-17
11. 1 Chronicles 17:12-14; Daniel 7:14; Revelation 22:3-5
12. Revelation 1:3
13. Daniel 2:20-22; Romans 16:25-26
14. 2 Chronicles 20:17; Deuteronomy 31:6; 2 Corinthians 10:3-4; Ephesians 6:12; 2 Corinthians 10:5-6
15. Ephesians 6:17; Hebrews 4:12; Isaiah 45:23-25
16. Mark 1:15
17. Ezekiel 31:3; Ezekiel 31:4
18. Ephesians 2:10; James 1:18; Ephesians 2:10; 1 Corinthians 6:19-20; 1 Corinthians 13:7 (ESV); Deuteronomy 30:19
19. 2 Peter 1:4
20. John 16:33; 1 John 4:4; 2 Corinthians 4:18
21. Revelation 10:5-6
22. Revelation 10:7
23. Revelation 11:15
24. 1 Thessalonians 4:16
25. 1 Thessalonians 4-17

Back Cover

1. 1 John 1:1; Proverbs 8:22-23; Ecclesiastes 3:15; John 16:22; Ecclesiastes 3:11; Romans 16:25-26; Revelation 1:3

Made in the USA
Charleston, SC
12 April 2014